POSTAL™

CREATED BY MATT HAWKINS

VOLU

PUBLISHED BY TOP COW PRODUCTIONS, INC.
LOS ANGELES

POSTAL

CREATED BY MATT HAWKINS

BRYAN HILL
WRITER

ISAAC GOODHART
ARTIST

K. MICHAEL RUSSELL
COLORIST

TROY PETERI
LETTERER

ELENA SALCEDO &
MATT HAWKINS
EDITORS

COVER ART FOR THIS EDITION BY
ISAAC GOODHART
& K. MICHAEL RUSSELL

BOOK DESIGN & LAYOUT BY
CAREY HALL

To find the comic shop
nearest you, call:
1-888-COMICBOOK

Want more info? Check out:
www.topcow.com
for news & exclusive Top Cow merchan

For Top Cow Productions, Inc.
For Top Cow Productions, Inc.
Marc Silvestri - CEO
Matt Hawkins - President & COO
Elena Salcedo - Vice President of Operations
Henry Barajas - Director of Operations
Vincent Valentine - Production Manager
Dylan Gray - Marketing Director

IMAGE COMICS, INC.
Robert Kirkman—Chief Operating Officer
Erik Larsen—Chief Financial Officer
Todd McFarlane—President
Marc Silvestri—Chief Executive Officer
Jim Valentino—Vice President

Eric Stephenson—Publisher
Corey Hart—Director of Sales
Jeff Boison—Director of Publishing Planning
& Book Trade Sales
Chris Ross—Director of Digital Sales
Jeff Stang—Director of Specialty Sales
Kat Salazar—Director of PR & Marketing
Drew Gill—Art Director
Heather Doornink—Production Director
Branwyn Bigglestone—Controller
IMAGECOMICS.COM

POSTAL

THE STORY SO FAR…

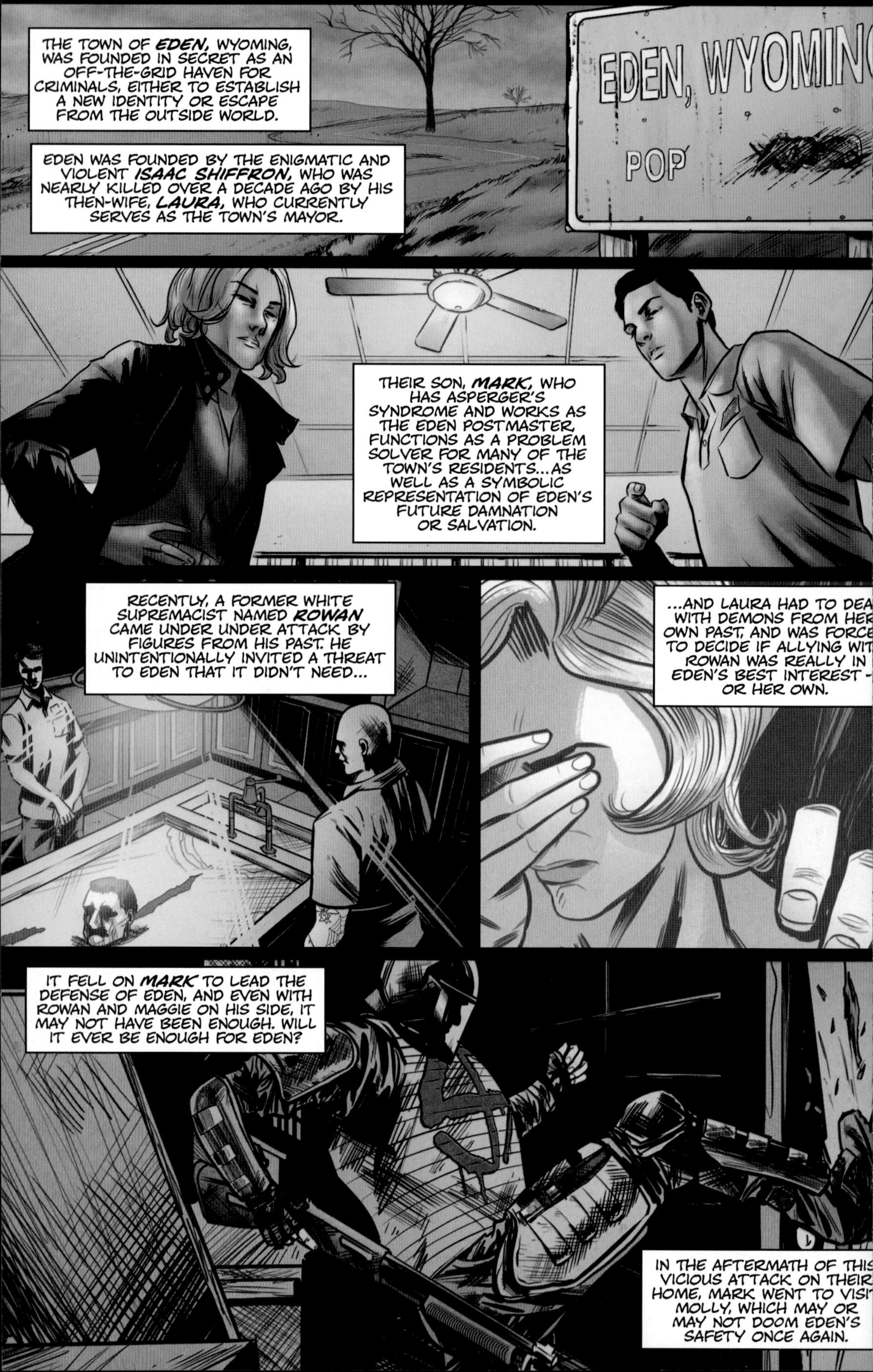
THE TOWN OF EDEN, WYOMING, WAS FOUNDED IN SECRET AS AN OFF-THE-GRID HAVEN FOR CRIMINALS, EITHER TO ESTABLISH A NEW IDENTITY OR ESCAPE FROM THE OUTSIDE WORLD.
EDEN, WYOMIN
POP
EDEN WAS FOUNDED BY THE ENIGMATIC AND VIOLENT ISAAC SHIFFRON, WHO WAS NEARLY KILLED OVER A DECADE AGO BY HIS THEN-WIFE, LAURA, WHO CURRENTLY SERVES AS THE TOWN'S MAYOR.
THEIR SON, MARK, WHO HAS ASPERGER'S SYNDROME AND WORKS AS THE EDEN POSTMASTER, FUNCTIONS AS A PROBLEM SOLVER FOR MANY OF THE TOWN'S RESIDENTS…AS WELL AS A SYMBOLIC REPRESENTATION OF EDEN'S FUTURE DAMNATION OR SALVATION.
RECENTLY, A FORMER WHITE SUPREMACIST NAMED ROWAN CAME UNDER UNDER ATTACK BY FIGURES FROM HIS PAST. HE UNINTENTIONALLY INVITED A THREAT TO EDEN THAT IT DIDN'T NEED…
…AND LAURA HAD TO DEA WITH DEMONS FROM HER OWN PAST, AND WAS FORCE TO DECIDE IF ALLYING WIT ROWAN WAS REALLY IN EDEN'S BEST INTEREST – OR HER OWN.
IT FELL ON MARK TO LEAD THE DEFENSE OF EDEN, AND EVEN WITH ROWAN AND MAGGIE ON HIS SIDE, IT MAY NOT HAVE BEEN ENOUGH. WILL IT EVER BE ENOUGH FOR EDEN?
IN THE AFTERMATH OF THIS VICIOUS ATTACK ON THEIR HOME, MARK WENT TO VISI MOLLY, WHICH MAY OR MAY NOT DOOM EDEN'S SAFETY ONCE AGAIN.

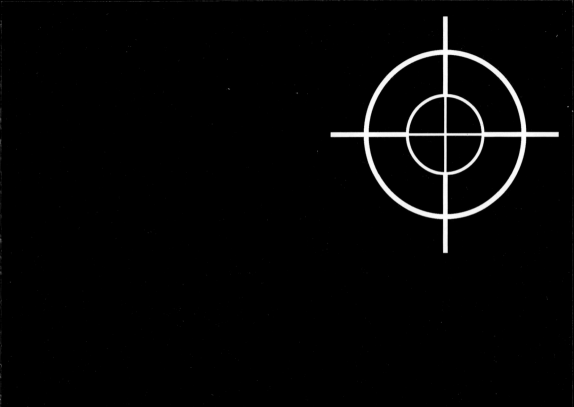

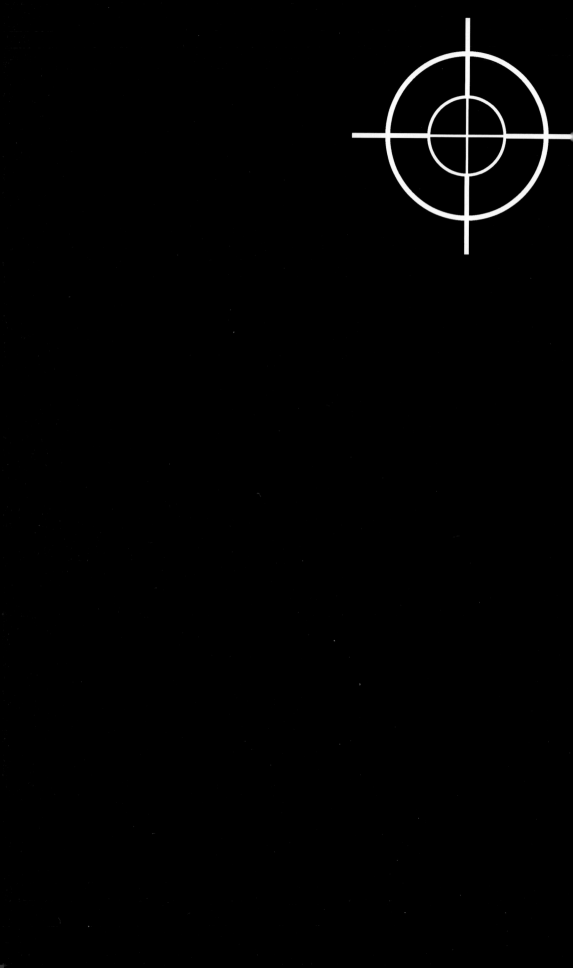

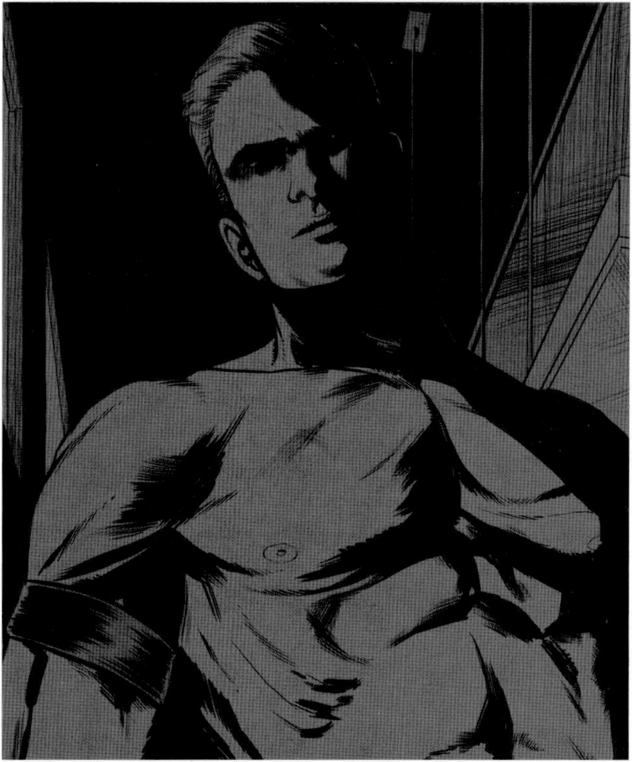

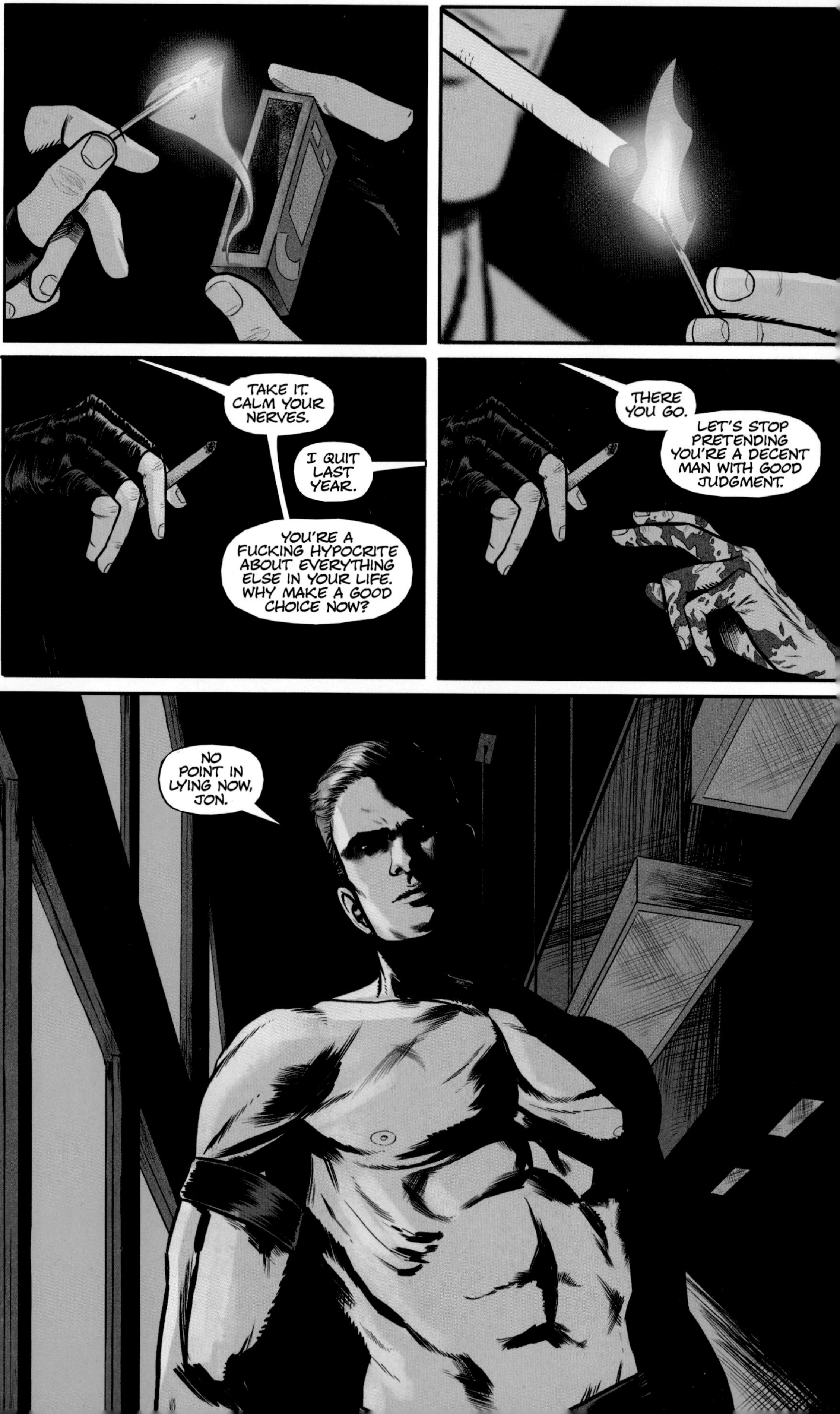
TAKE IT. CALM YOUR NERVES.
I QUIT LAST YEAR.
YOU'RE A FUCKING HYPOCRITE ABOUT EVERYTHING ELSE IN YOUR LIFE. WHY MAKE A GOOD CHOICE NOW?
THERE YOU GO.
LET'S STOP PRETENDING YOU'RE A DECENT MAN WITH GOOD JUDGMENT.
NO POINT IN LYING NOW, JON.

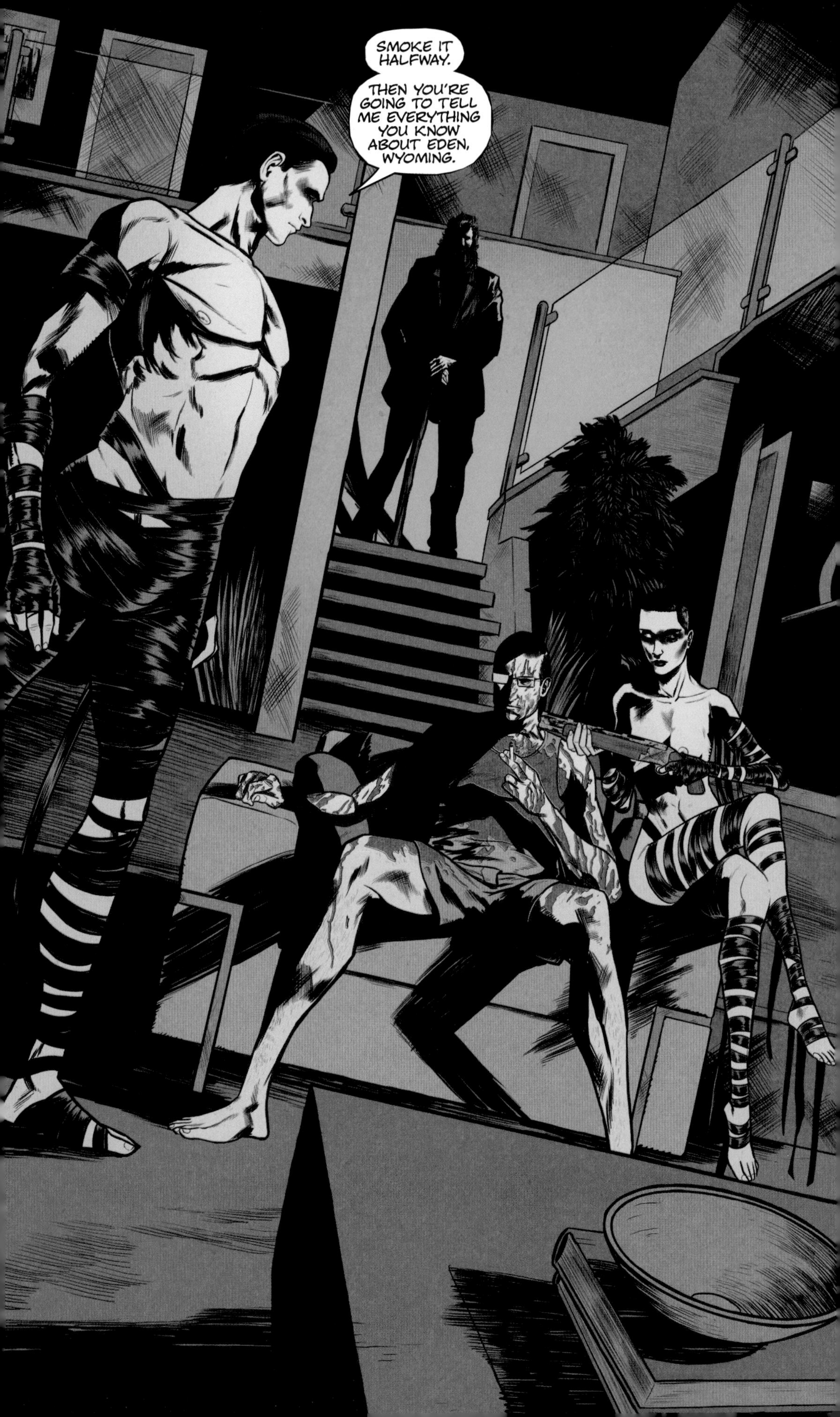
SMOKE IT HALFWAY.
THEN YOU'RE GOING TO TELL ME EVERYTHING YOU KNOW ABOUT EDEN, WYOMING.

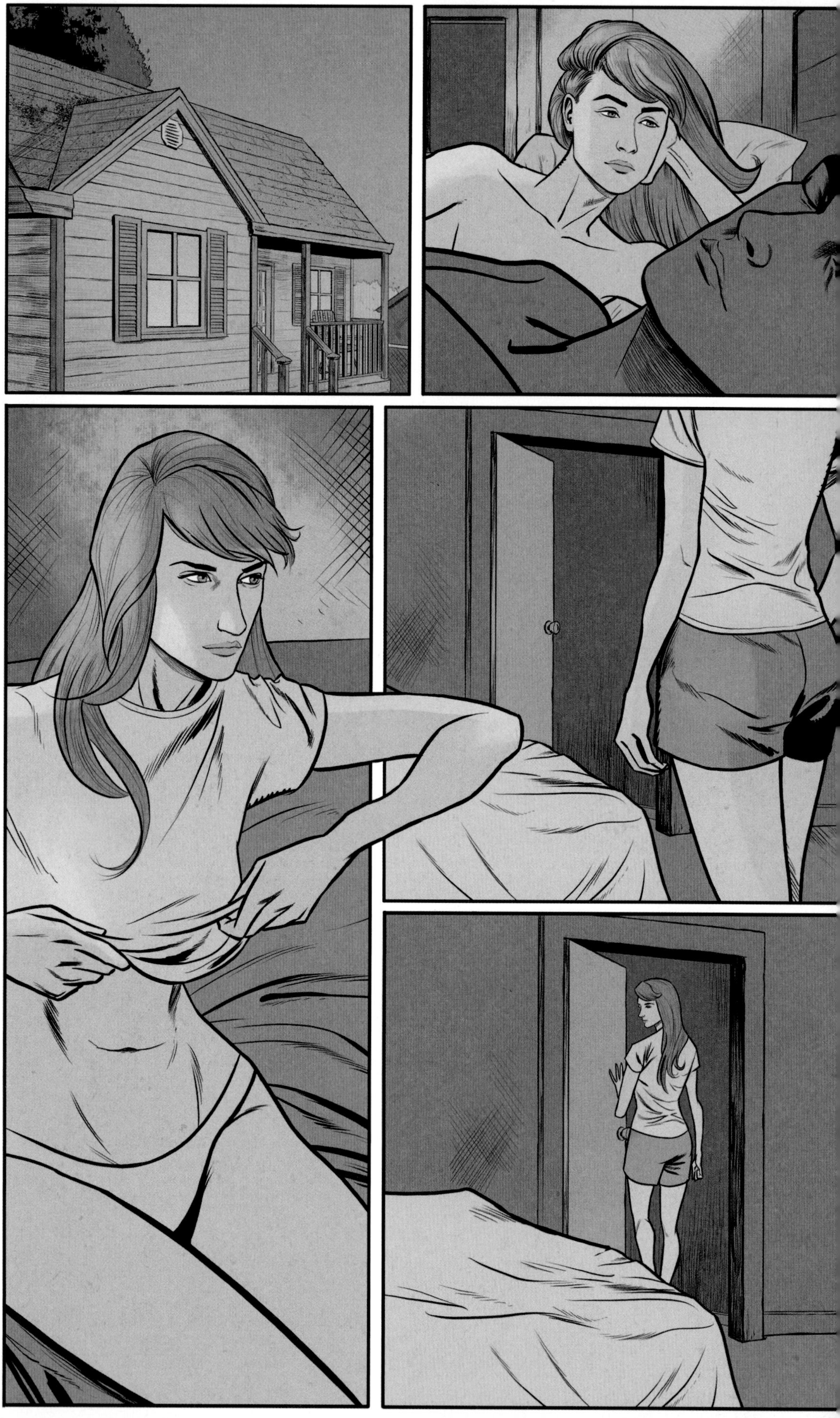

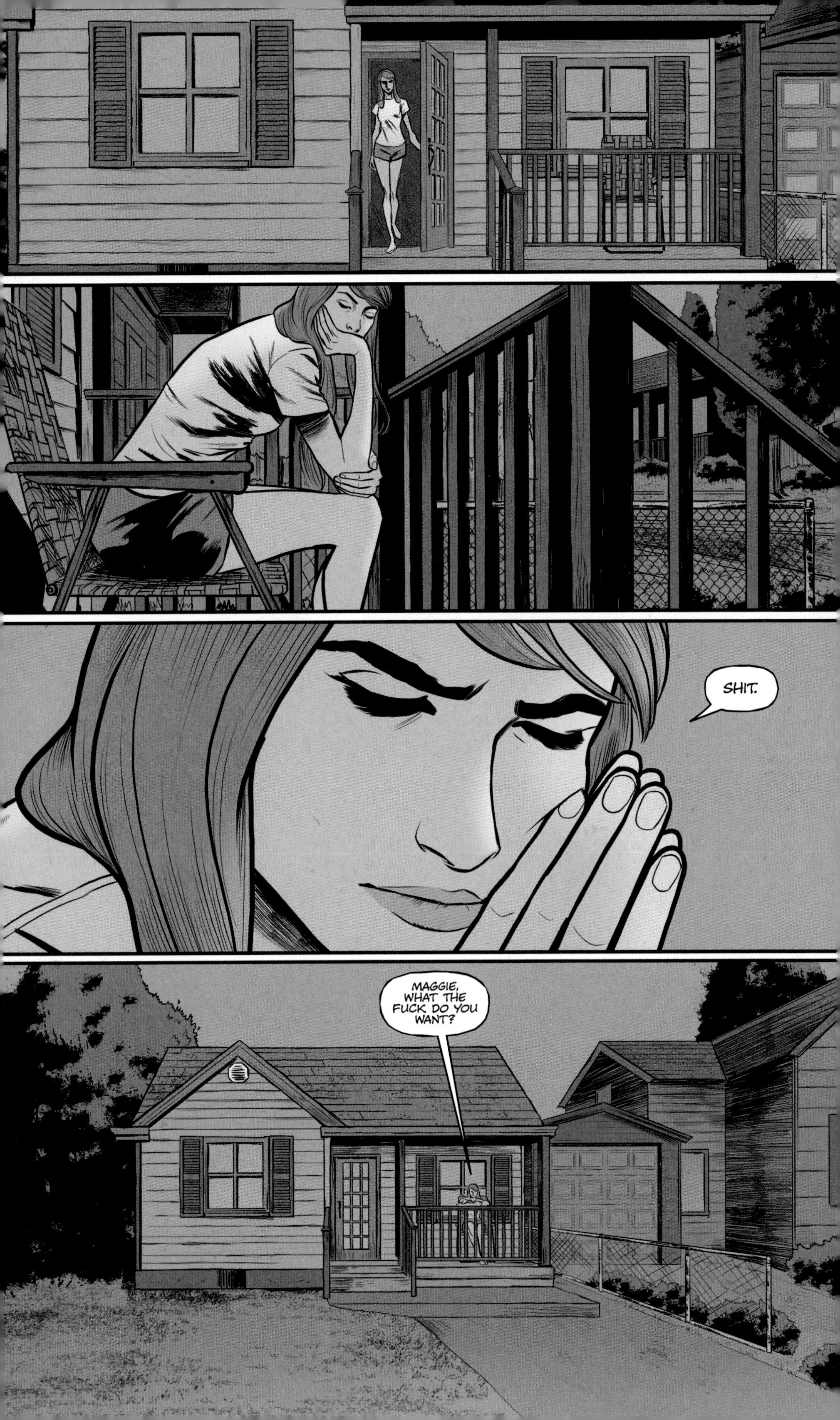
SHIT.
MAGGIE, WHAT THE FUCK DO YOU WANT?

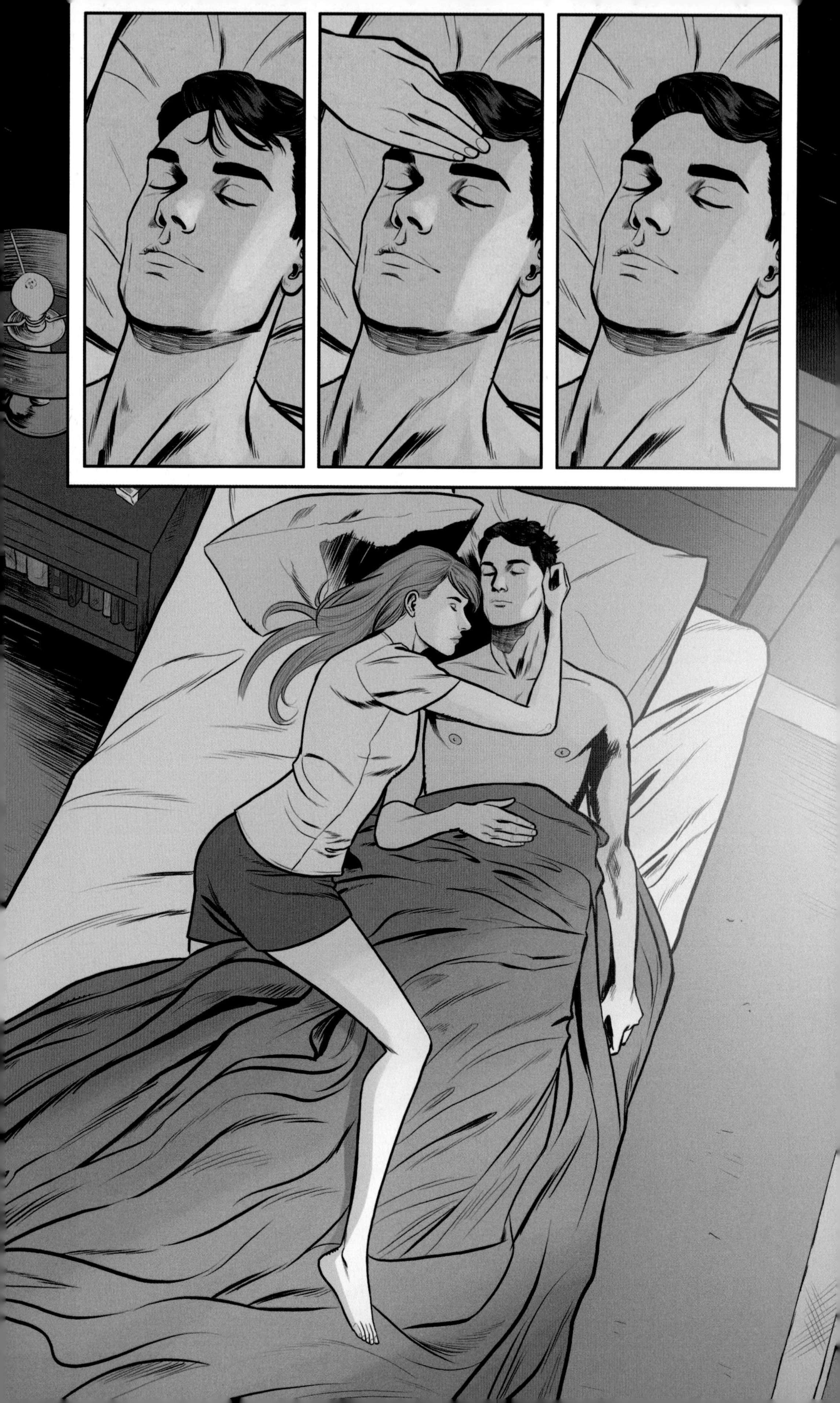

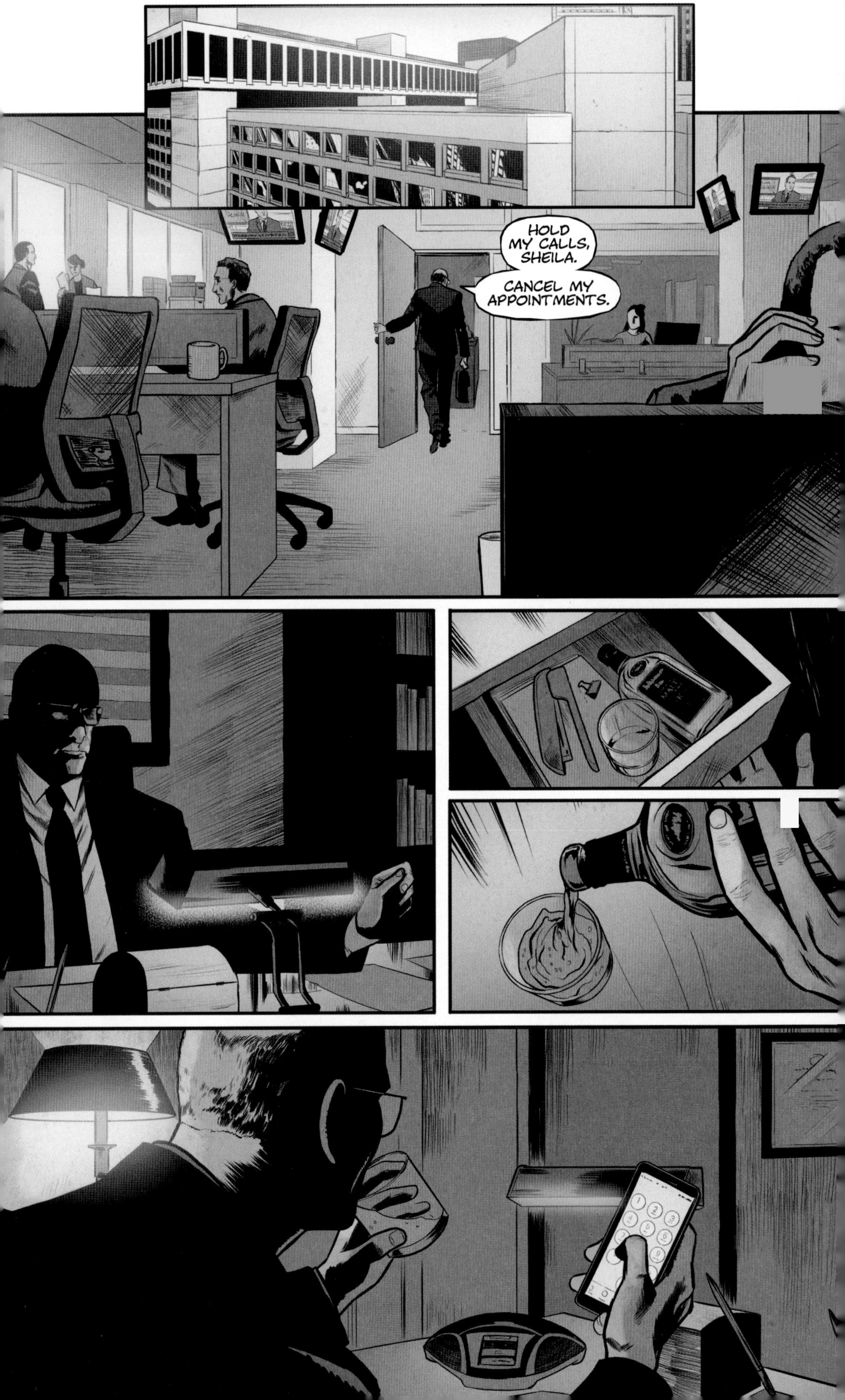
HOLD MY CALLS, SHEILA.
CANCEL MY APPOINTMENTS.

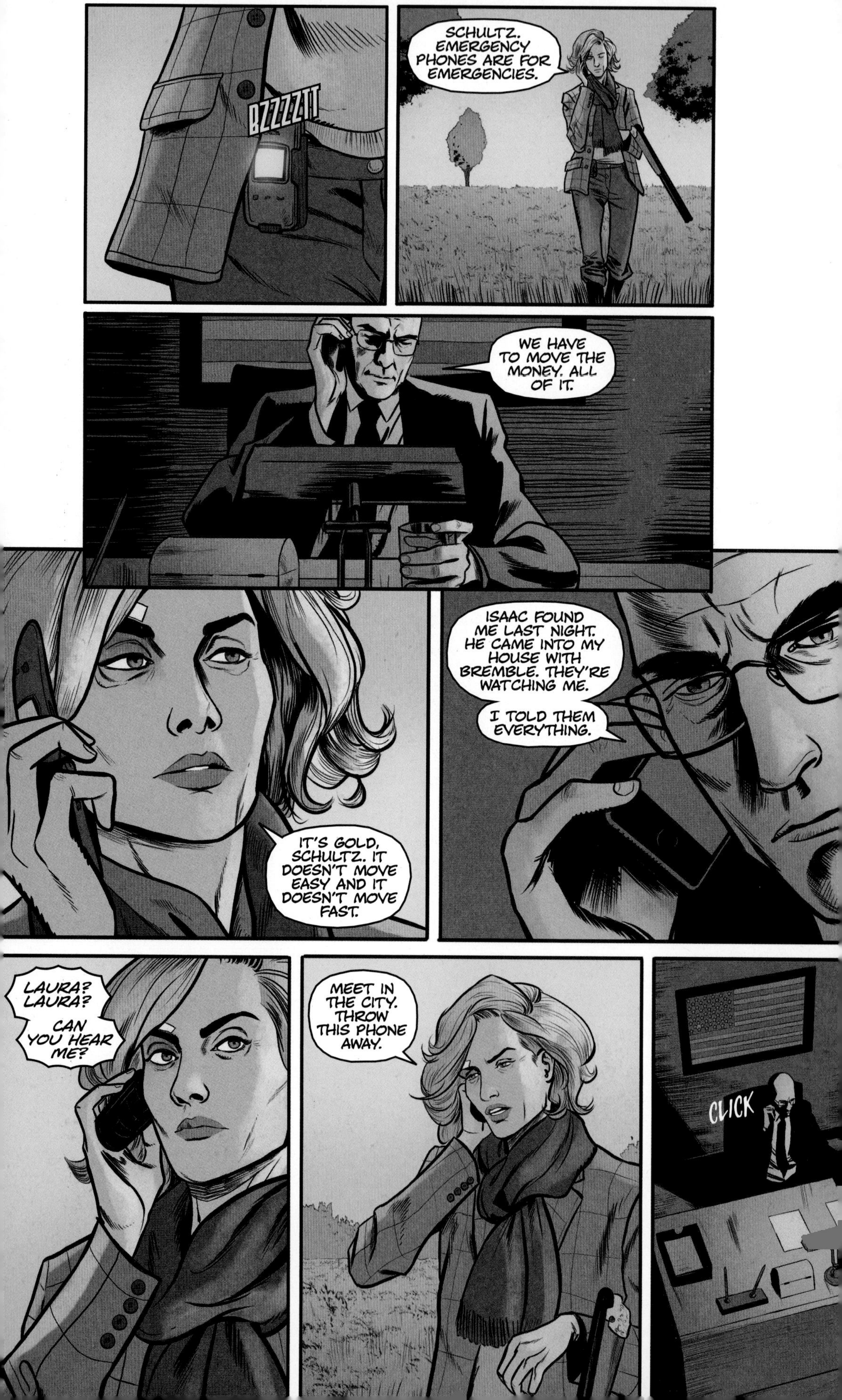
BZZZZZTT
SCHULTZ. EMERGENCY PHONES ARE FOR EMERGENCIES.
WE HAVE TO MOVE THE MONEY. ALL OF IT.
IT'S GOLD, SCHULTZ. IT DOESN'T MOVE EASY AND IT DOESN'T MOVE FAST.
ISAAC FOUND ME LAST NIGHT. HE CAME INTO MY HOUSE WITH BREMBLE. THEY'RE WATCHING ME.
I TOLD THEM EVERYTHING.
LAURA? LAURA?
CAN YOU HEAR ME?
MEET IN THE CITY. THROW THIS PHONE AWAY.
CLICK

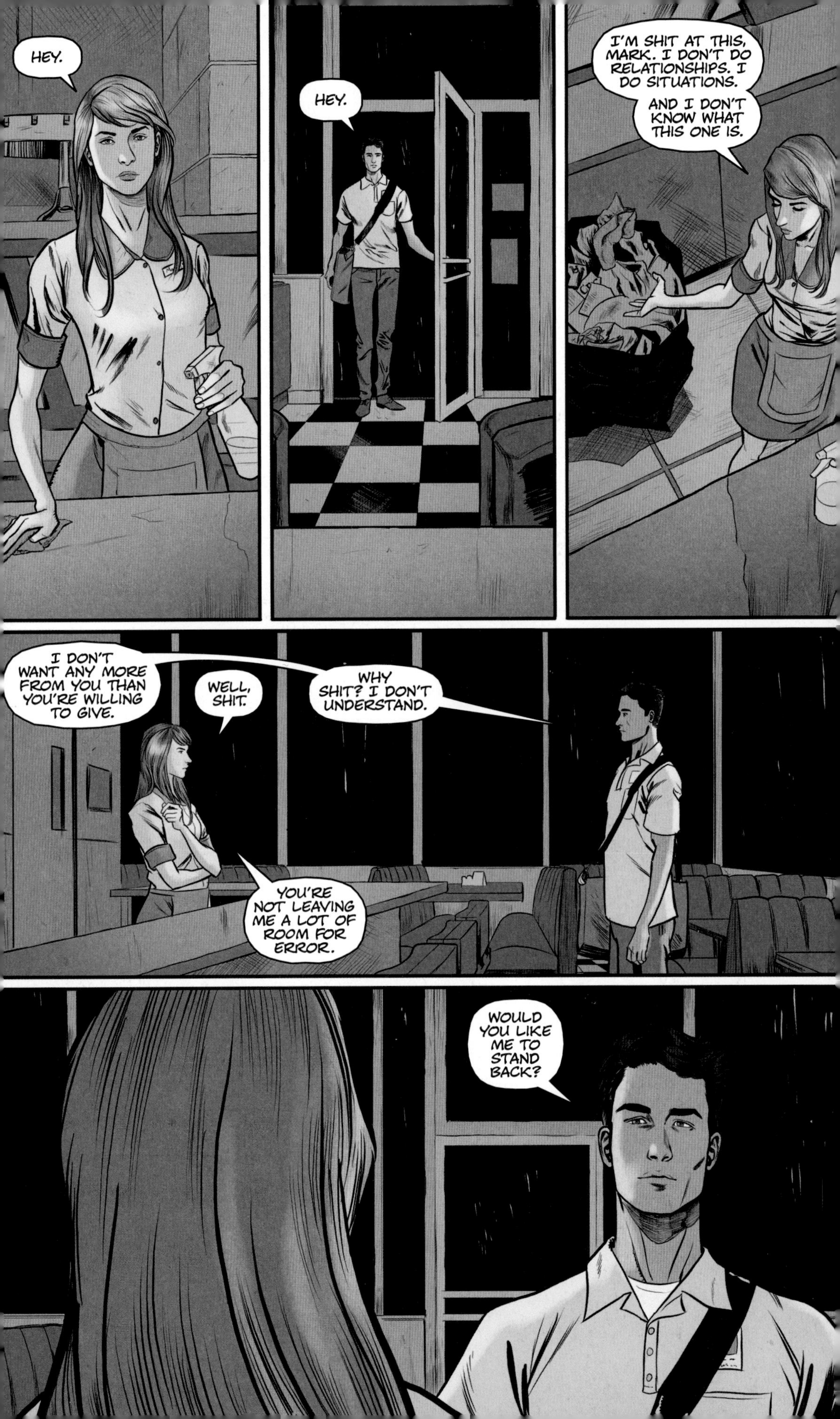
HEY.
HEY.
I'M SHIT AT THIS, MARK. I DON'T DO RELATIONSHIPS. I DO SITUATIONS.
AND I DON'T KNOW WHAT THIS ONE IS.
I DON'T WANT ANY MORE FROM YOU THAN YOU'RE WILLING TO GIVE.
WELL, SHIT.
WHY SHIT? I DON'T UNDERSTAND.
YOU'RE NOT LEAVING ME A LOT OF ROOM FOR ERROR.
WOULD YOU LIKE ME TO STAND BACK?

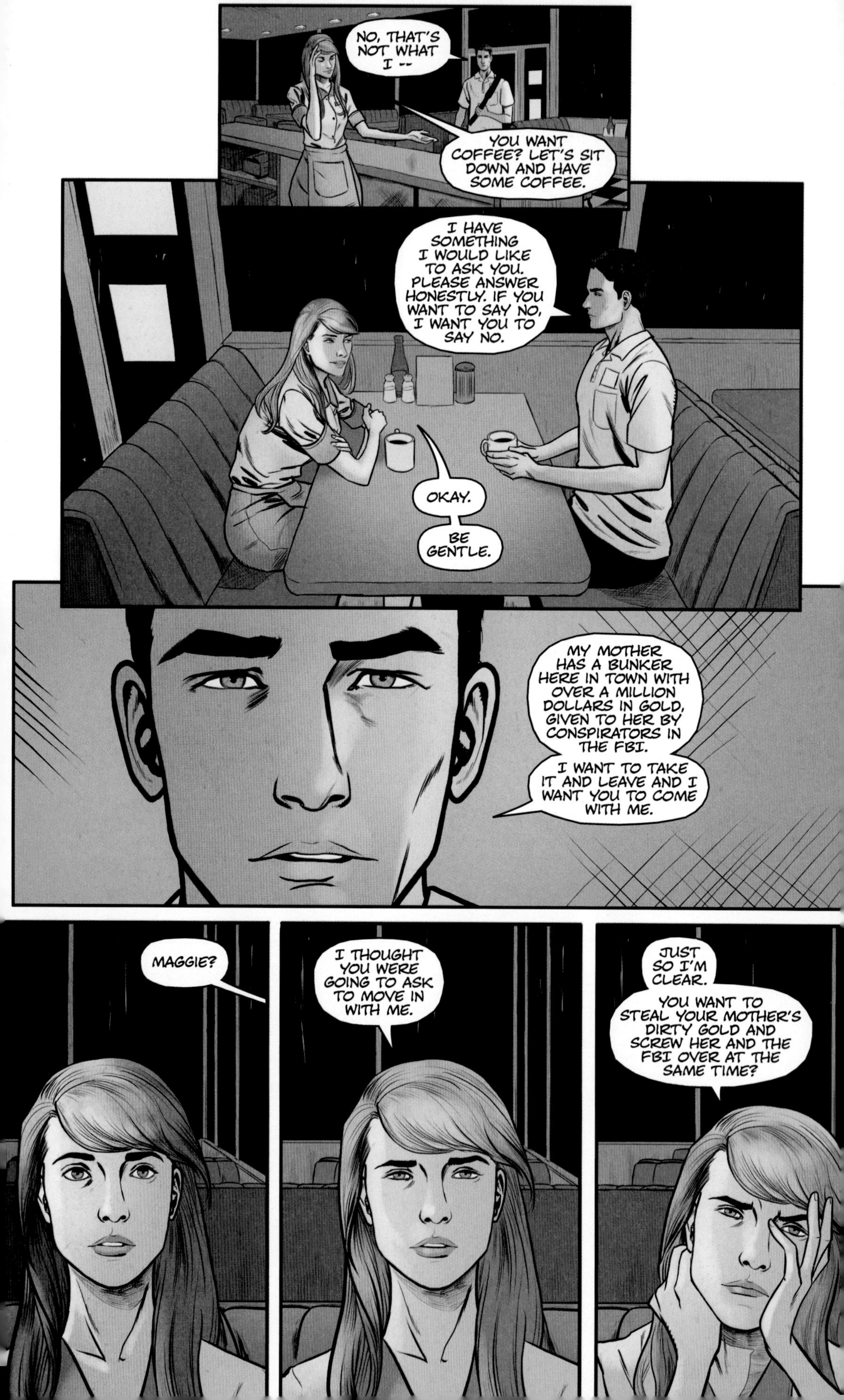
NO, THAT'S NOT WHAT I --
YOU WANT COFFEE? LET'S SIT DOWN AND HAVE SOME COFFEE.
I HAVE SOMETHING I WOULD LIKE TO ASK YOU. PLEASE ANSWER HONESTLY. IF YOU WANT TO SAY NO, I WANT YOU TO SAY NO.
OKAY.
BE GENTLE.
MY MOTHER HAS A BUNKER HERE IN TOWN WITH OVER A MILLION DOLLARS IN GOLD, GIVEN TO HER BY CONSPIRATORS IN THE FBI.
I WANT TO TAKE IT AND LEAVE AND I WANT YOU TO COME WITH ME.
MAGGIE?
I THOUGHT YOU WERE GOING TO ASK TO MOVE IN WITH ME.
JUST SO I'M CLEAR.
YOU WANT TO STEAL YOUR MOTHER'S DIRTY GOLD AND SCREW HER AND THE FBI OVER AT THE SAME TIME?

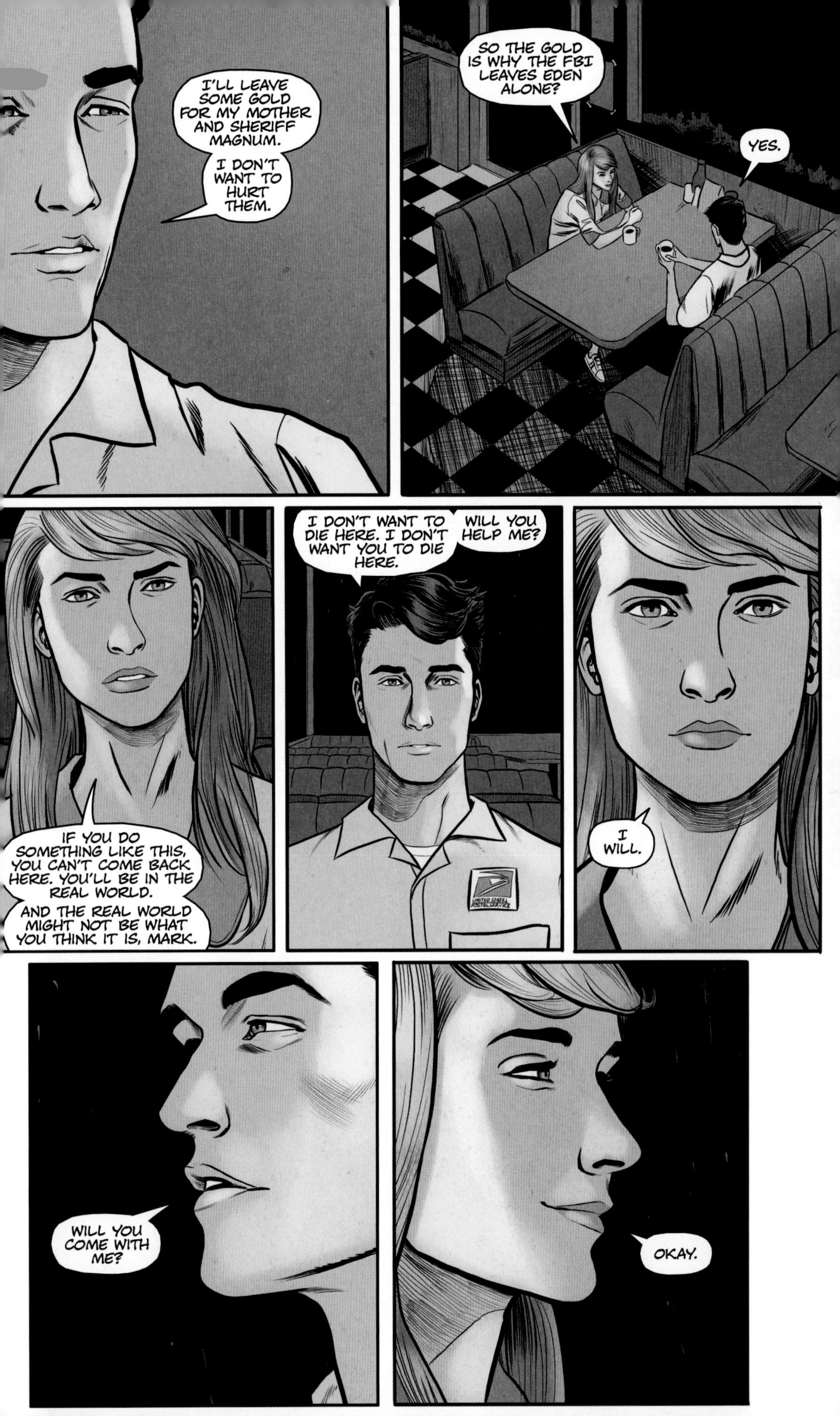
I'LL LEAVE SOME GOLD FOR MY MOTHER AND SHERIFF MAGNUM.
I DON'T WANT TO HURT THEM.
SO THE GOLD IS WHY THE FBI LEAVES EDEN ALONE?
YES.
IF YOU DO SOMETHING LIKE THIS, YOU CAN'T COME BACK HERE. YOU'LL BE IN THE REAL WORLD.
AND THE REAL WORLD MIGHT NOT BE WHAT YOU THINK IT IS, MARK.
I DON'T WANT TO DIE HERE. I DON'T WANT YOU TO DIE HERE.
WILL YOU HELP ME?
I WILL.
WILL YOU COME WITH ME?
OKAY.

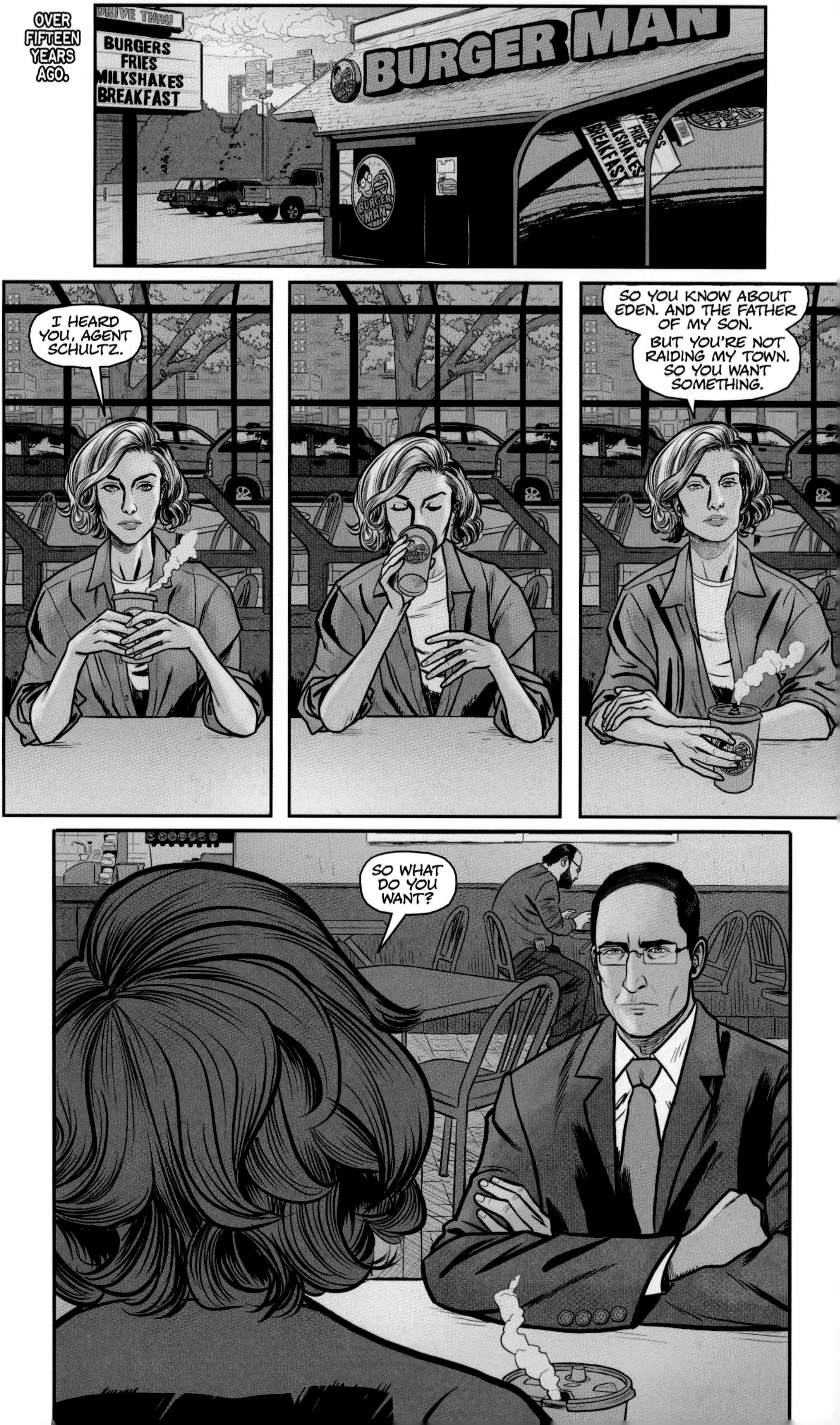
OVER FIFTEEN YEARS AGO.
DRIVE THRU
BURGERS
FRIES
MILKSHAKES
BREAKFAST
BURGER MAN
BURGER MAN
I HEARD YOU, AGENT SCHULTZ.
SO YOU KNOW ABOUT EDEN. AND THE FATHER OF MY SON.
BUT YOU'RE NOT RAIDING MY TOWN. SO YOU WANT SOMETHING.
SO WHAT DO YOU WANT?

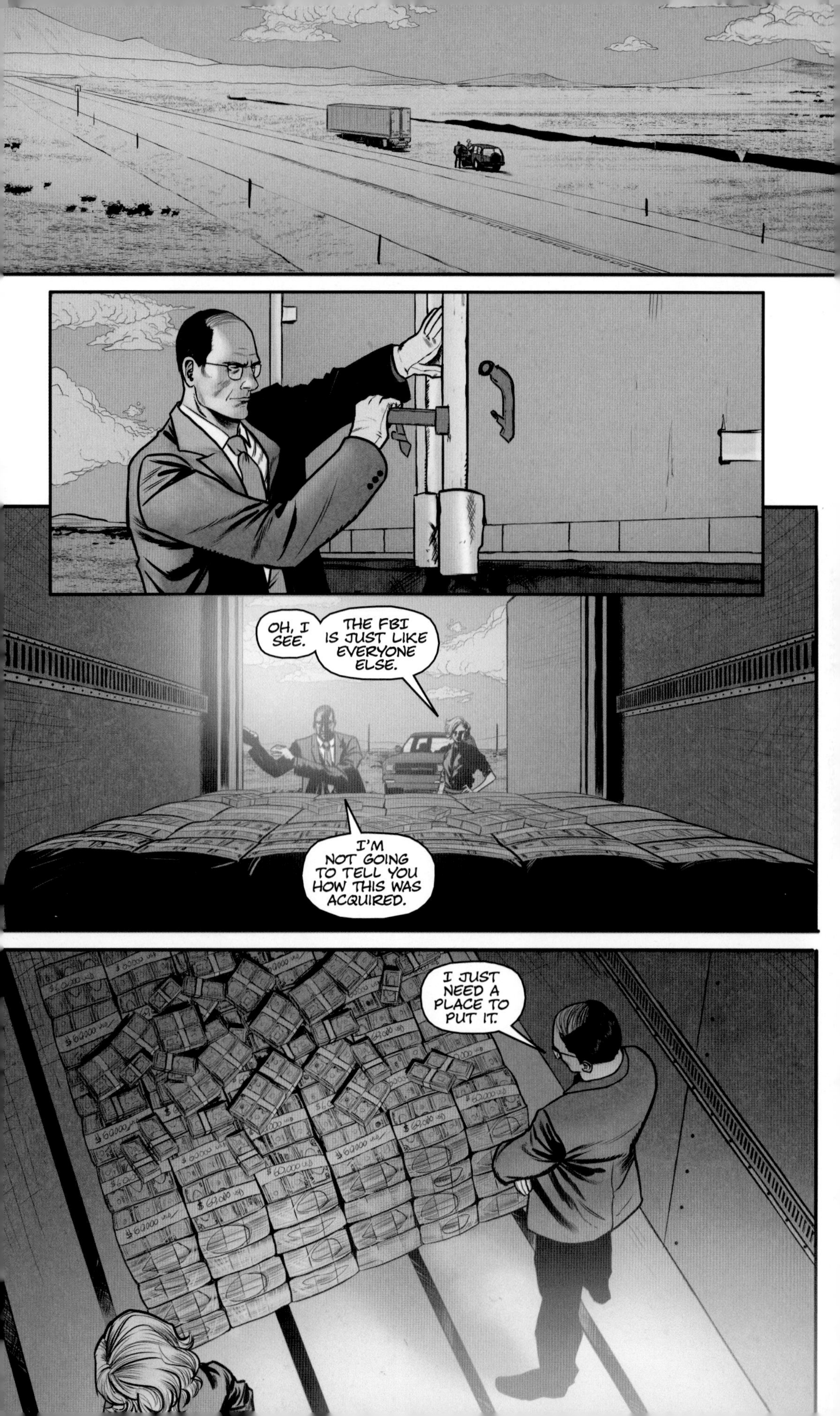
OH, I SEE.
THE FBI IS JUST LIKE EVERYONE ELSE.
I'M NOT GOING TO TELL YOU HOW THIS WAS ACQUIRED.
I JUST NEED A PLACE TO PUT IT.

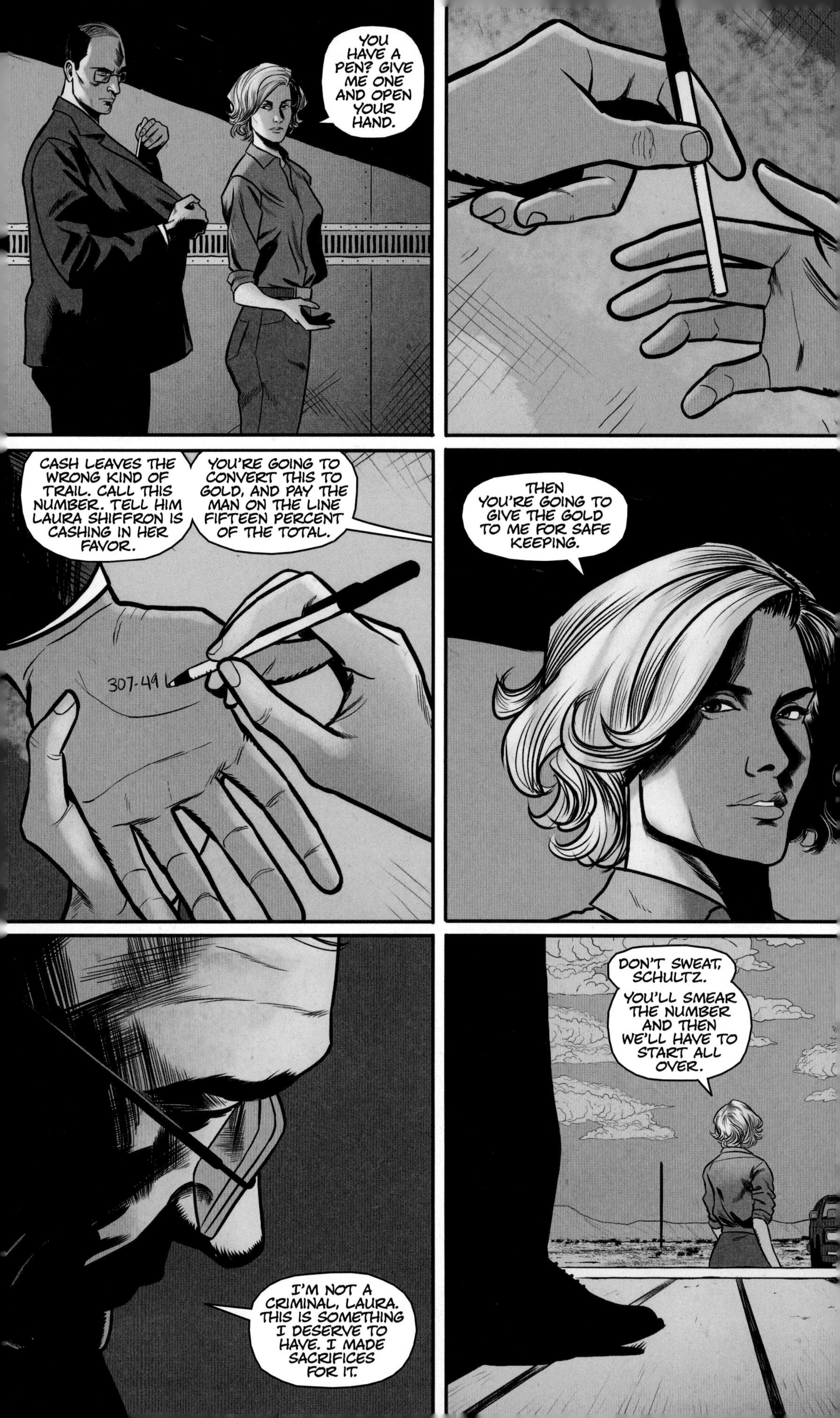
YOU HAVE A PEN? GIVE ME ONE AND OPEN YOUR HAND.
CASH LEAVES THE WRONG KIND OF TRAIL. CALL THIS NUMBER. TELL HIM LAURA SHIFFRON IS CASHING IN HER FAVOR.
YOU'RE GOING TO CONVERT THIS TO GOLD, AND PAY THE MAN ON THE LINE FIFTEEN PERCENT OF THE TOTAL.
307-49
THEN YOU'RE GOING TO GIVE THE GOLD TO ME FOR SAFE KEEPING.
I'M NOT A CRIMINAL, LAURA. THIS IS SOMETHING I DESERVE TO HAVE. I MADE SACRIFICES FOR IT.
DON'T SWEAT, SCHULTZ.
YOU'LL SMEAR THE NUMBER AND THEN WE'LL HAVE TO START ALL OVER.

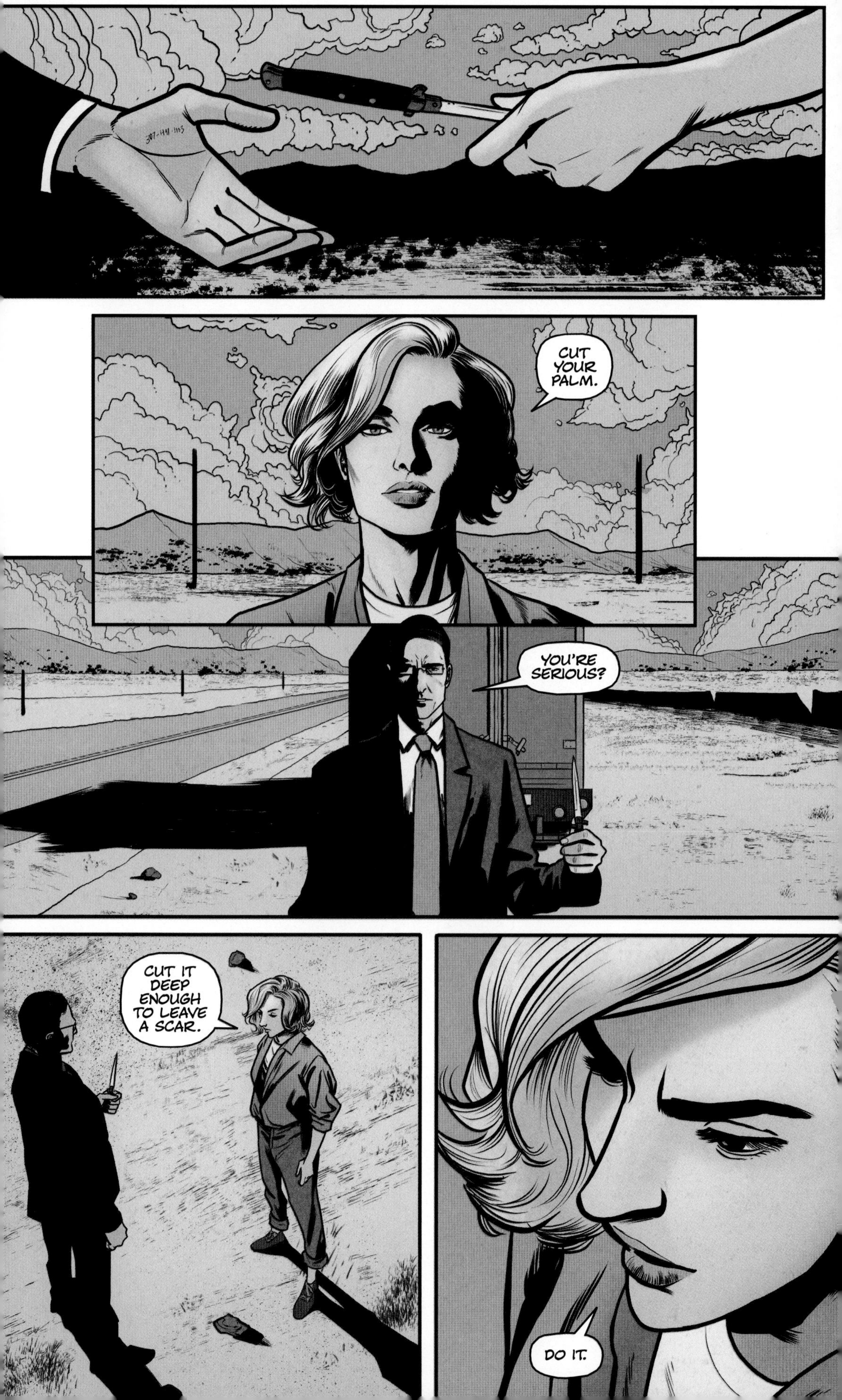
CUT YOUR PALM.
YOU'RE SERIOUS?
CUT IT DEEP ENOUGH TO LEAVE A SCAR.
DO IT.

PAY ATTENTION, SCHULTZ.

WHEN YOU REMEMBER YOUR MONEY, AND OUR BARGAIN --

REMEMBER WHAT I'M KEEPING FOR YOU.

THE GOLD --

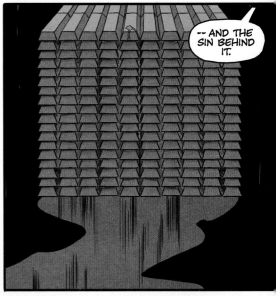

-- AND THE SIN BEHIND IT.

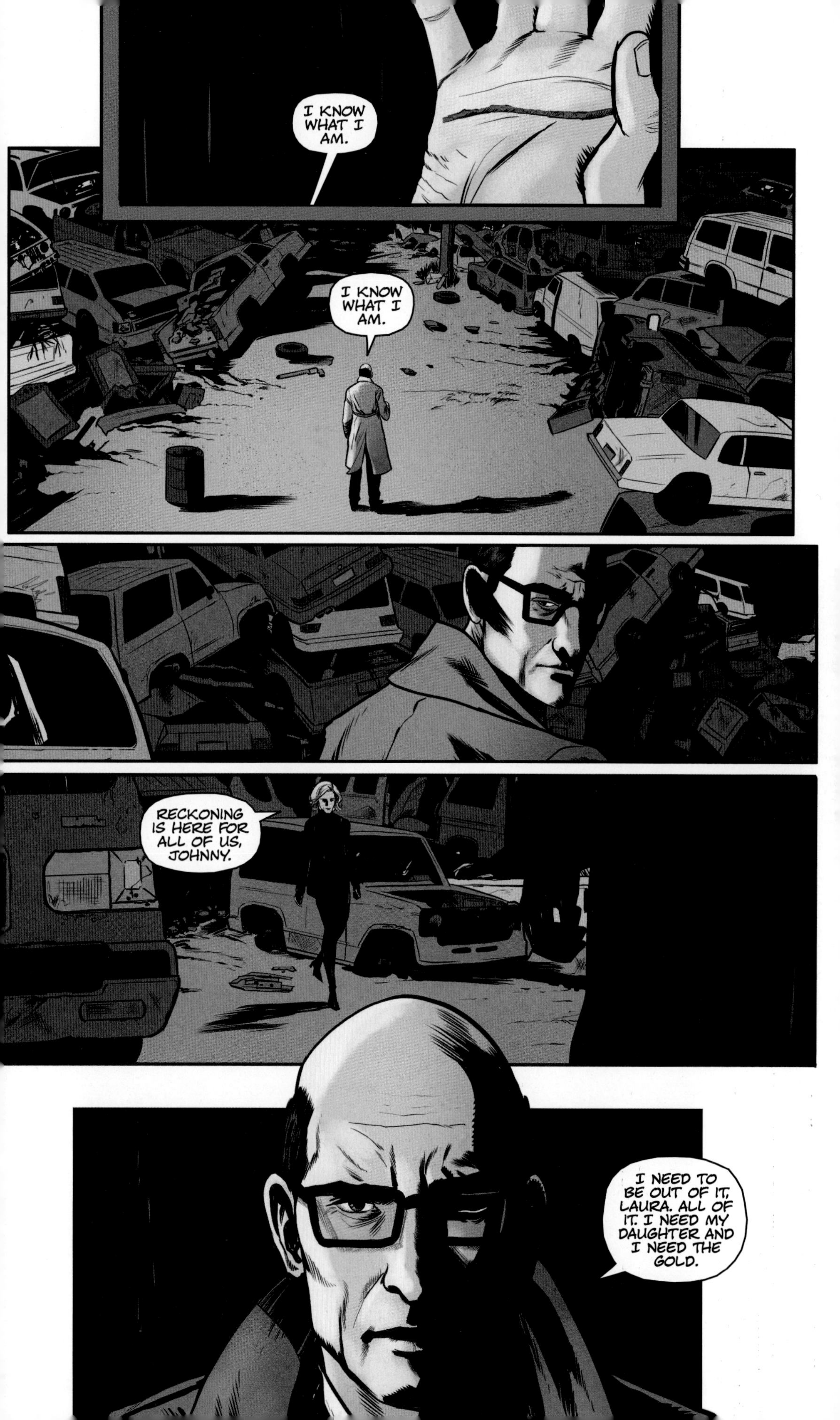
I KNOW WHAT I AM.
I KNOW WHAT I AM.
RECKONING IS HERE FOR ALL OF US, JOHNNY.
I NEED TO BE OUT OF IT, LAURA. ALL OF IT. I NEED MY DAUGHTER AND I NEED THE GOLD.

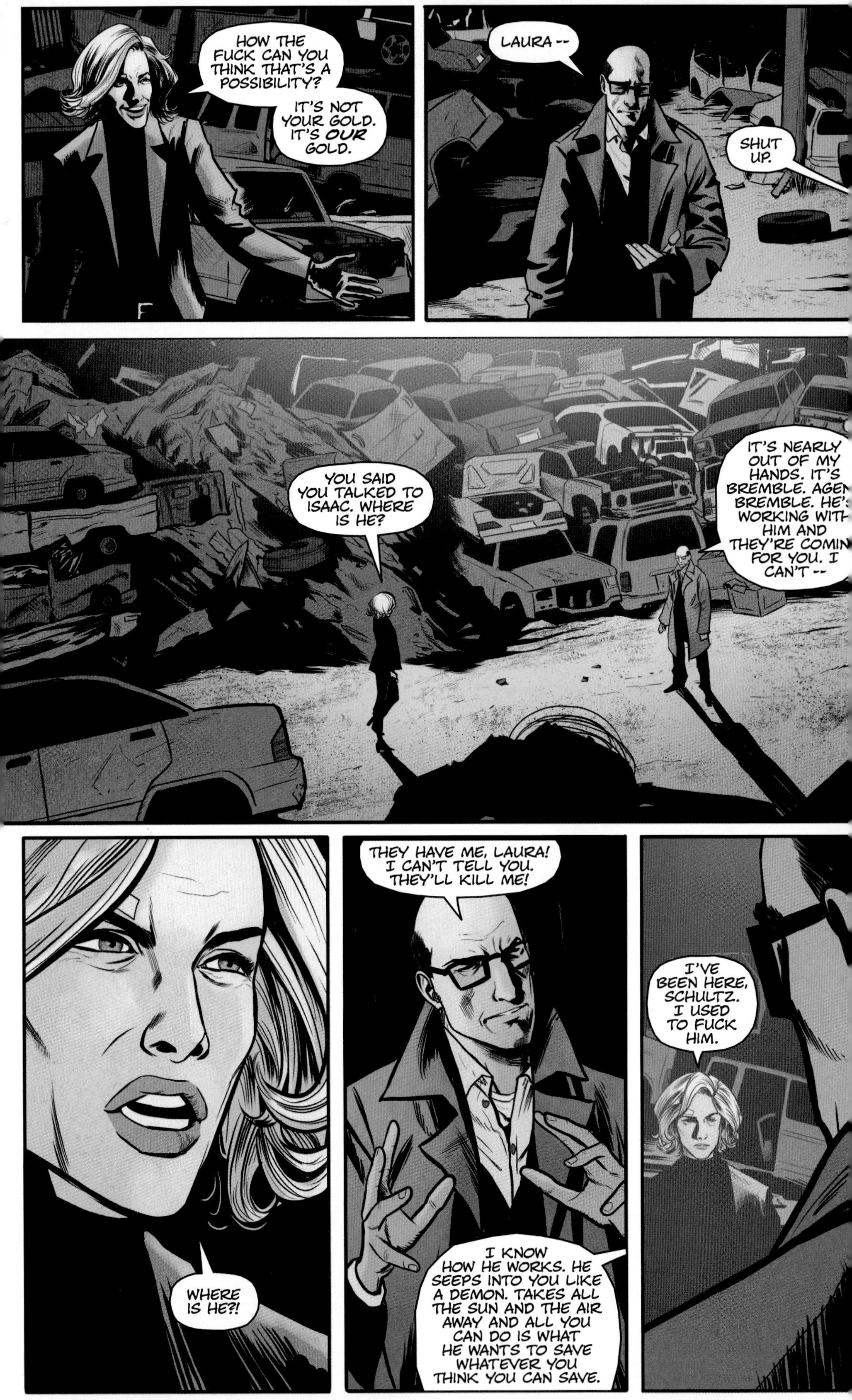
HOW THE FUCK CAN YOU THINK THAT'S A POSSIBILITY?
IT'S NOT YOUR GOLD. IT'S *OUR* GOLD.
LAURA --
SHUT UP.
YOU SAID YOU TALKED TO ISAAC. WHERE IS HE?
IT'S NEARLY OUT OF MY HANDS. IT'S BREMBLE. AGEN BREMBLE. HE'S WORKING WITH HIM AND THEY'RE COMIN FOR YOU. I CAN'T --
WHERE IS HE?!
THEY HAVE ME, LAURA! I CAN'T TELL YOU. THEY'LL KILL ME!
I KNOW HOW HE WORKS. HE SEEPS INTO YOU LIKE A DEMON. TAKES ALL THE SUN AND THE AIR AWAY AND ALL YOU CAN DO IS WHAT HE WANTS TO SAVE WHATEVER YOU THINK YOU CAN SAVE.
I'VE BEEN HERE, SCHULTZ. I USED TO FUCK HIM.

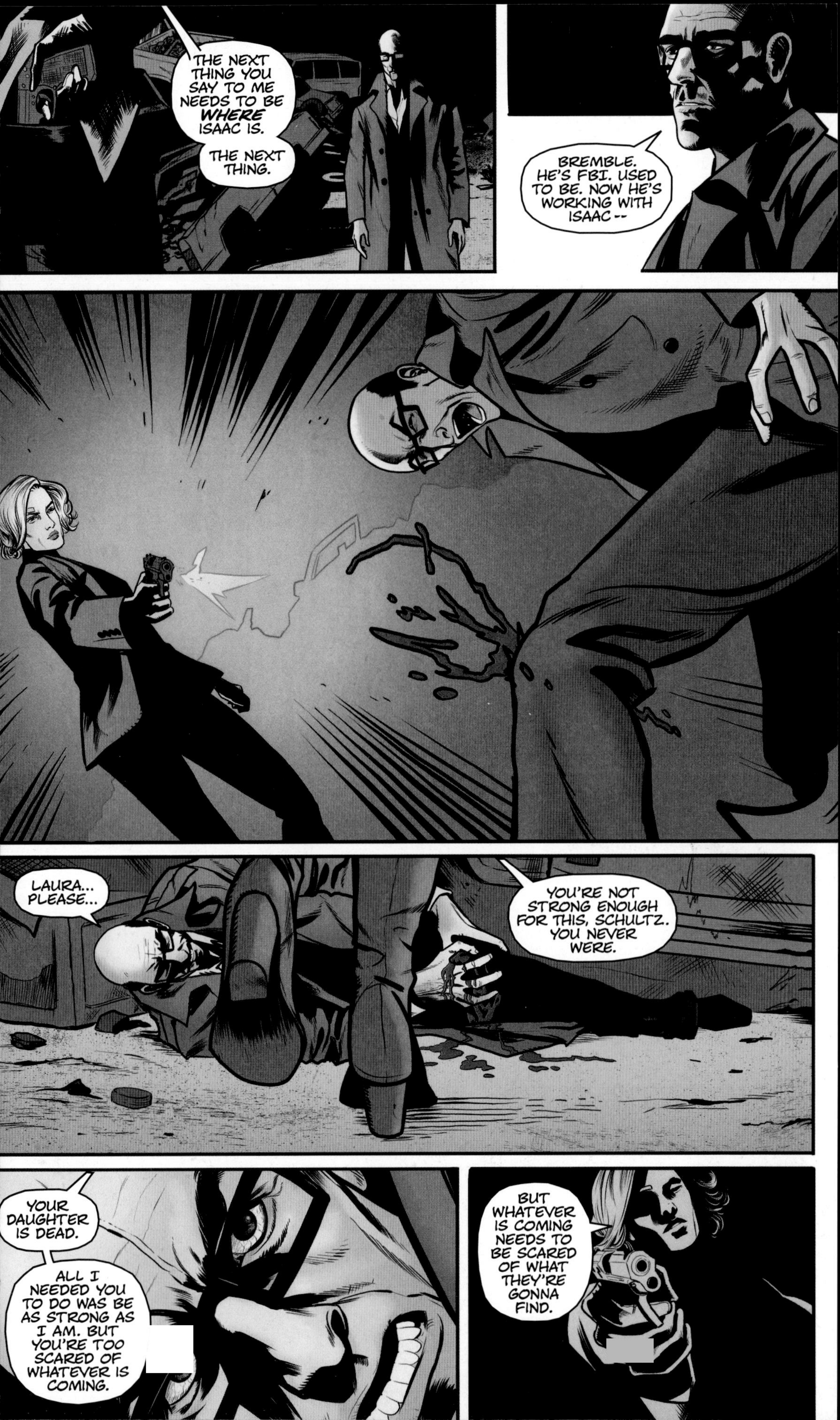
THE NEXT THING YOU SAY TO ME NEEDS TO BE *WHERE* ISAAC IS.
THE NEXT THING.
BREMBLE. HE'S FBI. USED TO BE. NOW HE'S WORKING WITH ISAAC --
LAURA... PLEASE...
YOU'RE NOT STRONG ENOUGH FOR THIS, SCHULTZ. YOU NEVER WERE.
YOUR DAUGHTER IS DEAD.
ALL I NEEDED YOU TO DO WAS BE AS STRONG AS I AM. BUT YOU'RE TOO SCARED OF WHATEVER IS COMING.
BUT WHATEVER IS COMING NEEDS TO BE SCARED OF WHAT THEY'RE GONNA FIND.

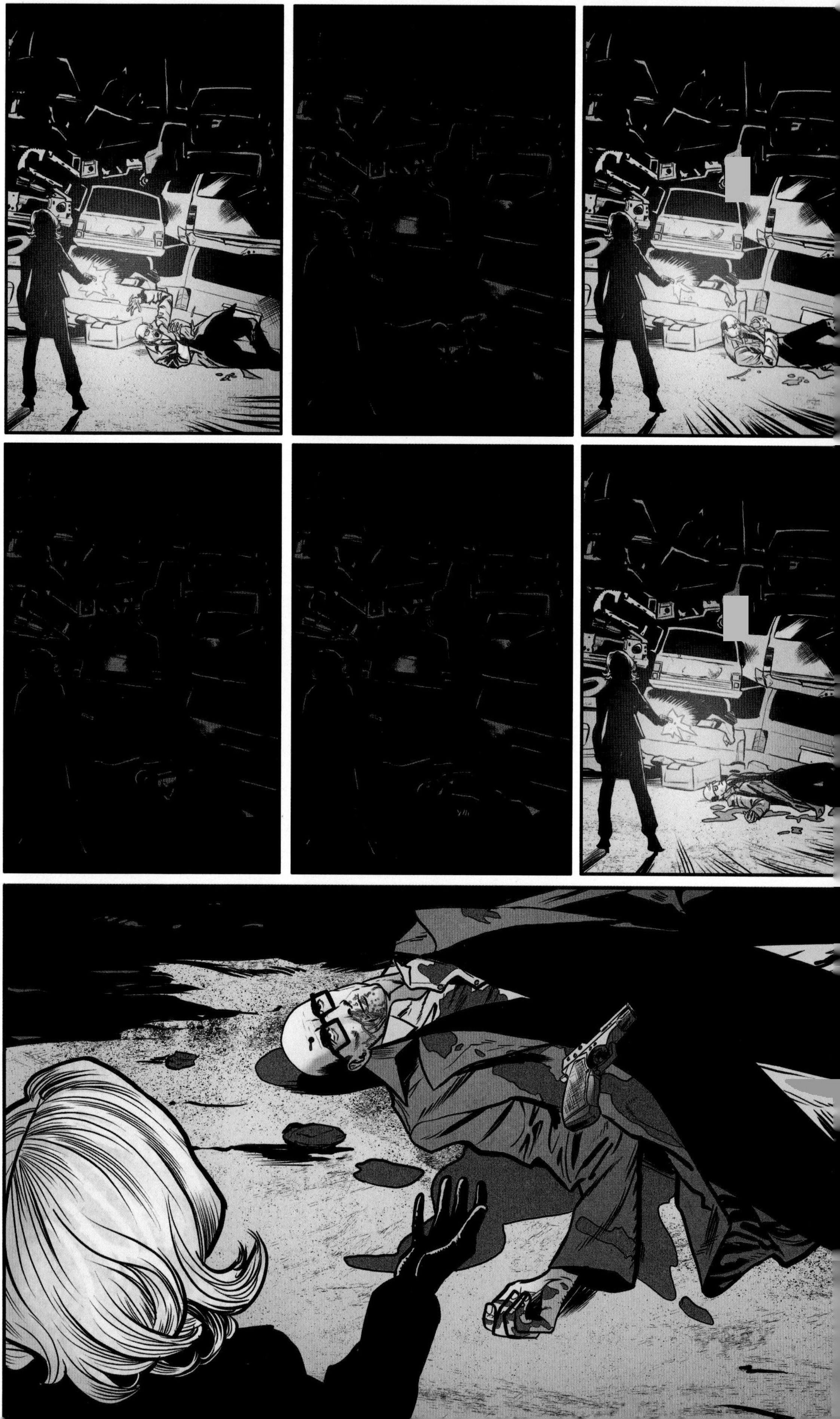

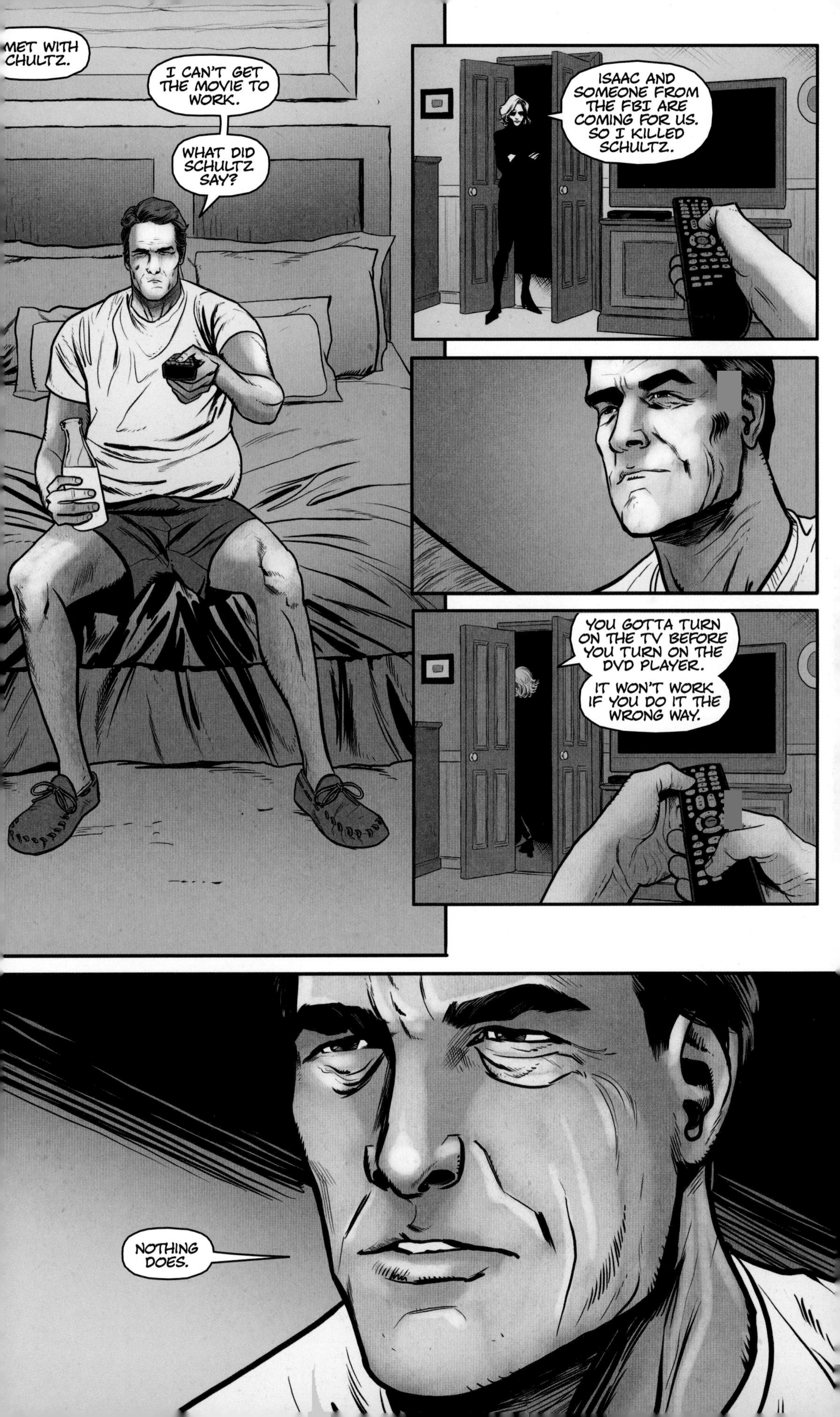
MET WITH
CHULTZ.
I CAN'T GET THE MOVIE TO WORK.
WHAT DID SCHULTZ SAY?
ISAAC AND SOMEONE FROM THE FBI ARE COMING FOR US. SO I KILLED SCHULTZ.
YOU GOTTA TURN ON THE TV BEFORE YOU TURN ON THE DVD PLAYER.
IT WON'T WORK IF YOU DO IT THE WRONG WAY.
NOTHING DOES.

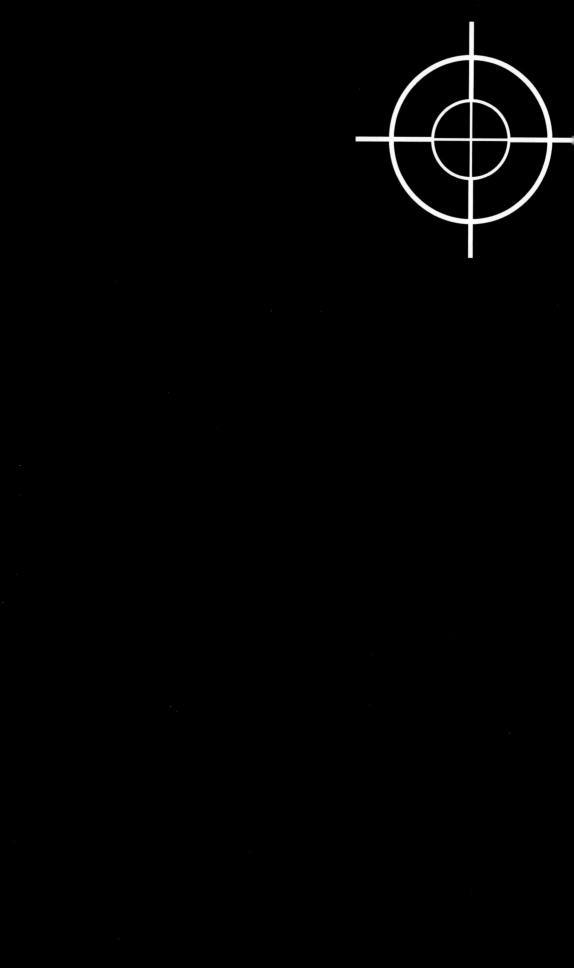

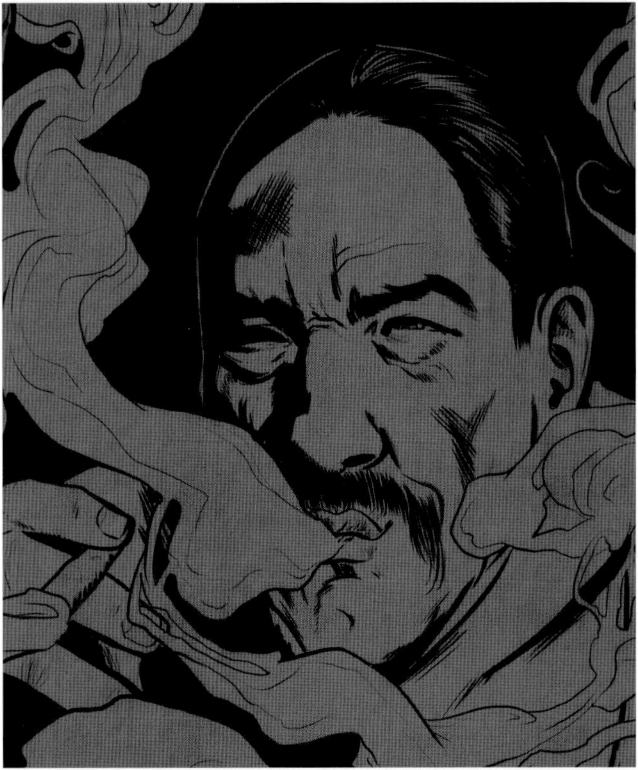

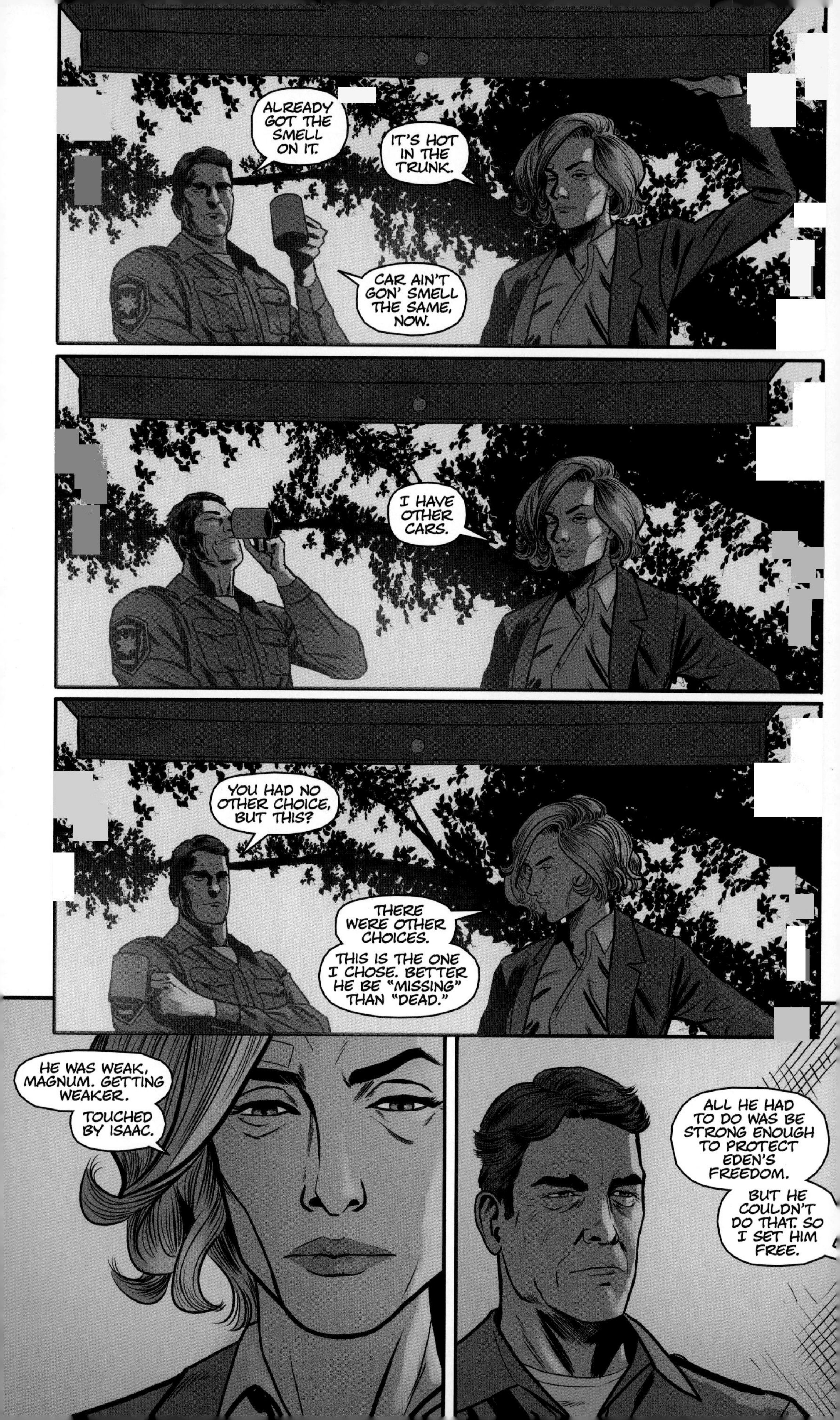
ALREADY GOT THE SMELL ON IT.
IT'S HOT IN THE TRUNK.
CAR AIN'T GON' SMELL THE SAME, NOW.
I HAVE OTHER CARS.
YOU HAD NO OTHER CHOICE, BUT THIS?
THERE WERE OTHER CHOICES.
THIS IS THE ONE I CHOSE. BETTER HE BE "MISSING" THAN "DEAD."
HE WAS WEAK, MAGNUM. GETTING WEAKER.
TOUCHED BY ISAAC.
ALL HE HAD TO DO WAS BE STRONG ENOUGH TO PROTECT EDEN'S FREEDOM.
BUT HE COULDN'T DO THAT. SO I SET HIM FREE.

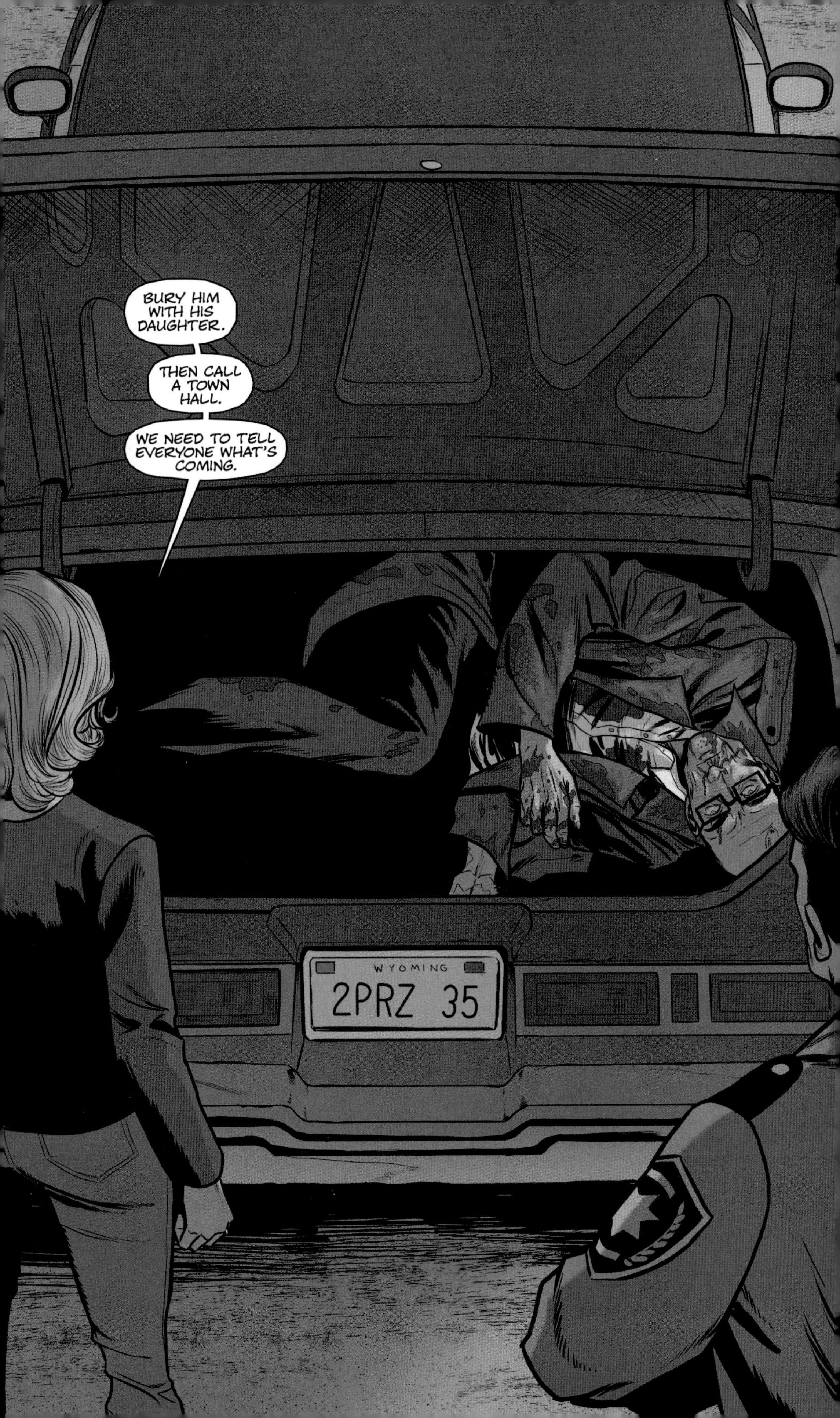
BURY HIM WITH HIS DAUGHTER.
THEN CALL A TOWN HALL.
WE NEED TO TELL EVERYONE WHAT'S COMING.
WYOMING
2PRZ 35

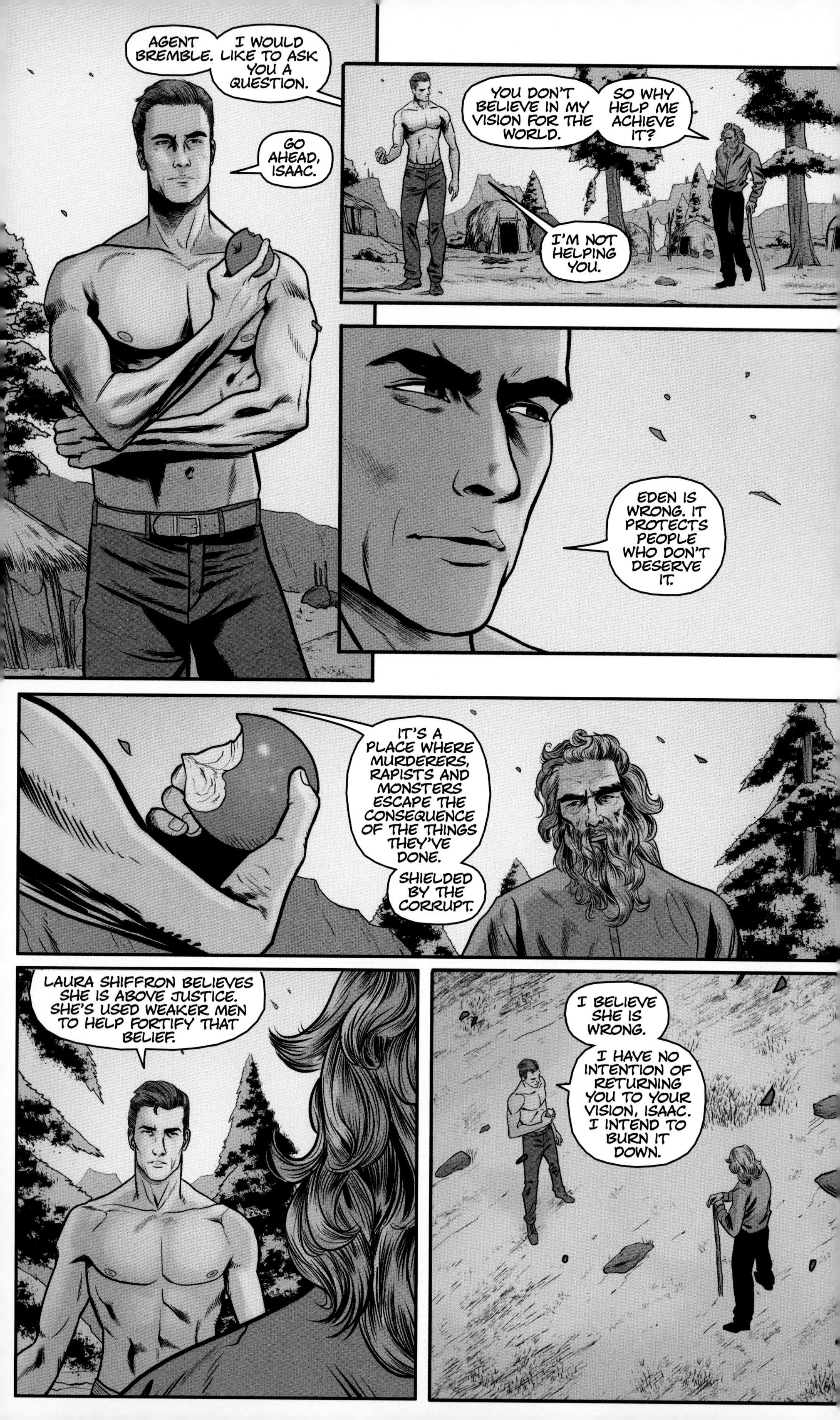
AGENT BREMBLE.
I WOULD LIKE TO ASK YOU A QUESTION.
GO AHEAD, ISAAC.
YOU DON'T BELIEVE IN MY VISION FOR THE WORLD.
SO WHY HELP ME ACHIEVE IT?
I'M NOT HELPING YOU.
EDEN IS WRONG. IT PROTECTS PEOPLE WHO DON'T DESERVE IT.
IT'S A PLACE WHERE MURDERERS, RAPISTS AND MONSTERS ESCAPE THE CONSEQUENCE OF THE THINGS THEY'VE DONE.
SHIELDED BY THE CORRUPT.
LAURA SHIFFRON BELIEVES SHE IS ABOVE JUSTICE. SHE'S USED WEAKER MEN TO HELP FORTIFY THAT BELIEF.
I BELIEVE SHE IS WRONG.
I HAVE NO INTENTION OF RETURNING YOU TO YOUR VISION, ISAAC. I INTEND TO BURN IT DOWN.

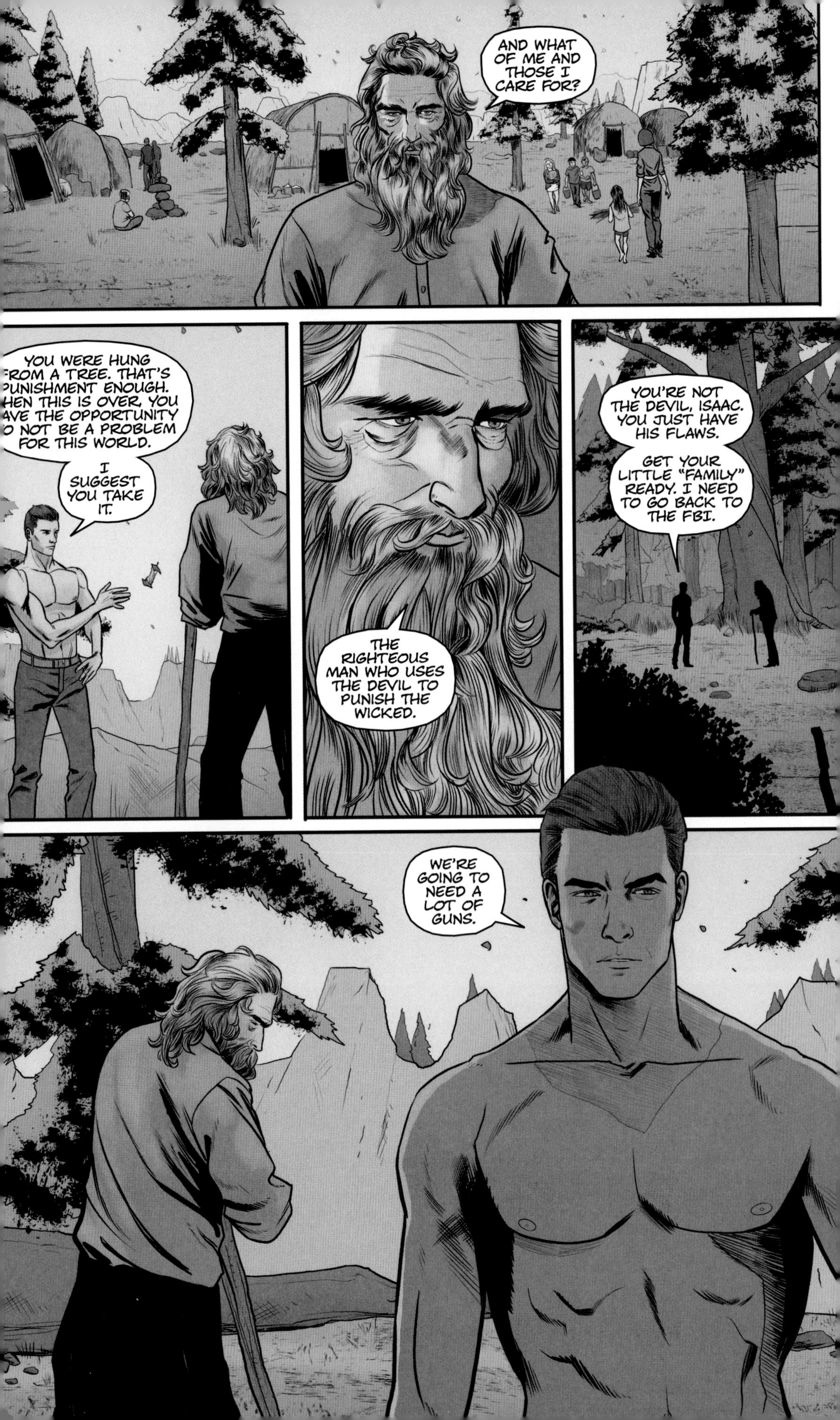
AND WHAT OF ME AND THOSE I CARE FOR?
YOU WERE HUNG FROM A TREE. THAT'S PUNISHMENT ENOUGH. WHEN THIS IS OVER, YOU HAVE THE OPPORTUNITY TO NOT BE A PROBLEM FOR THIS WORLD.
I SUGGEST YOU TAKE IT.
THE RIGHTEOUS MAN WHO USES THE DEVIL TO PUNISH THE WICKED.
YOU'RE NOT THE DEVIL, ISAAC. YOU JUST HAVE HIS FLAWS.
GET YOUR LITTLE "FAMILY" READY. I NEED TO GO BACK TO THE FBI.
WE'RE GOING TO NEED A LOT OF GUNS.

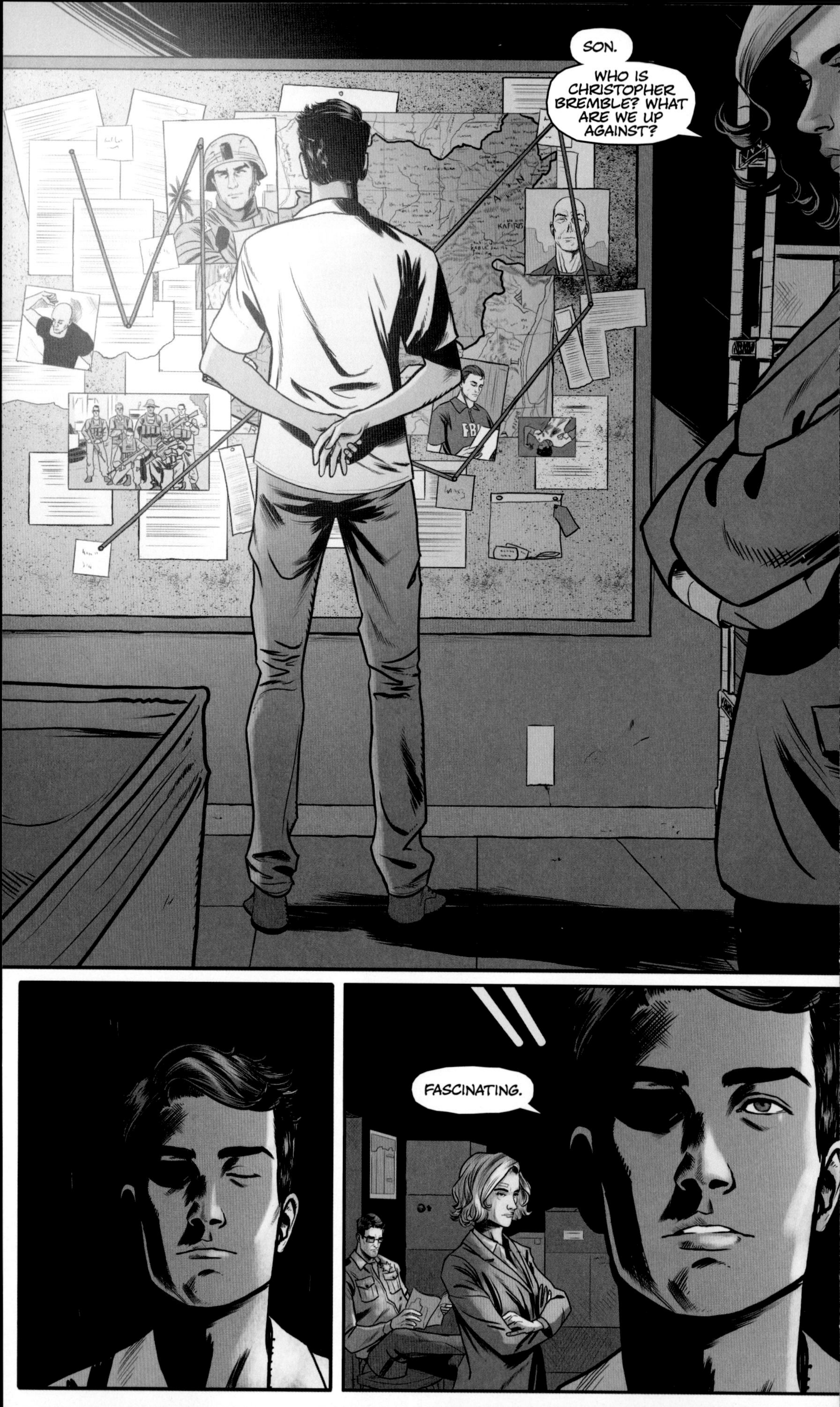
SON.
WHO IS CHRISTOPHER BREMBLE? WHAT ARE WE UP AGAINST?
FASCINATING.

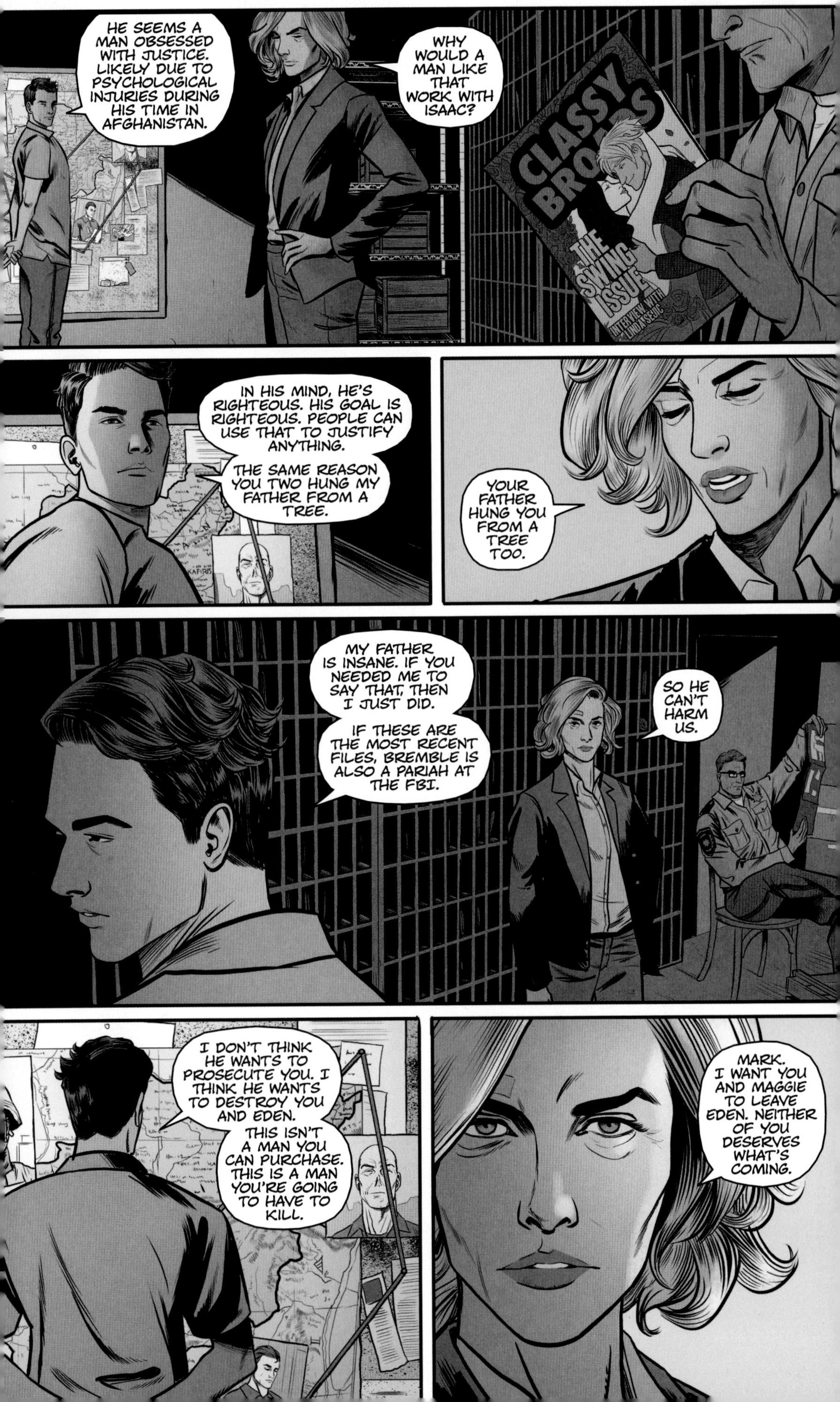

HE SEEMS A MAN OBSESSED WITH JUSTICE. LIKELY DUE TO PSYCHOLOGICAL INJURIES DURING HIS TIME IN AFGHANISTAN.
WHY WOULD A MAN LIKE THAT WORK WITH ISAAC?
THE SWING ISSUE
IN HIS MIND, HE'S RIGHTEOUS. HIS GOAL IS RIGHTEOUS. PEOPLE CAN USE THAT TO JUSTIFY ANYTHING.
THE SAME REASON YOU TWO HUNG MY FATHER FROM A TREE.
YOUR FATHER HUNG YOU FROM A TREE TOO.
MY FATHER IS INSANE. IF YOU NEEDED ME TO SAY THAT, THEN I JUST DID.
IF THESE ARE THE MOST RECENT FILES, BREMBLE IS ALSO A PARIAH AT THE FBI.
SO HE CAN'T HARM US.
I DON'T THINK HE WANTS TO PROSECUTE YOU. I THINK HE WANTS TO DESTROY YOU AND EDEN.
THIS ISN'T A MAN YOU CAN PURCHASE. THIS IS A MAN YOU'RE GOING TO HAVE TO KILL.
MARK. I WANT YOU AND MAGGIE TO LEAVE EDEN. NEITHER OF YOU DESERVES WHAT'S COMING.

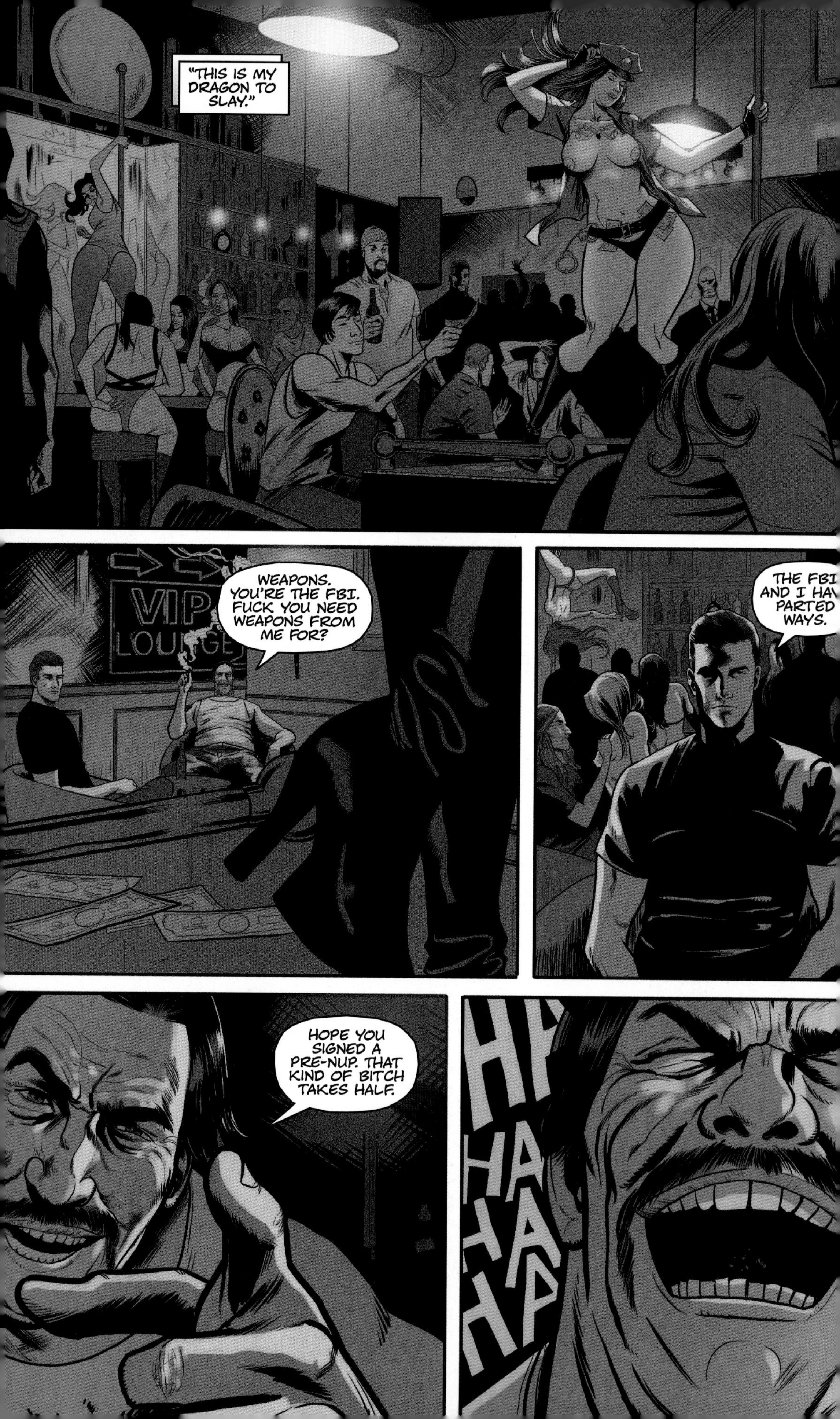
"THIS IS MY DRAGON TO SLAY."
VIP LOUNGE
WEAPONS. YOU'RE THE FBI. FUCK YOU NEED WEAPONS FROM ME FOR?
THE FBI AND I HAV PARTED WAYS.
HOPE YOU SIGNED A PRE-NUP. THAT KIND OF BITCH TAKES HALF.
HA HA HA HA

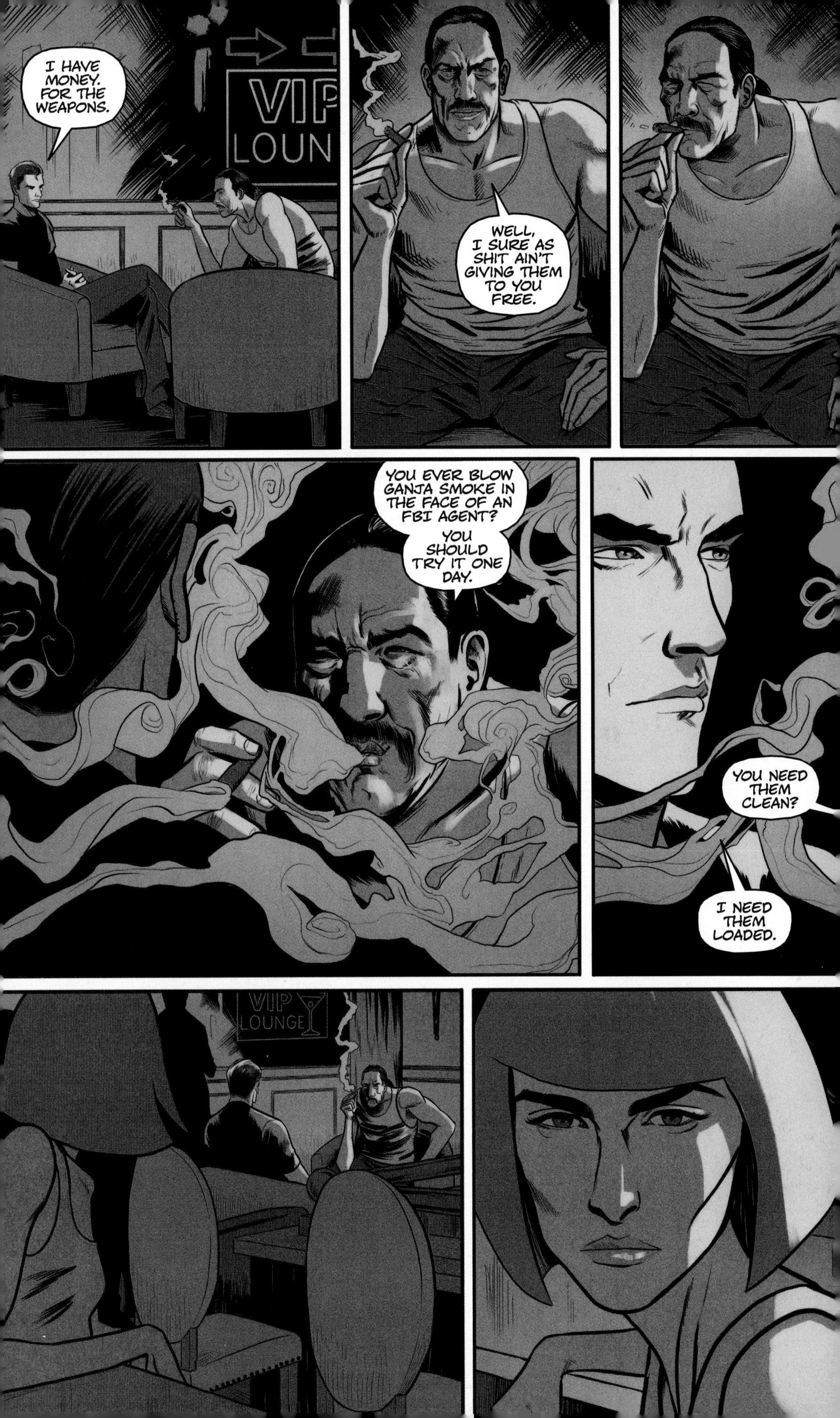
VIP
LOUNGE
I HAVE MONEY. FOR THE WEAPONS.
WELL, I SURE AS SHIT AIN'T GIVING THEM TO YOU FREE.
YOU EVER BLOW GANJA SMOKE IN THE FACE OF AN FBI AGENT?
YOU SHOULD TRY IT ONE DAY.
YOU NEED THEM CLEAN?
I NEED THEM LOADED.
VIP
LOUNGE

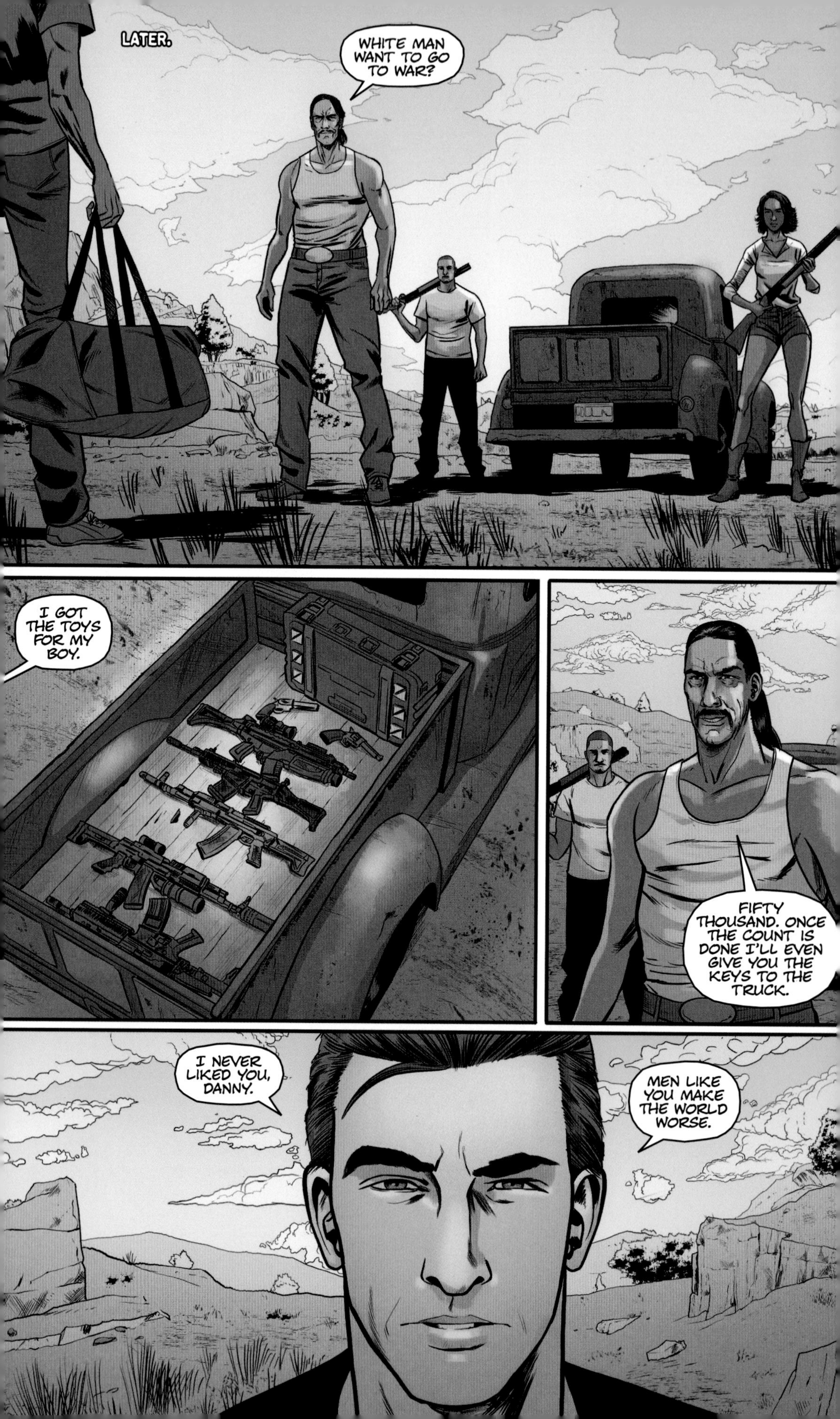
LATER.
WHITE MAN WANT TO GO TO WAR?
I GOT THE TOYS FOR MY BOY.
FIFTY THOUSAND. ONCE THE COUNT IS DONE I'LL EVEN GIVE YOU THE KEYS TO THE TRUCK.
I NEVER LIKED YOU, DANNY.
MEN LIKE YOU MAKE THE WORLD WORSE.

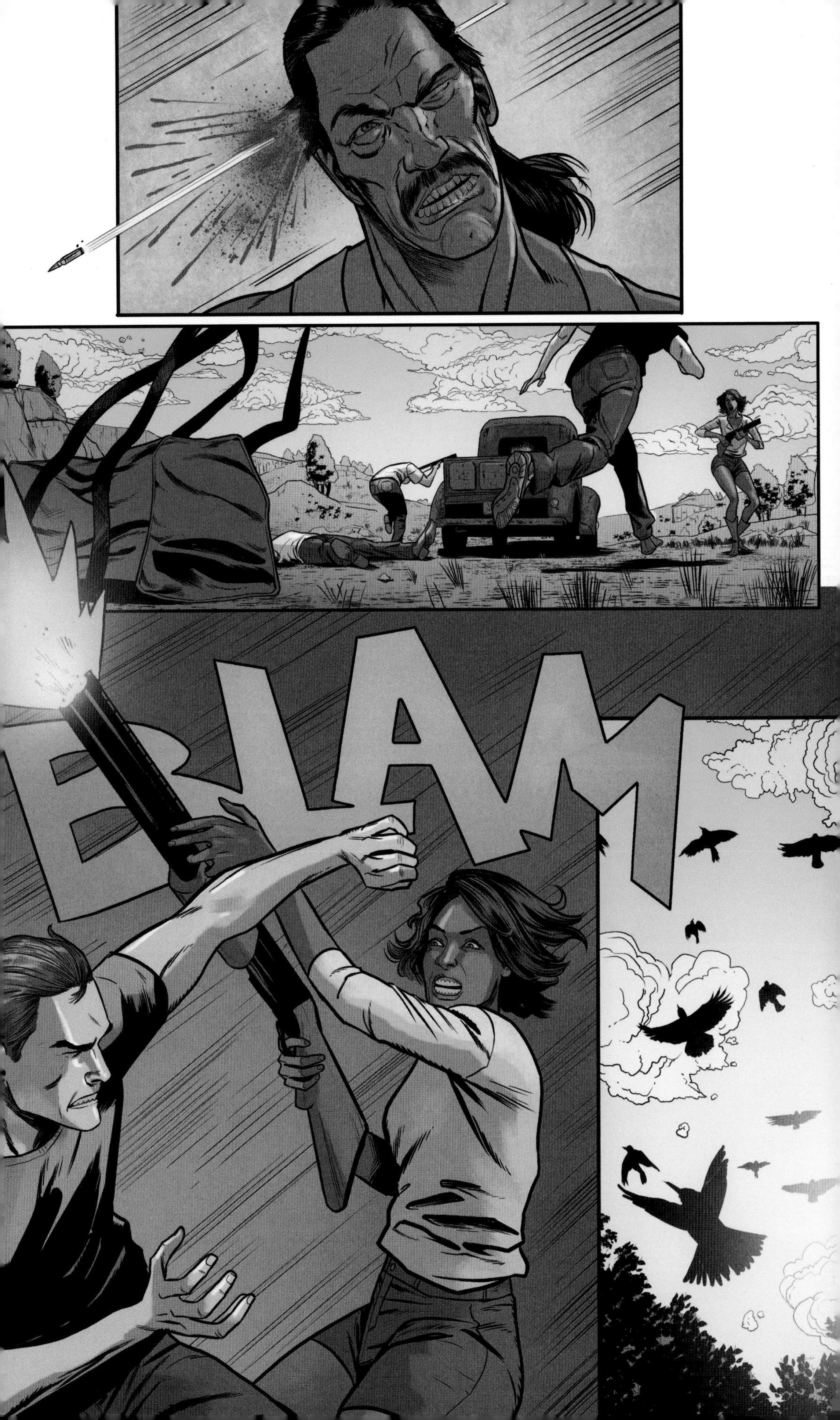
BLAM

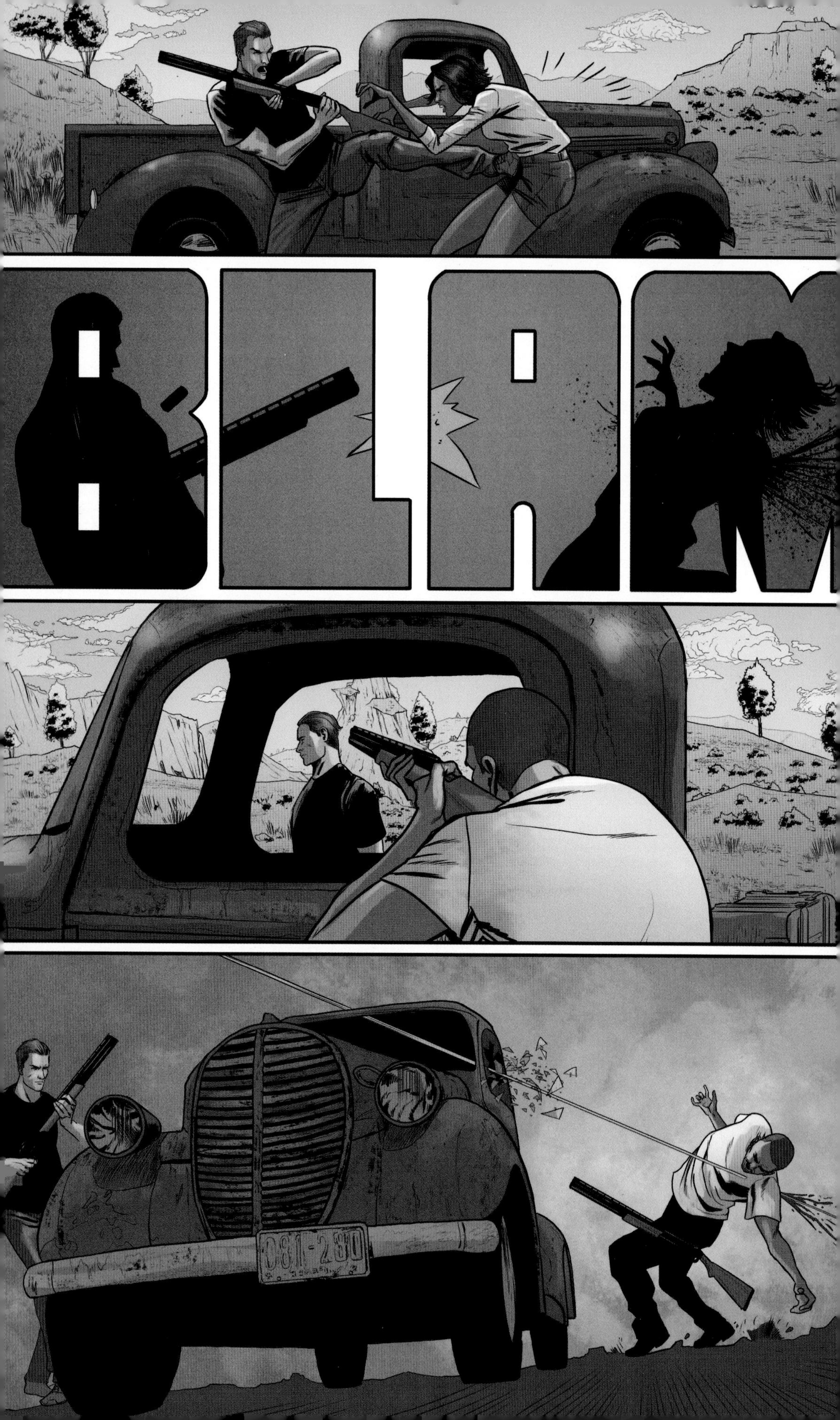
BLAM
081-280

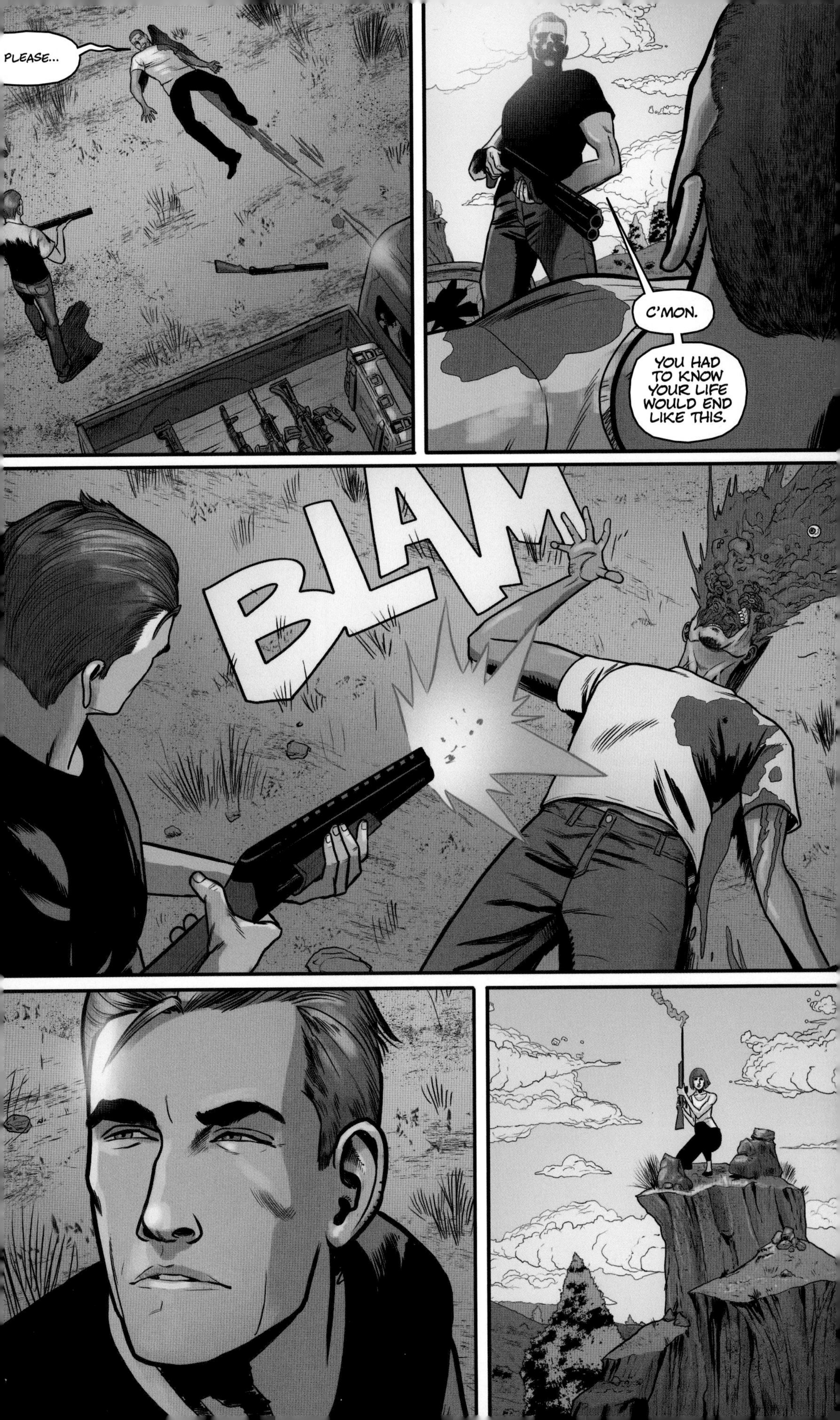
PLEASE...
C'MON.
YOU HAD TO KNOW YOUR LIFE WOULD END LIKE THIS.
BLAM

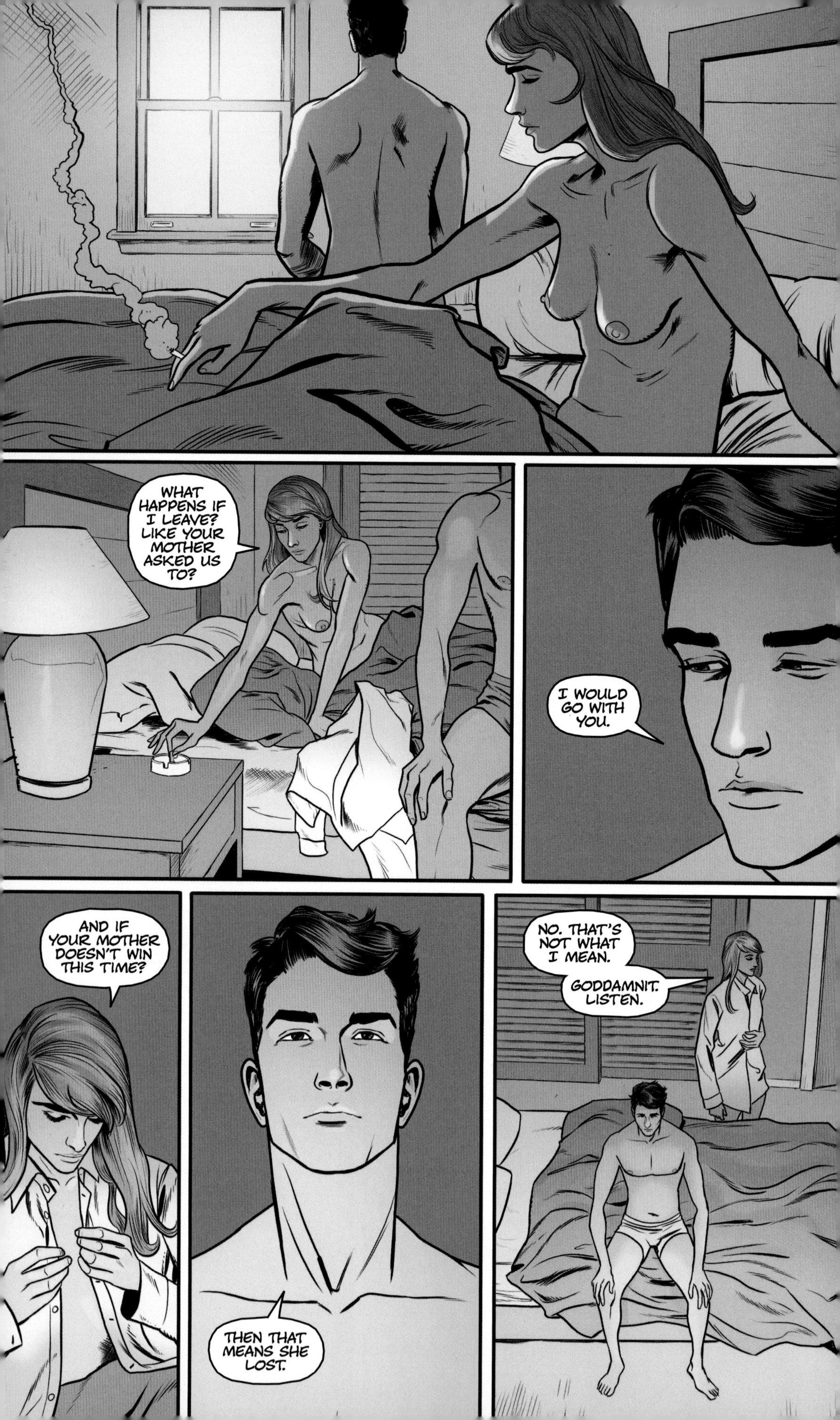
WHAT HAPPENS IF I LEAVE? LIKE YOUR MOTHER ASKED US TO?
I WOULD GO WITH YOU.
AND IF YOUR MOTHER DOESN'T WIN THIS TIME?
THEN THAT MEANS SHE LOST.
NO. THAT'S NOT WHAT I MEAN.
GODDAMNIT. LISTEN.

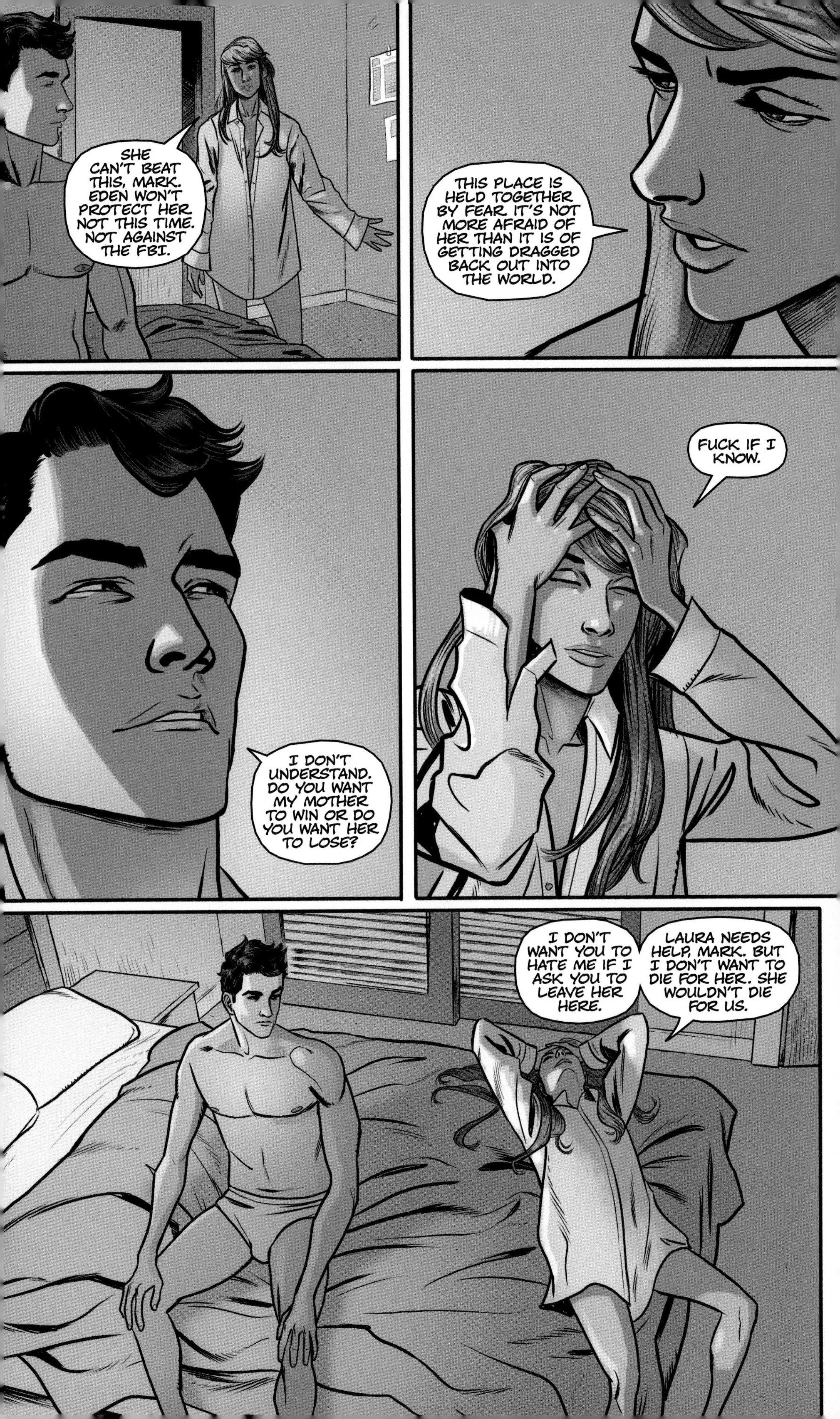
SHE CAN'T BEAT THIS, MARK. EDEN WON'T PROTECT HER NOT THIS TIME. NOT AGAINST THE FBI.
THIS PLACE IS HELD TOGETHER BY FEAR. IT'S NOT MORE AFRAID OF HER THAN IT IS OF GETTING DRAGGED BACK OUT INTO THE WORLD.
I DON'T UNDERSTAND. DO YOU WANT MY MOTHER TO WIN OR DO YOU WANT HER TO LOSE?
FUCK IF I KNOW.
LAURA NEEDS HELP, MARK. BUT I DON'T WANT TO DIE FOR HER. SHE WOULDN'T DIE FOR US.
I DON'T WANT YOU TO HATE ME IF I ASK YOU TO LEAVE HER HERE.

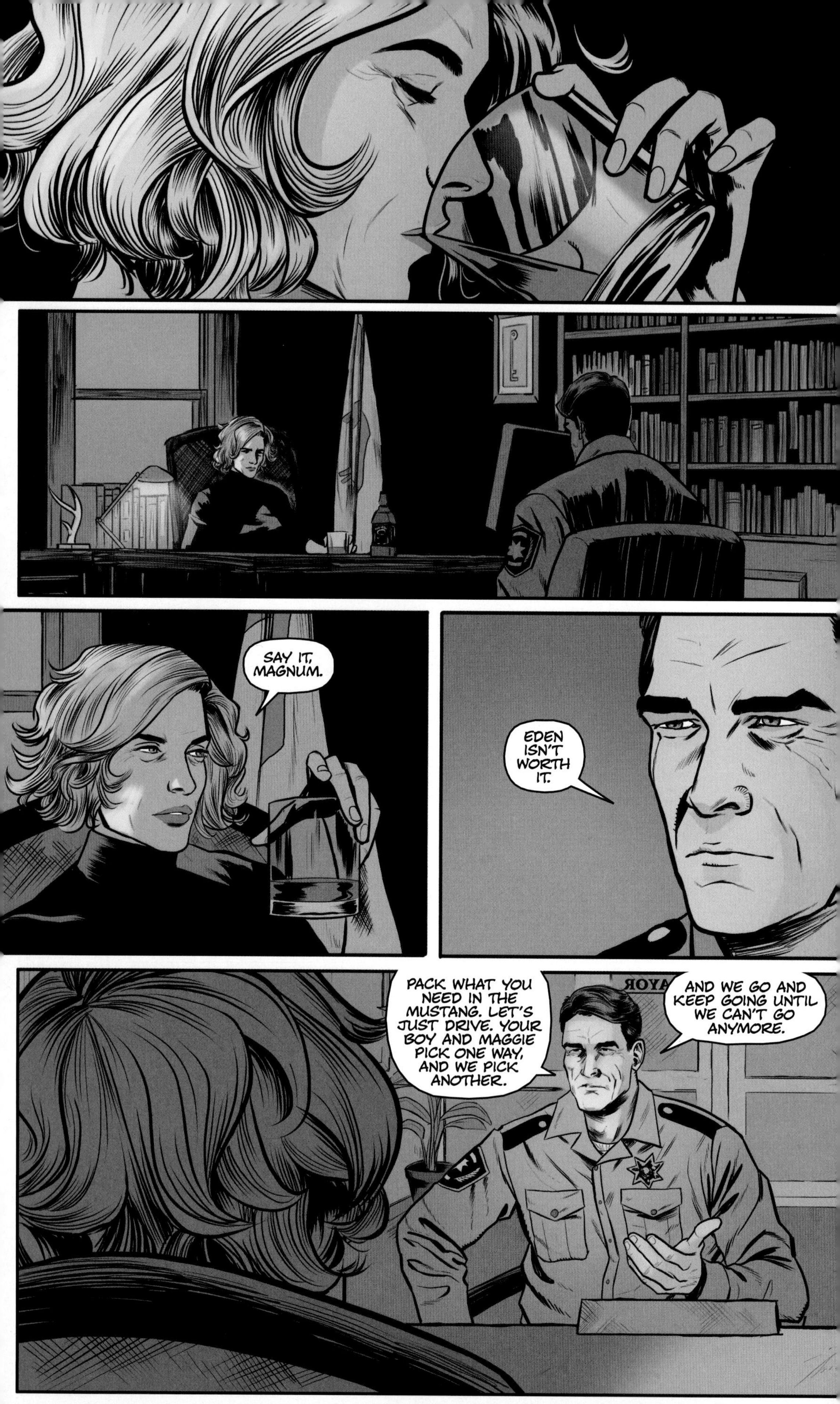
SAY IT, MAGNUM.
EDEN ISN'T WORTH IT.
PACK WHAT YOU NEED IN THE MUSTANG. LET'S JUST DRIVE. YOUR BOY AND MAGGIE PICK ONE WAY, AND WE PICK ANOTHER.
AND WE GO AND KEEP GOING UNTIL WE CAN'T GO ANYMORE.

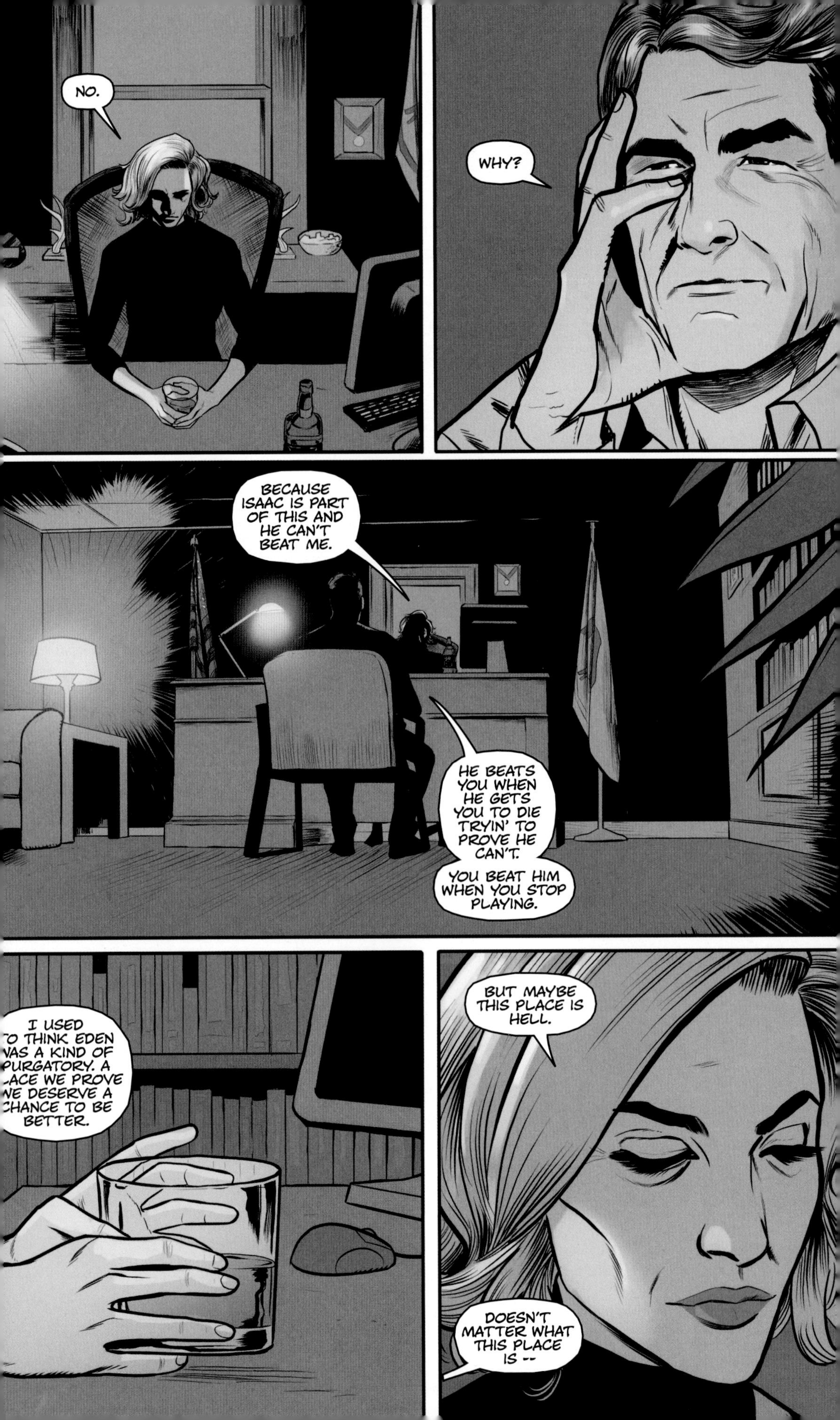

NO.
WHY?
BECAUSE ISAAC IS PART OF THIS AND HE CAN'T BEAT ME.
HE BEATS YOU WHEN HE GETS YOU TO DIE TRYIN' TO PROVE HE CAN'T.
YOU BEAT HIM WHEN YOU STOP PLAYING.
I USED TO THINK EDEN WAS A KIND OF PURGATORY. A PLACE WE PROVE WE DESERVE A CHANCE TO BE BETTER.
BUT MAYBE THIS PLACE IS HELL.
DOESN'T MATTER WHAT THIS PLACE IS --

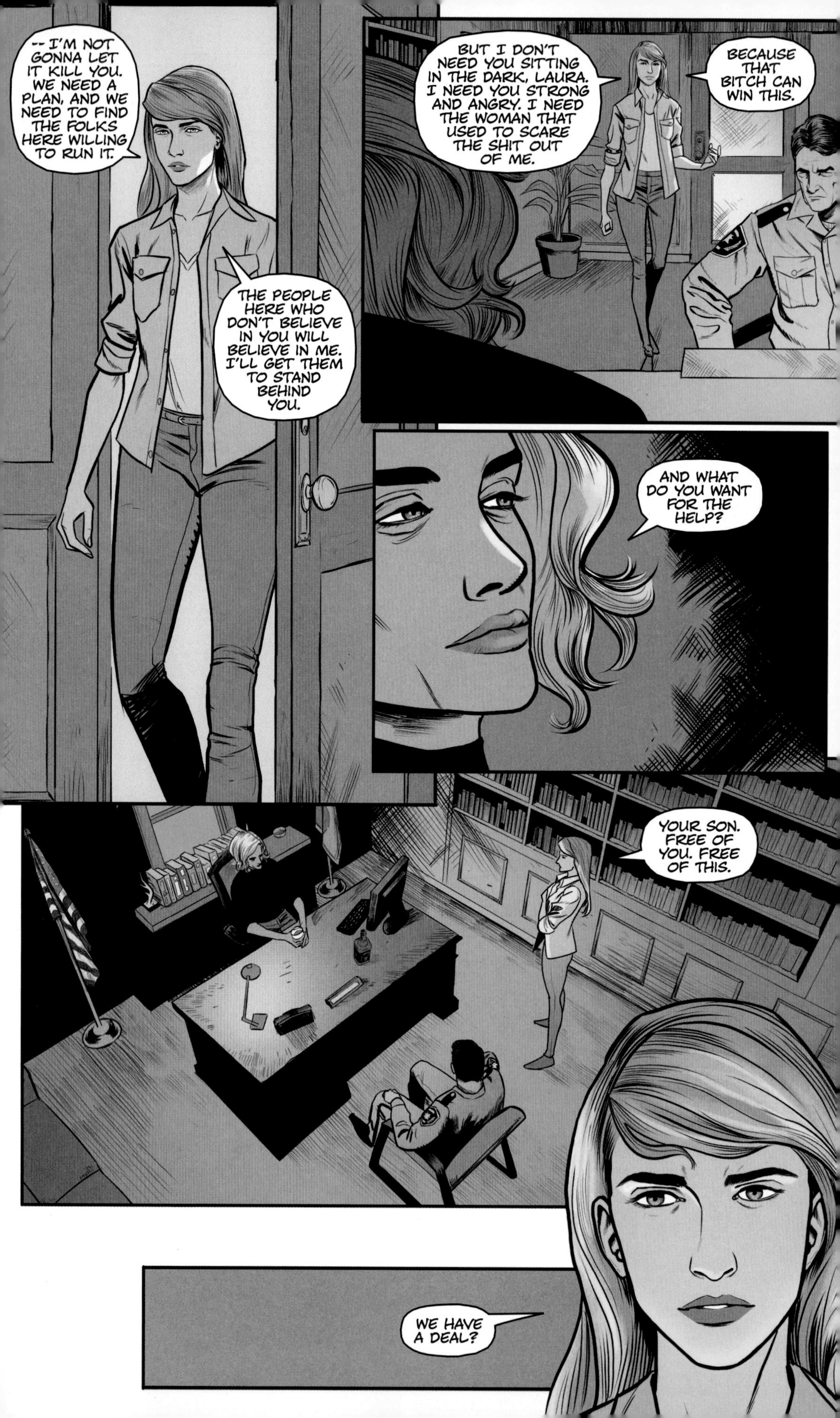

-- I'M NOT GONNA LET IT KILL YOU. WE NEED A PLAN, AND WE NEED TO FIND THE FOLKS HERE WILLING TO RUN IT.
THE PEOPLE HERE WHO DON'T BELIEVE IN YOU WILL BELIEVE IN ME. I'LL GET THEM TO STAND BEHIND YOU.
BUT I DON'T NEED YOU SITTING IN THE DARK, LAURA. I NEED YOU STRONG AND ANGRY. I NEED THE WOMAN THAT USED TO SCARE THE SHIT OUT OF ME.
BECAUSE THAT BITCH CAN WIN THIS.
AND WHAT DO YOU WANT FOR THE HELP?
YOUR SON. FREE OF YOU. FREE OF THIS.
WE HAVE A DEAL?

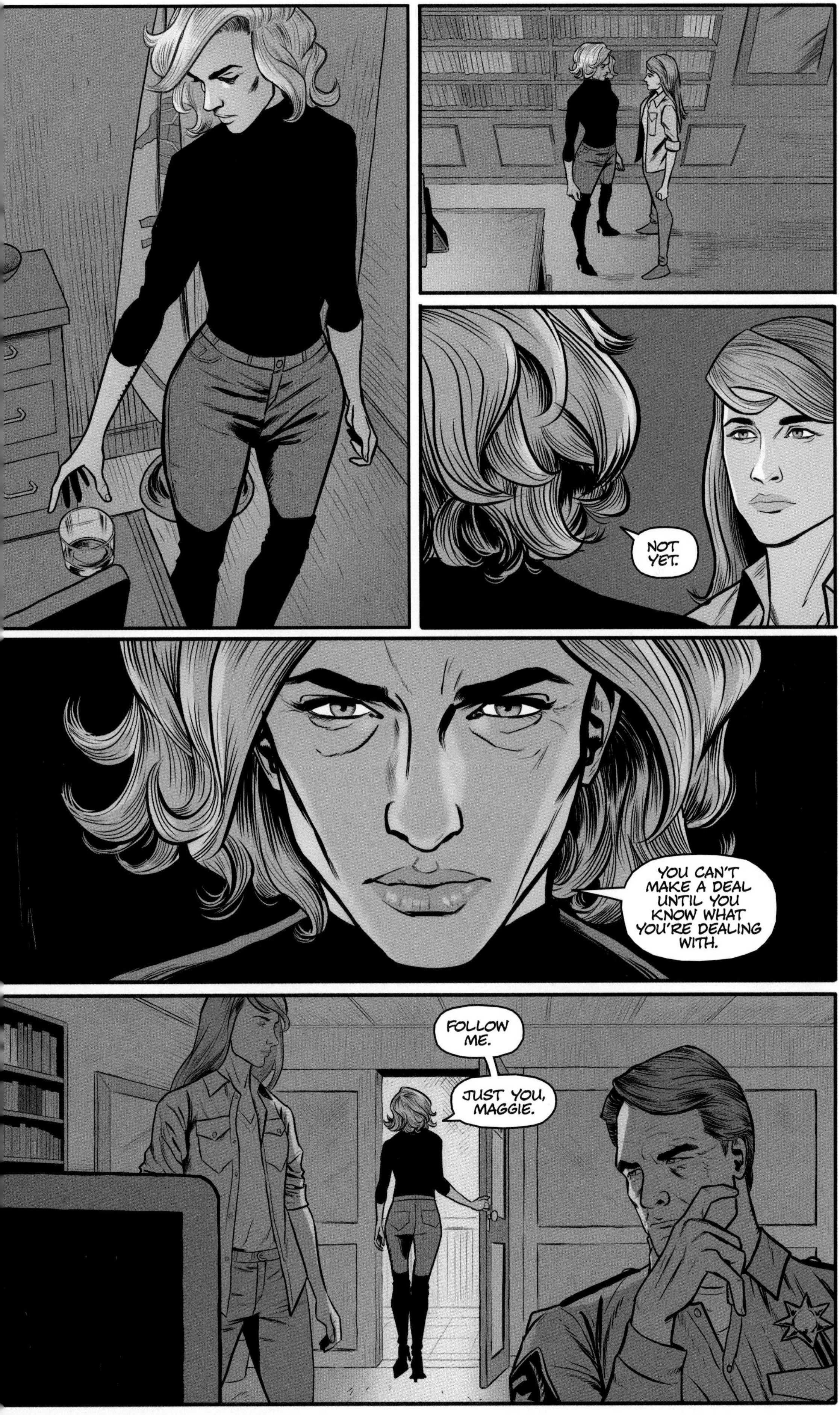
NOT YET.
YOU CAN'T MAKE A DEAL UNTIL YOU KNOW WHAT YOU'RE DEALING WITH.
FOLLOW ME.
JUST YOU, MAGGIE.

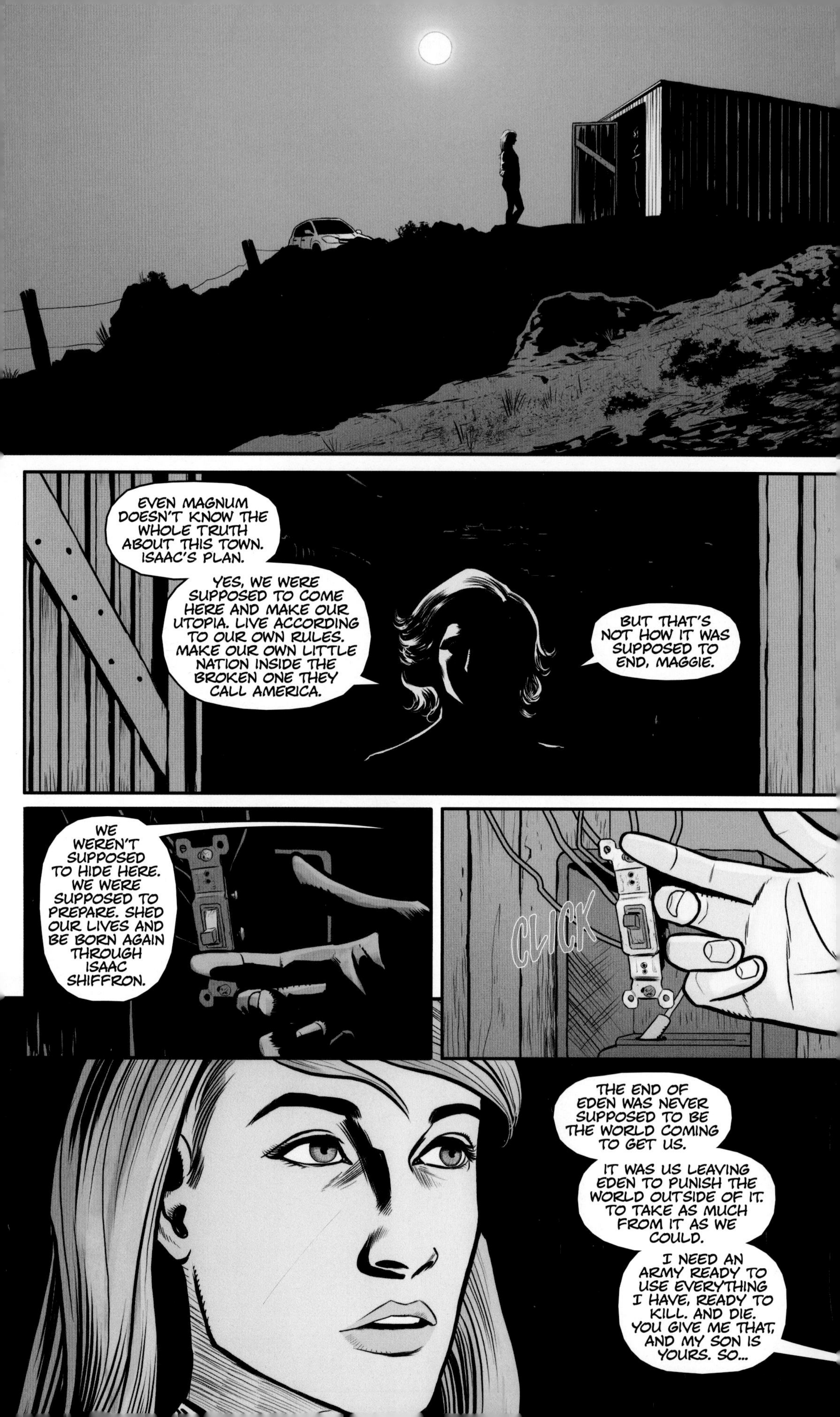
EVEN MAGNUM DOESN'T KNOW THE WHOLE TRUTH ABOUT THIS TOWN. ISAAC'S PLAN.
YES, WE WERE SUPPOSED TO COME HERE AND MAKE OUR UTOPIA. LIVE ACCORDING TO OUR OWN RULES. MAKE OUR OWN LITTLE NATION INSIDE THE BROKEN ONE THEY CALL AMERICA.
BUT THAT'S NOT HOW IT WAS SUPPOSED TO END, MAGGIE.
WE WEREN'T SUPPOSED TO HIDE HERE. WE WERE SUPPOSED TO PREPARE. SHED OUR LIVES AND BE BORN AGAIN THROUGH ISAAC SHIFFRON.
CLICK
THE END OF EDEN WAS NEVER SUPPOSED TO BE THE WORLD COMING TO GET US.
IT WAS US LEAVING EDEN TO PUNISH THE WORLD OUTSIDE OF IT. TO TAKE AS MUCH FROM IT AS WE COULD.
I NEED AN ARMY READY TO USE EVERYTHING I HAVE, READY TO KILL. AND DIE. YOU GIVE ME THAT, AND MY SON IS YOURS. SO...

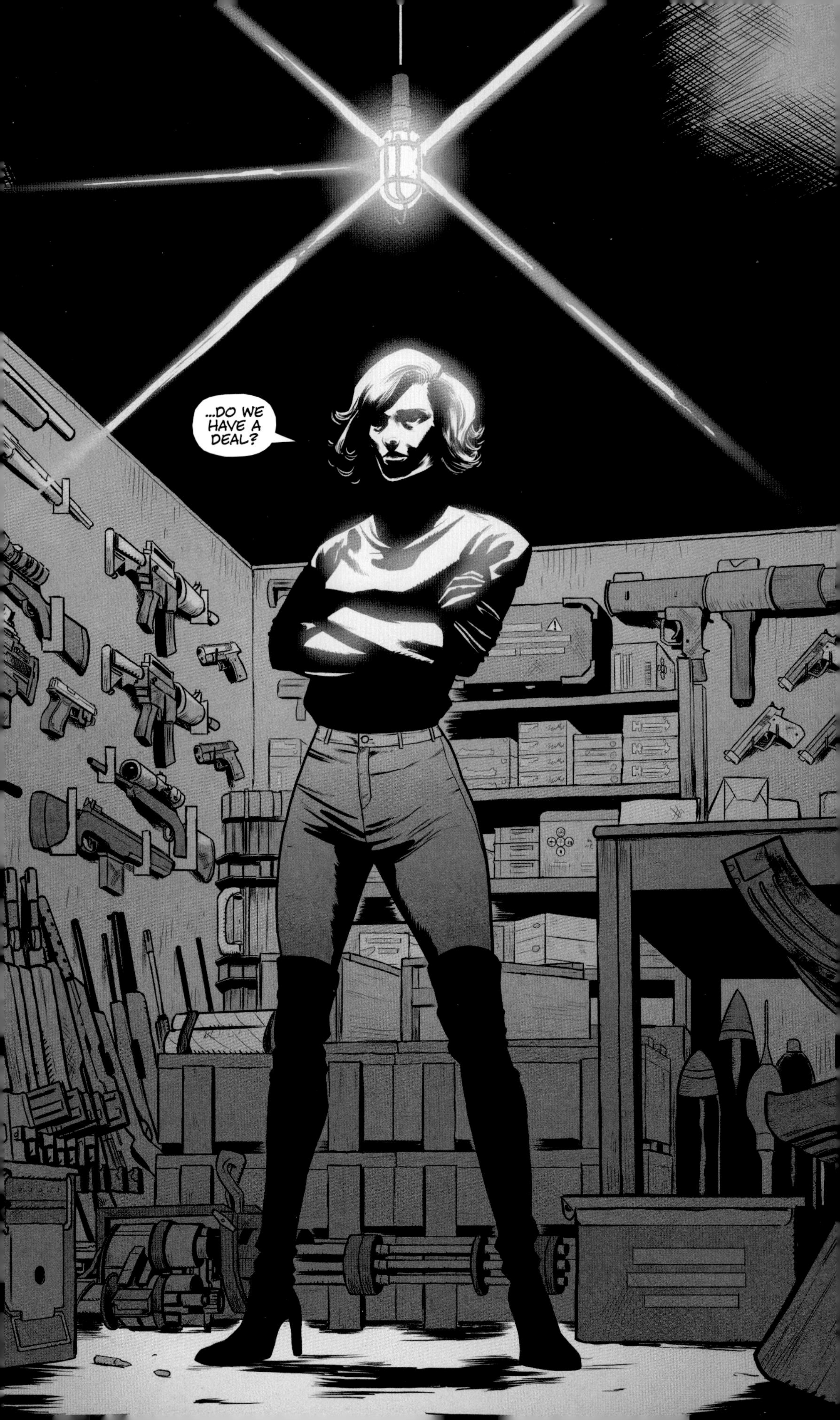
...DO WE HAVE A DEAL?

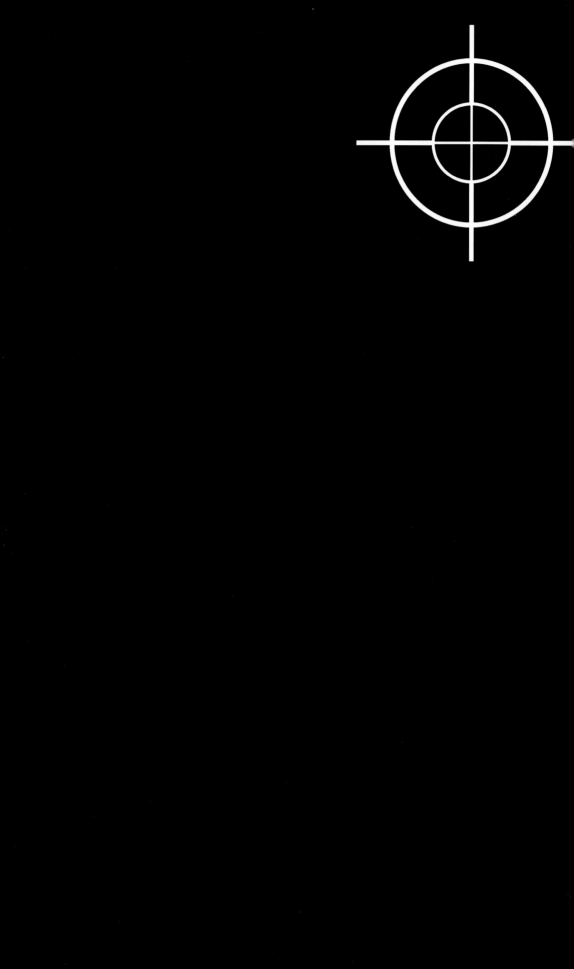

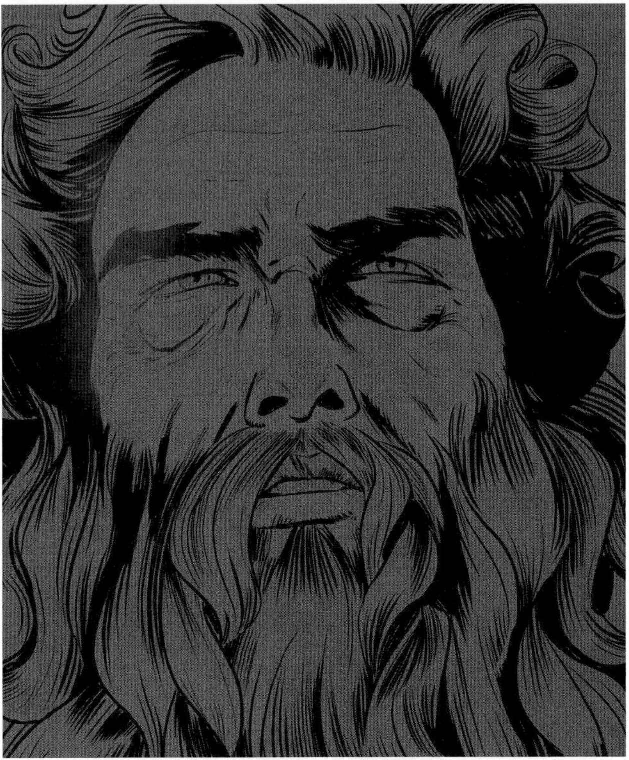

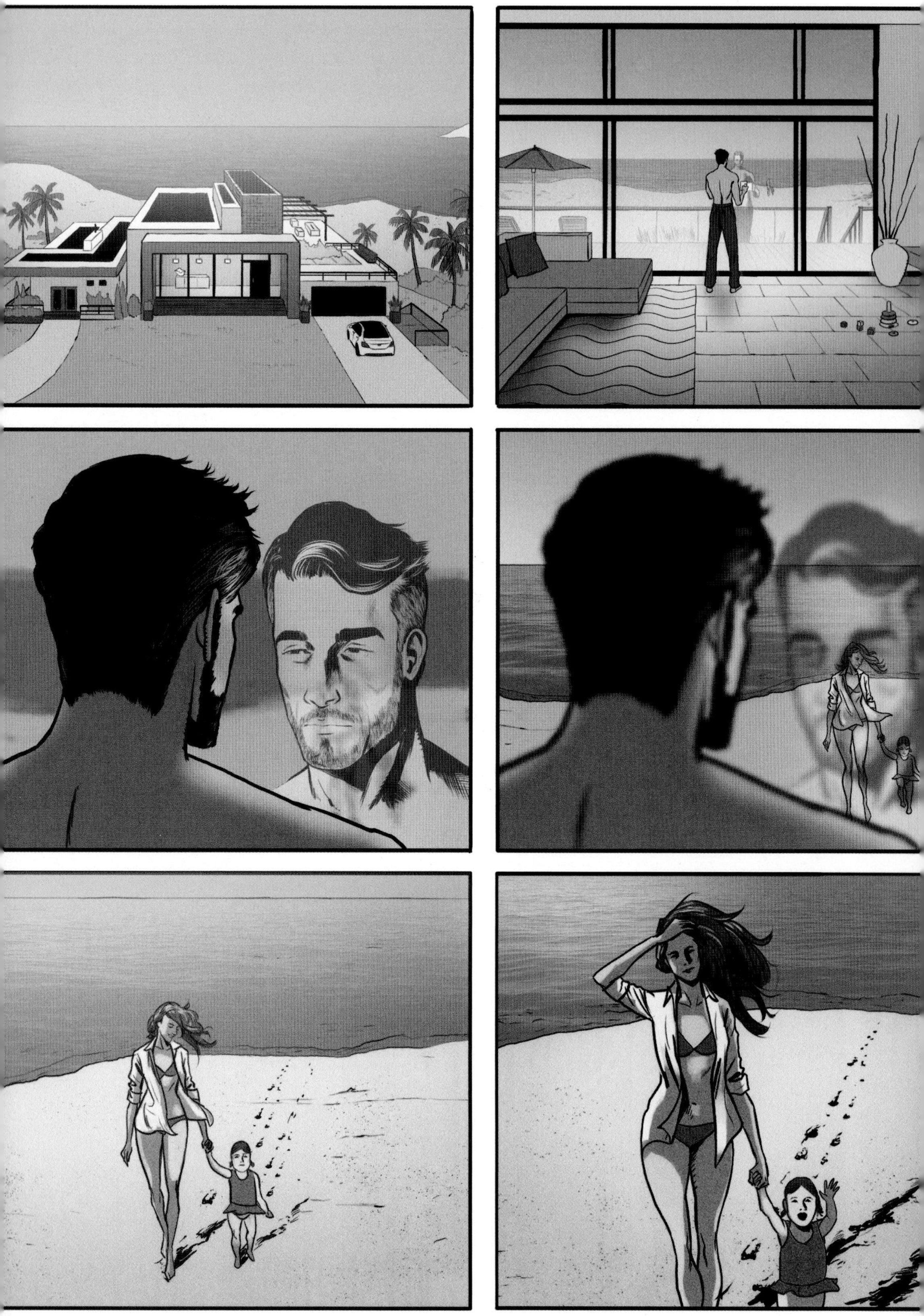

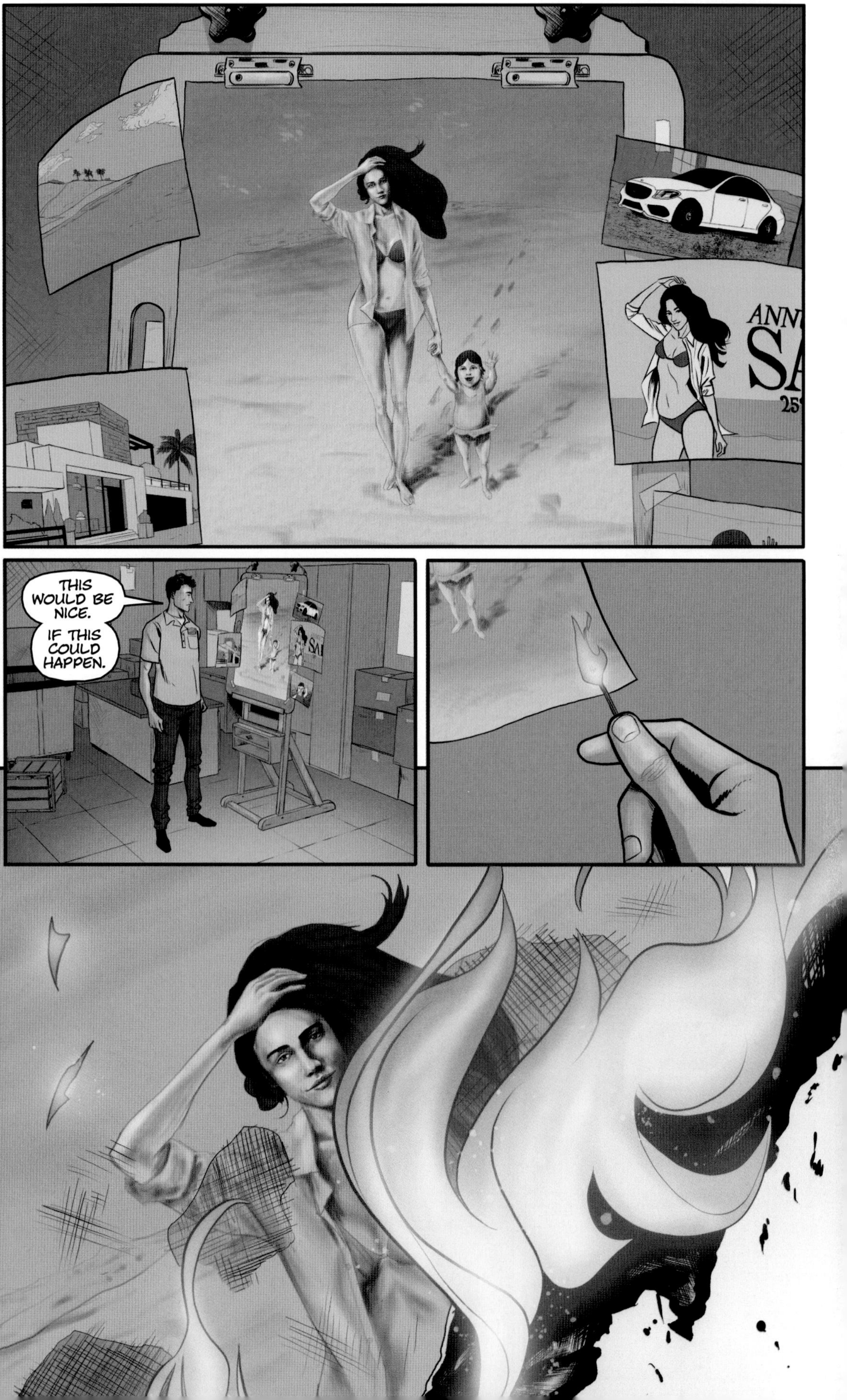
THIS WOULD BE NICE.
IF THIS COULD HAPPEN.

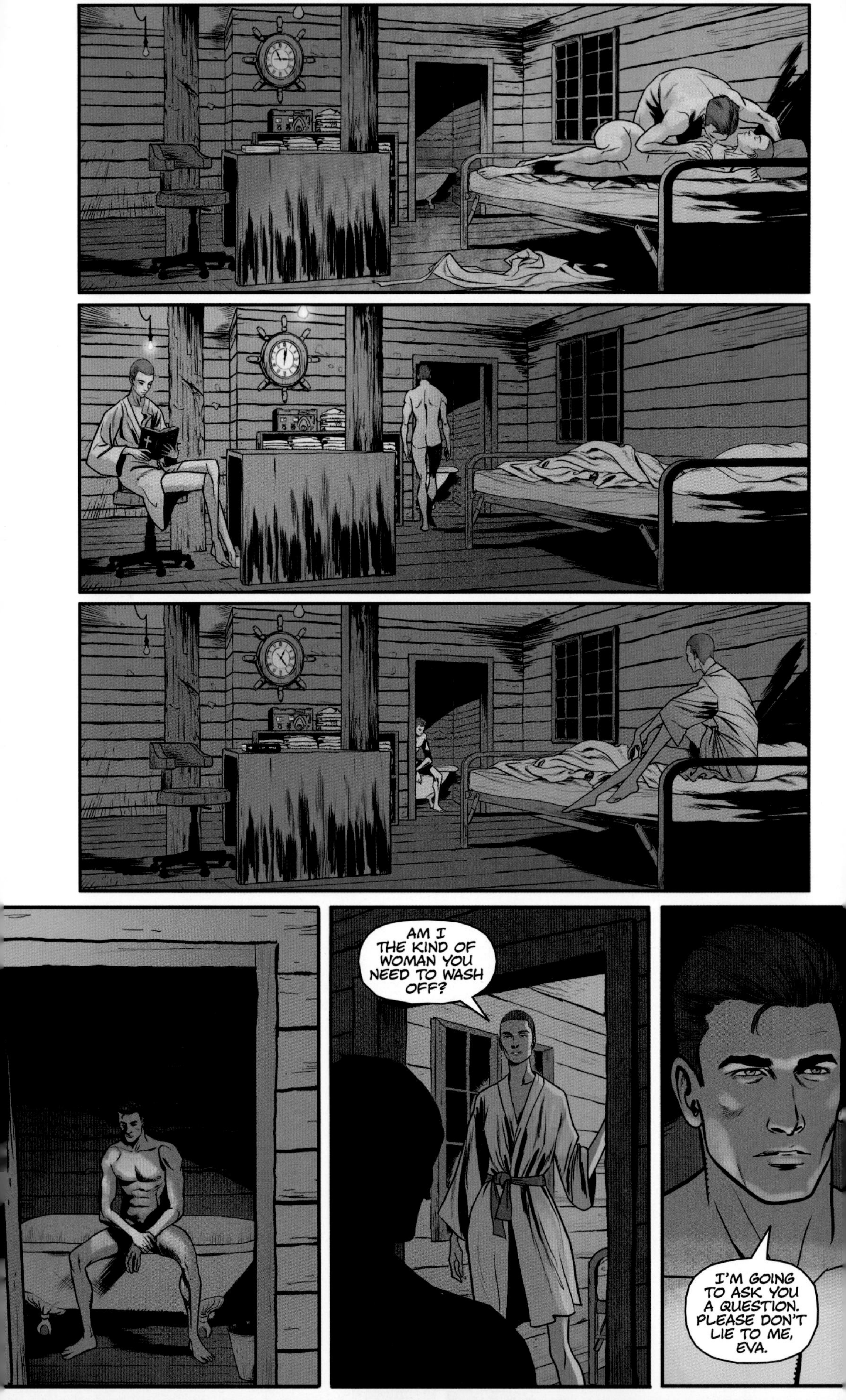
AM I THE KIND OF WOMAN YOU NEED TO WASH OFF?
I'M GOING TO ASK YOU A QUESTION. PLEASE DON'T LIE TO ME, EVA.

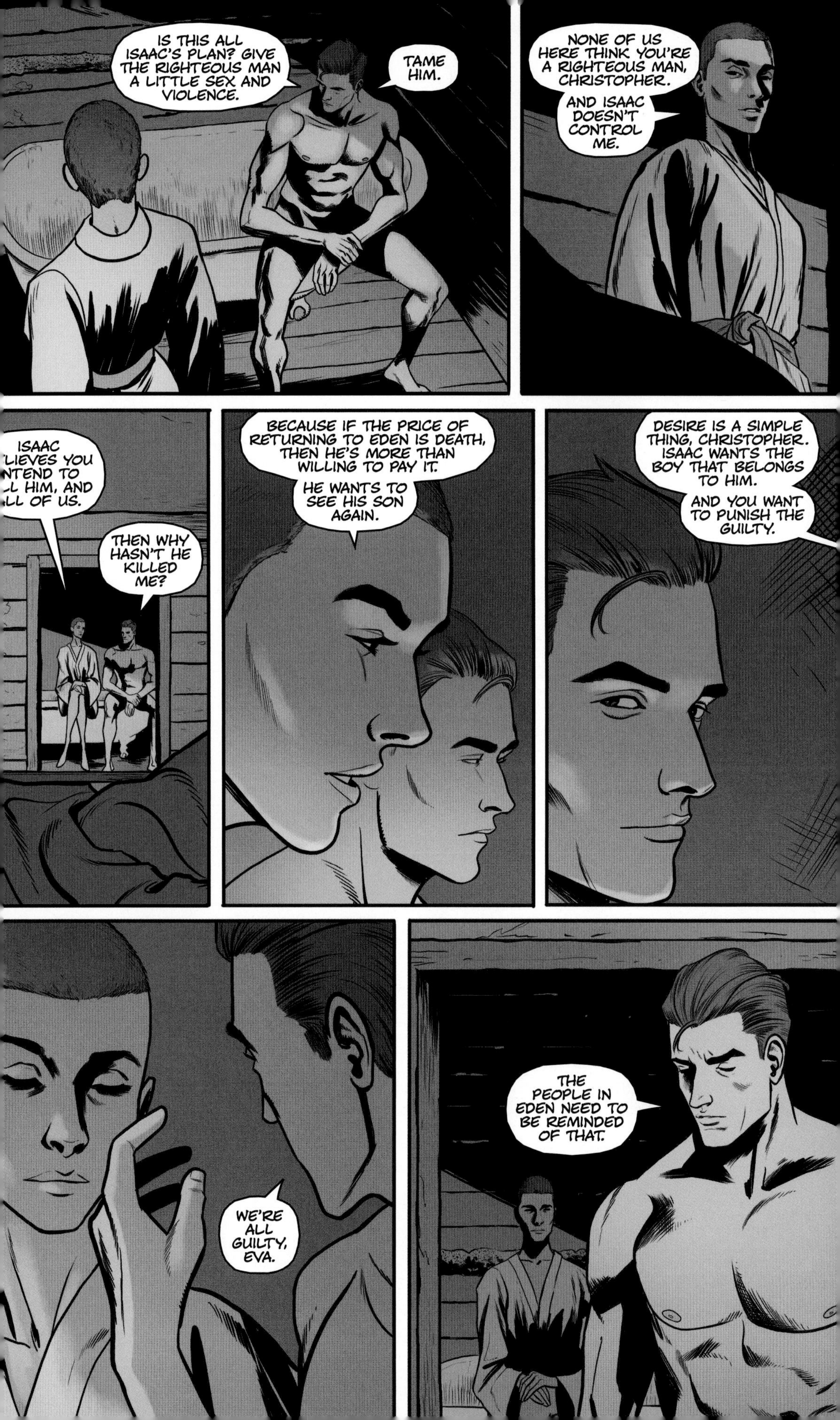
IS THIS ALL ISAAC'S PLAN? GIVE THE RIGHTEOUS MAN A LITTLE SEX AND VIOLENCE.
TAME HIM.
NONE OF US HERE THINK YOU'RE A RIGHTEOUS MAN, CHRISTOPHER.
AND ISAAC DOESN'T CONTROL ME.
ISAAC LIEVES YOU NTEND TO L HIM, AND LL OF US.
THEN WHY HASN'T HE KILLED ME?
BECAUSE IF THE PRICE OF RETURNING TO EDEN IS DEATH, THEN HE'S MORE THAN WILLING TO PAY IT.
HE WANTS TO SEE HIS SON AGAIN.
DESIRE IS A SIMPLE THING, CHRISTOPHER. ISAAC WANTS THE BOY THAT BELONGS TO HIM.
AND YOU WANT TO PUNISH THE GUILTY.
WE'RE ALL GUILTY, EVA.
THE PEOPLE IN EDEN NEED TO BE REMINDED OF THAT.

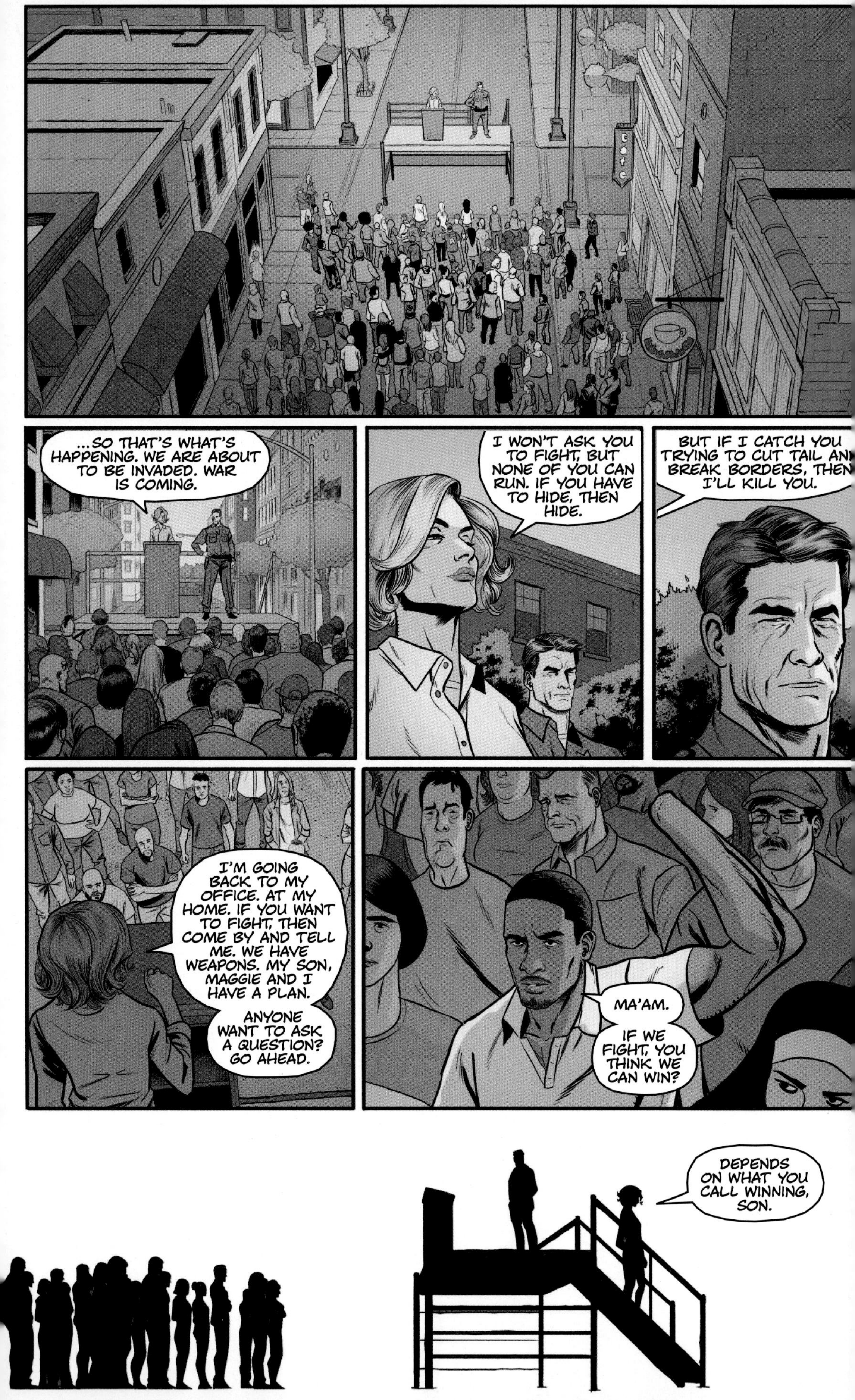
...SO THAT'S WHAT'S HAPPENING. WE ARE ABOUT TO BE INVADED. WAR IS COMING.
I WON'T ASK YOU TO FIGHT, BUT NONE OF YOU CAN RUN. IF YOU HAVE TO HIDE, THEN HIDE.
BUT IF I CATCH YOU TRYING TO CUT TAIL AN BREAK BORDERS, THEN I'LL KILL YOU.
I'M GOING BACK TO MY OFFICE. AT MY HOME. IF YOU WANT TO FIGHT, THEN COME BY AND TELL ME. WE HAVE WEAPONS. MY SON, MAGGIE AND I HAVE A PLAN.
ANYONE WANT TO ASK A QUESTION? GO AHEAD.
MA'AM.
IF WE FIGHT, YOU THINK WE CAN WIN?
DEPENDS ON WHAT YOU CALL WINNING, SON.

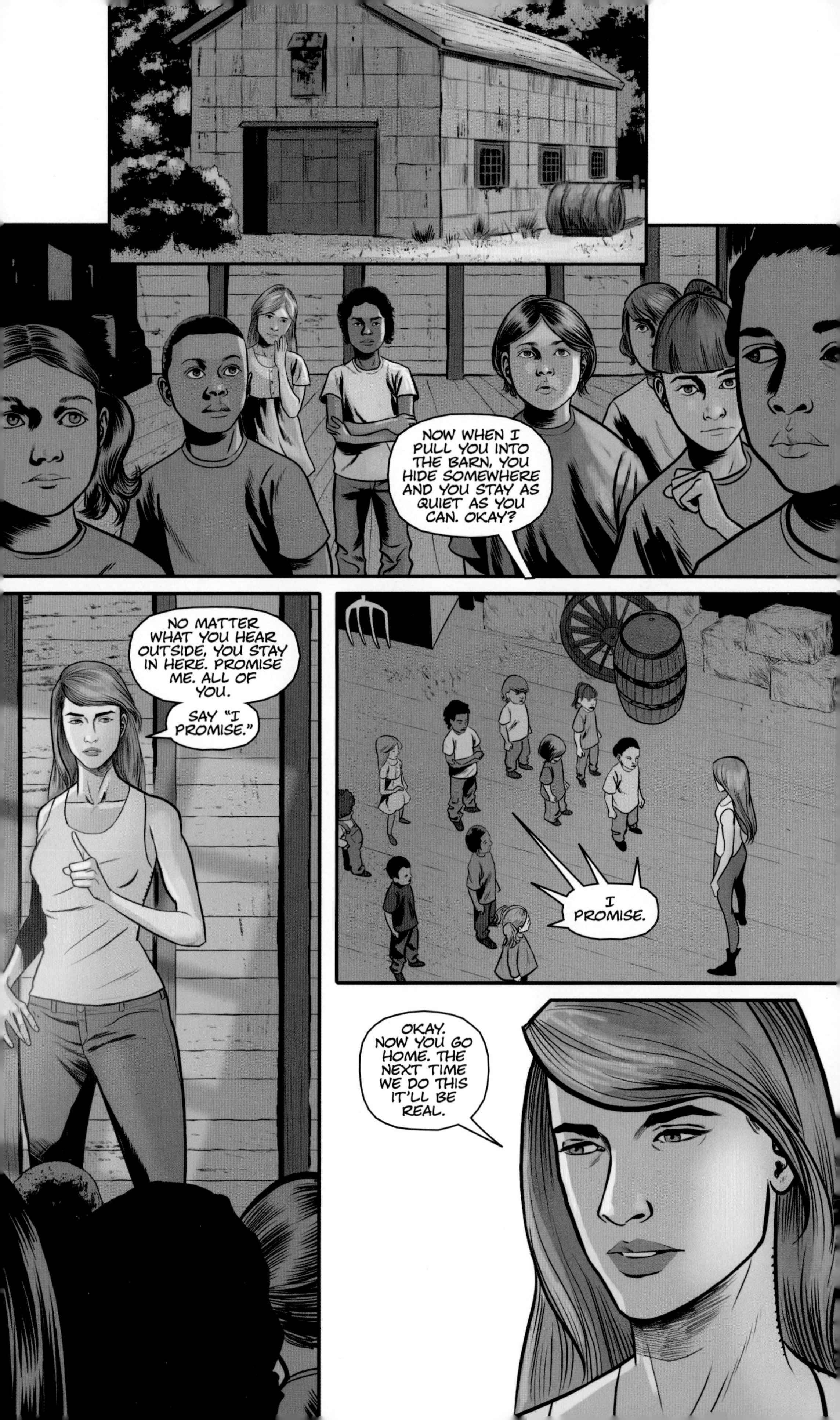
NOW WHEN I PULL YOU INTO THE BARN, YOU HIDE SOMEWHERE AND YOU STAY AS QUIET AS YOU CAN. OKAY?
NO MATTER WHAT YOU HEAR OUTSIDE, YOU STAY IN HERE. PROMISE ME. ALL OF YOU.
SAY "I PROMISE."
I PROMISE.
OKAY. NOW YOU GO HOME. THE NEXT TIME WE DO THIS IT'LL BE REAL.

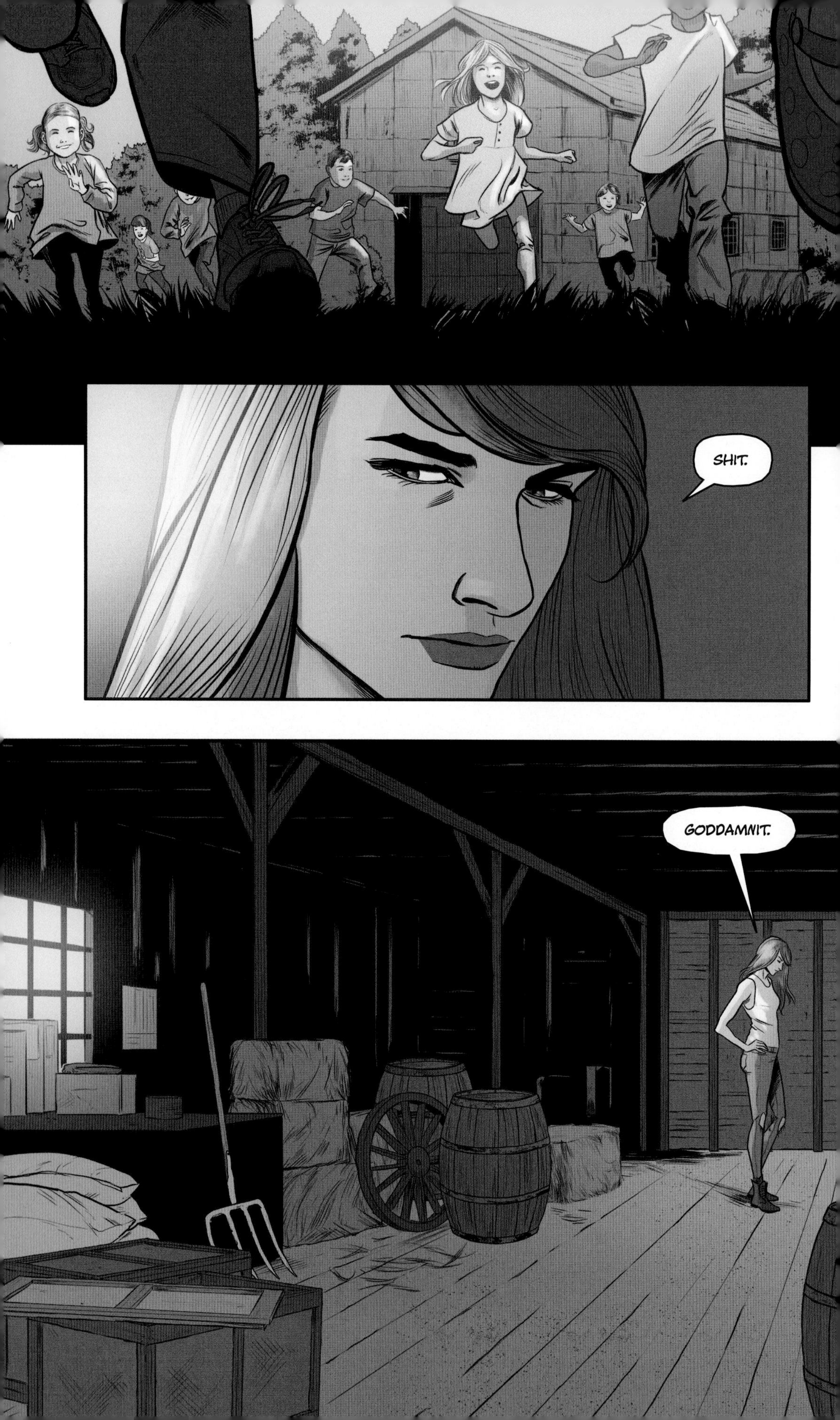
SHIT.
GODDAMNIT.

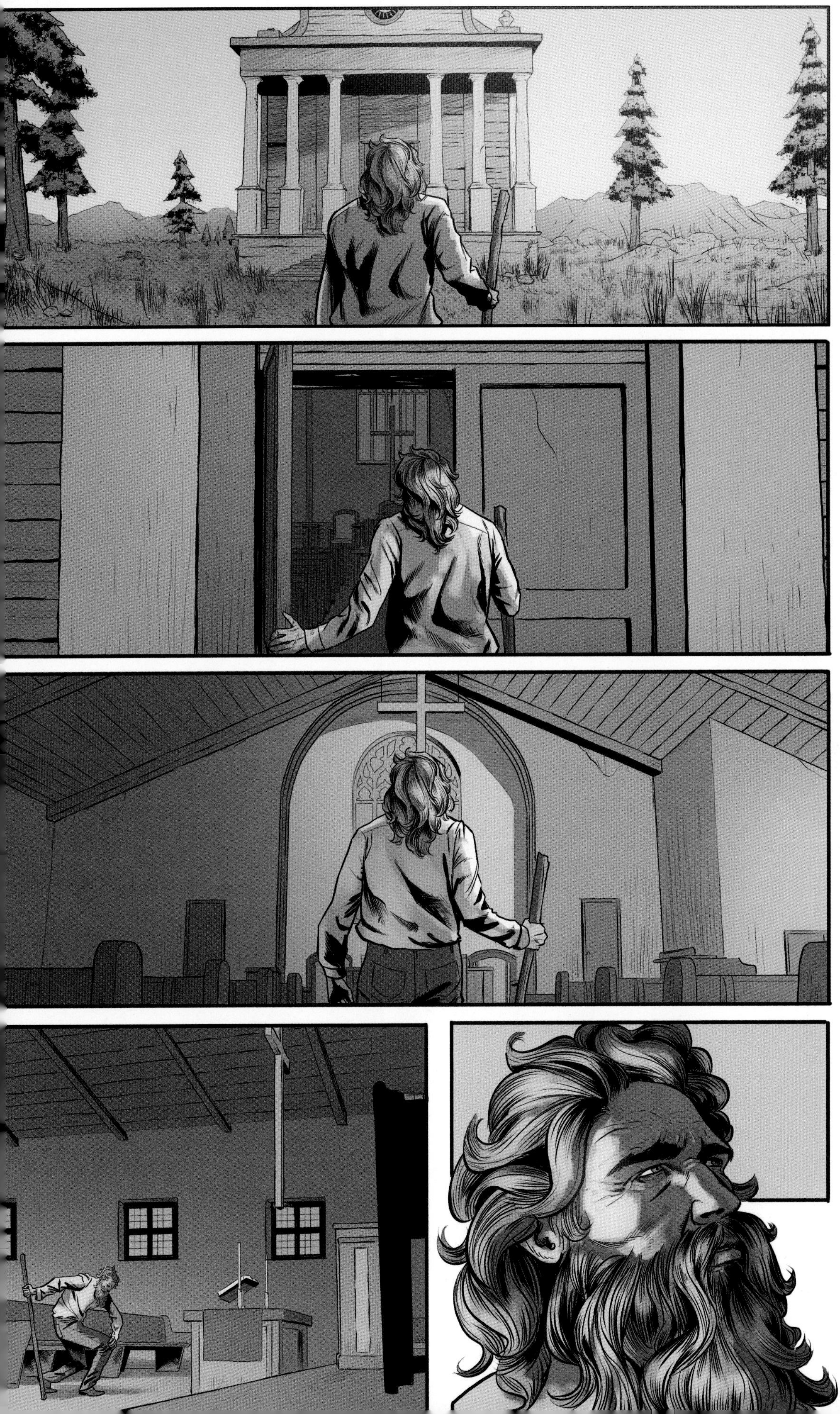

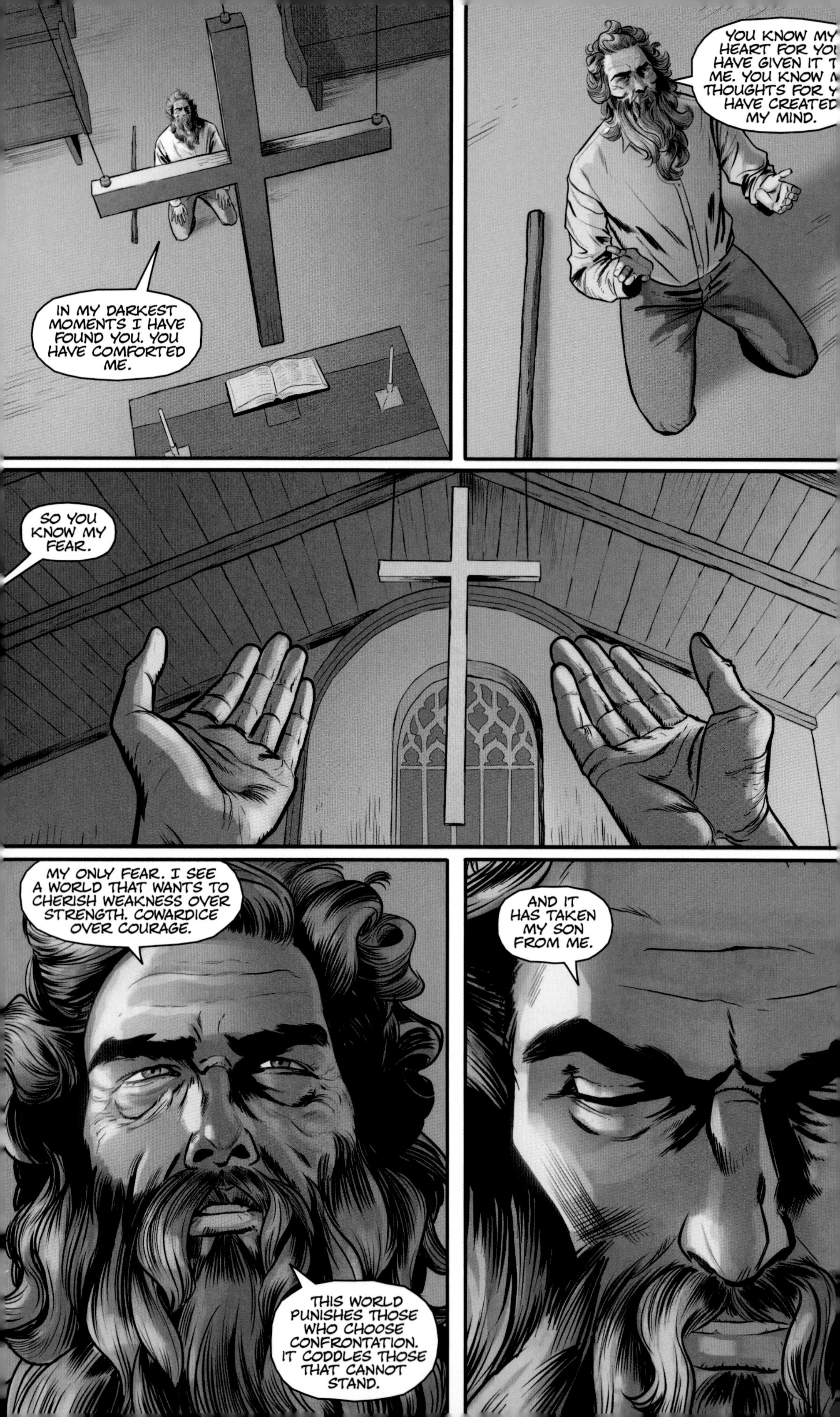
IN MY DARKEST MOMENTS I HAVE FOUND YOU. YOU HAVE COMFORTED ME.
YOU KNOW MY HEART FOR YOU HAVE GIVEN IT T ME. YOU KNOW M THOUGHTS FOR Y HAVE CREATED MY MIND.
SO YOU KNOW MY FEAR.
MY ONLY FEAR. I SEE A WORLD THAT WANTS TO CHERISH WEAKNESS OVER STRENGTH. COWARDICE OVER COURAGE.
THIS WORLD PUNISHES THOSE WHO CHOOSE CONFRONTATION. IT CODDLES THOSE THAT CANNOT STAND.
AND IT HAS TAKEN MY SON FROM ME.

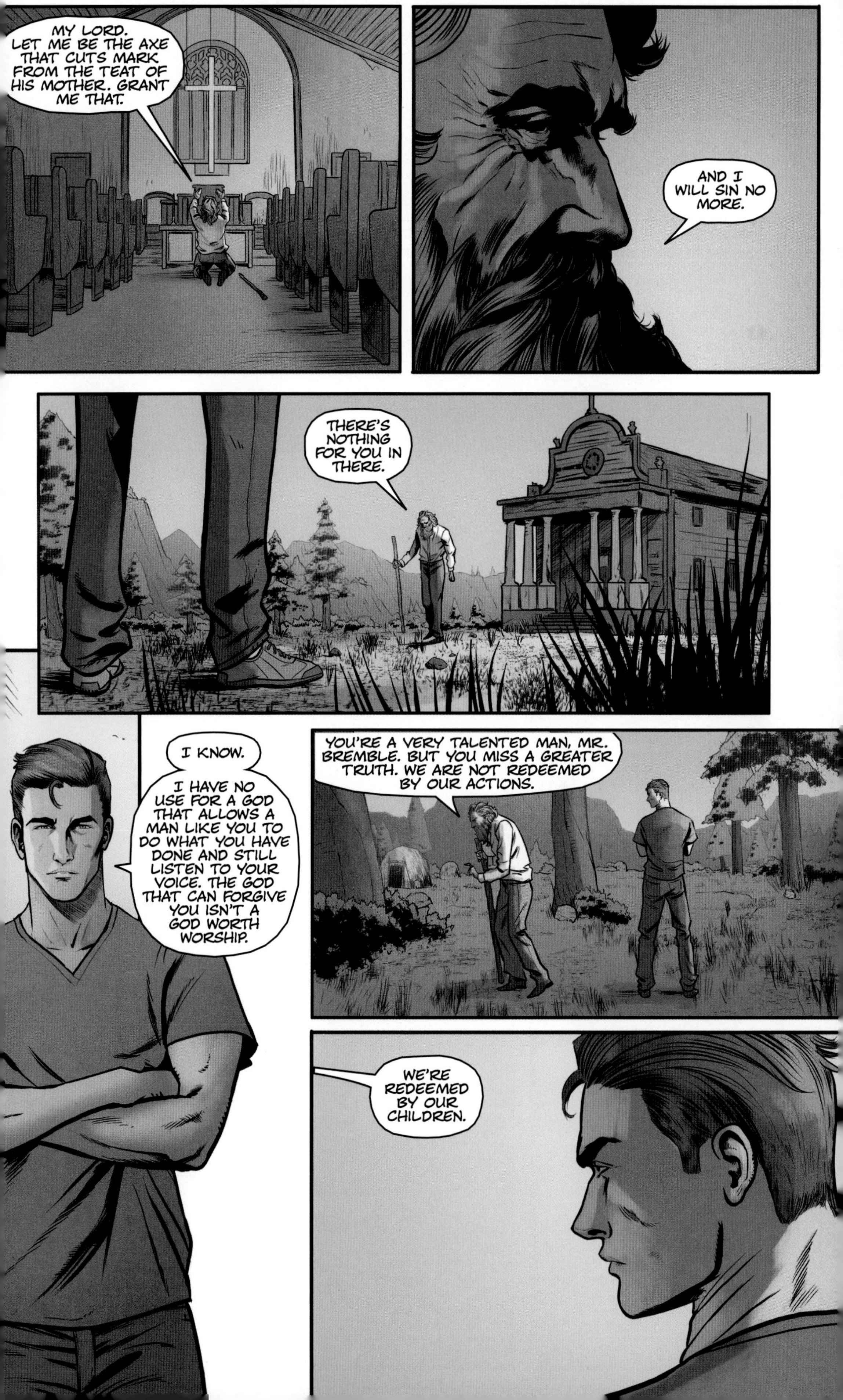

MY LORD. LET ME BE THE AXE THAT CUTS MARK FROM THE TEAT OF HIS MOTHER. GRANT ME THAT.
AND I WILL SIN NO MORE.
THERE'S NOTHING FOR YOU IN THERE.
I KNOW.
I HAVE NO USE FOR A GOD THAT ALLOWS A MAN LIKE YOU TO DO WHAT YOU HAVE DONE AND STILL LISTEN TO YOUR VOICE. THE GOD THAT CAN FORGIVE YOU ISN'T A GOD WORTH WORSHIP.
YOU'RE A VERY TALENTED MAN, MR. BREMBLE. BUT YOU MISS A GREATER TRUTH. WE ARE NOT REDEEMED BY OUR ACTIONS.
WE'RE REDEEMED BY OUR CHILDREN.

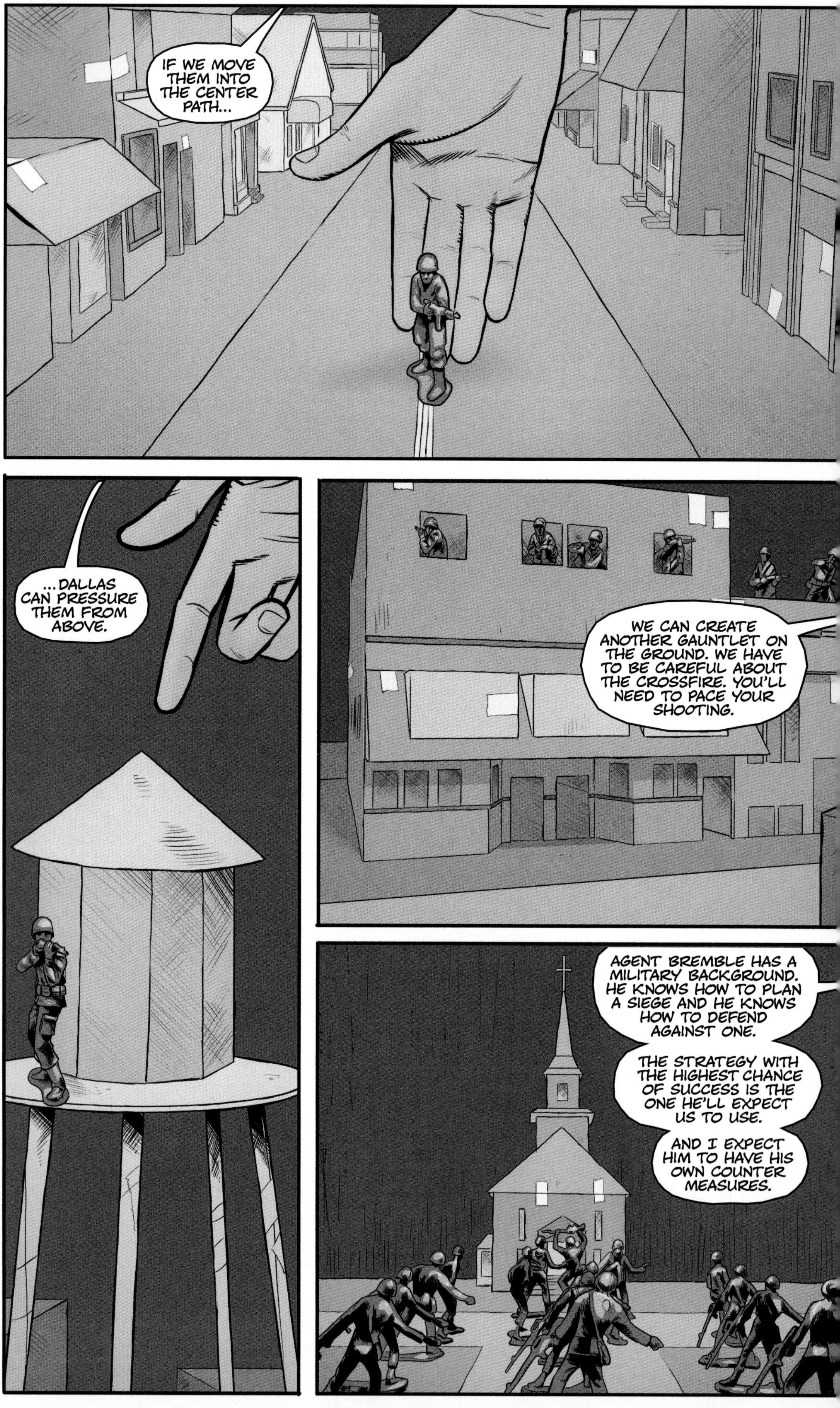
IF WE MOVE THEM INTO THE CENTER PATH...
...DALLAS CAN PRESSURE THEM FROM ABOVE.
WE CAN CREATE ANOTHER GAUNTLET ON THE GROUND. WE HAVE TO BE CAREFUL ABOUT THE CROSSFIRE. YOU'LL NEED TO PACE YOUR SHOOTING.
AGENT BREMBLE HAS A MILITARY BACKGROUND. HE KNOWS HOW TO PLAN A SIEGE AND HE KNOWS HOW TO DEFEND AGAINST ONE.
THE STRATEGY WITH THE HIGHEST CHANCE OF SUCCESS IS THE ONE HE'LL EXPECT US TO USE.
AND I EXPECT HIM TO HAVE HIS OWN COUNTER MEASURES.

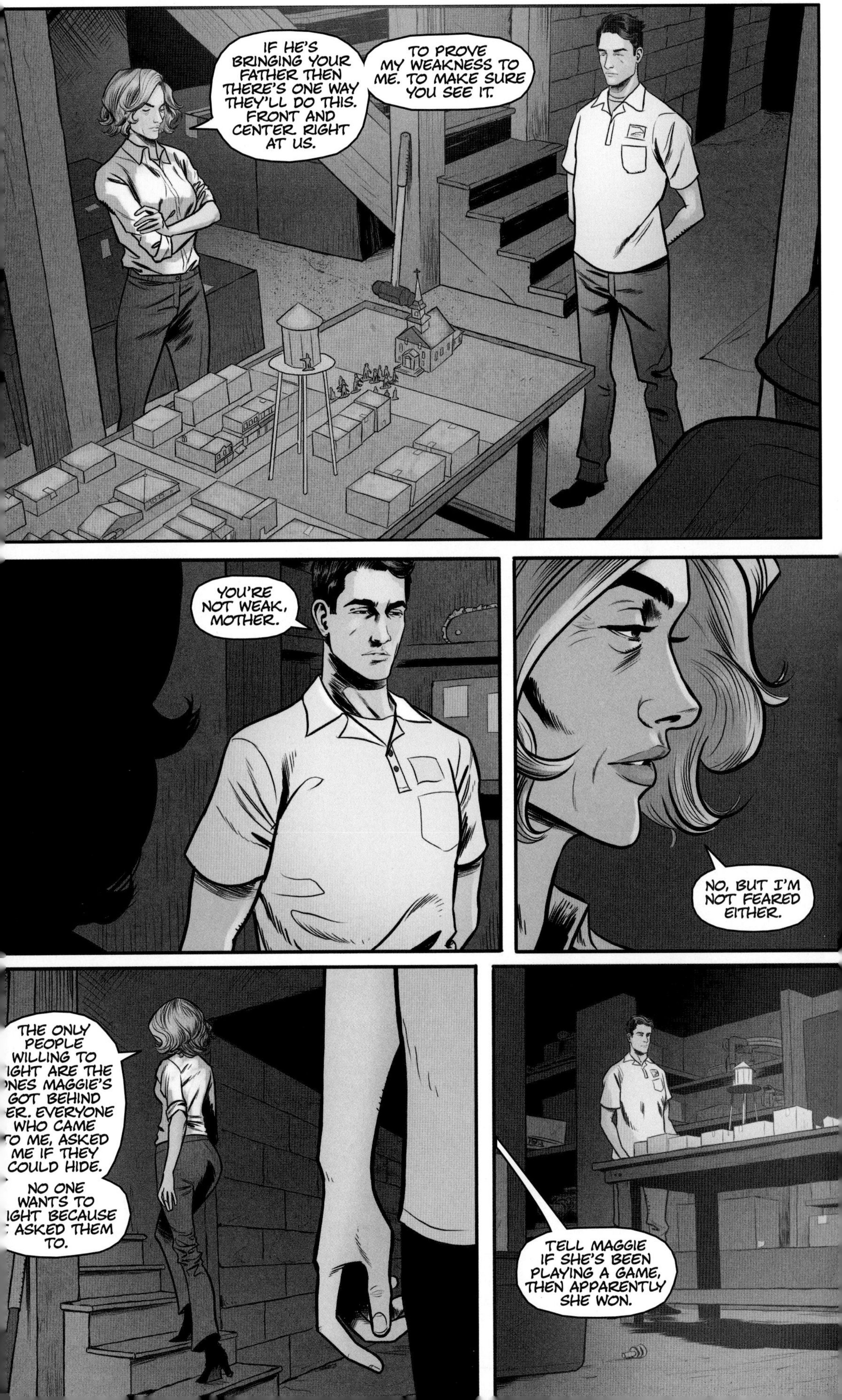
IF HE'S BRINGING YOUR FATHER THEN THERE'S ONE WAY THEY'LL DO THIS. FRONT AND CENTER RIGHT AT US.
TO PROVE MY WEAKNESS TO ME. TO MAKE SURE YOU SEE IT.
YOU'RE NOT WEAK, MOTHER.
NO, BUT I'M NOT FEARED EITHER.
THE ONLY PEOPLE WILLING TO IGHT ARE THE NES MAGGIE'S GOT BEHIND ER. EVERYONE WHO CAME O ME, ASKED ME IF THEY COULD HIDE.
NO ONE WANTS TO IGHT BECAUSE ASKED THEM TO.
TELL MAGGIE IF SHE'S BEEN PLAYING A GAME, THEN APPARENTLY SHE WON.

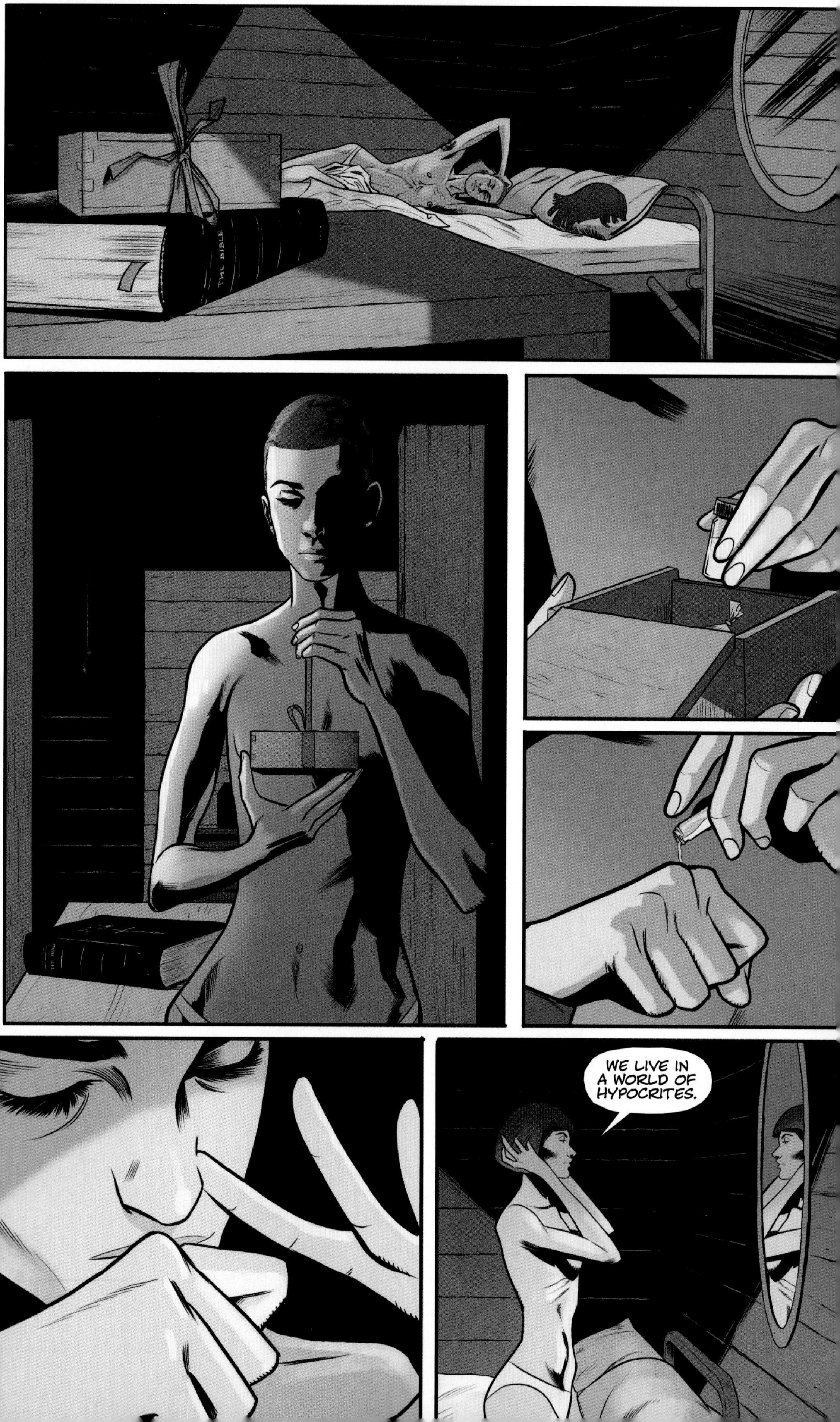
THE BIBLE
WE LIVE IN A WORLD OF HYPOCRITES.

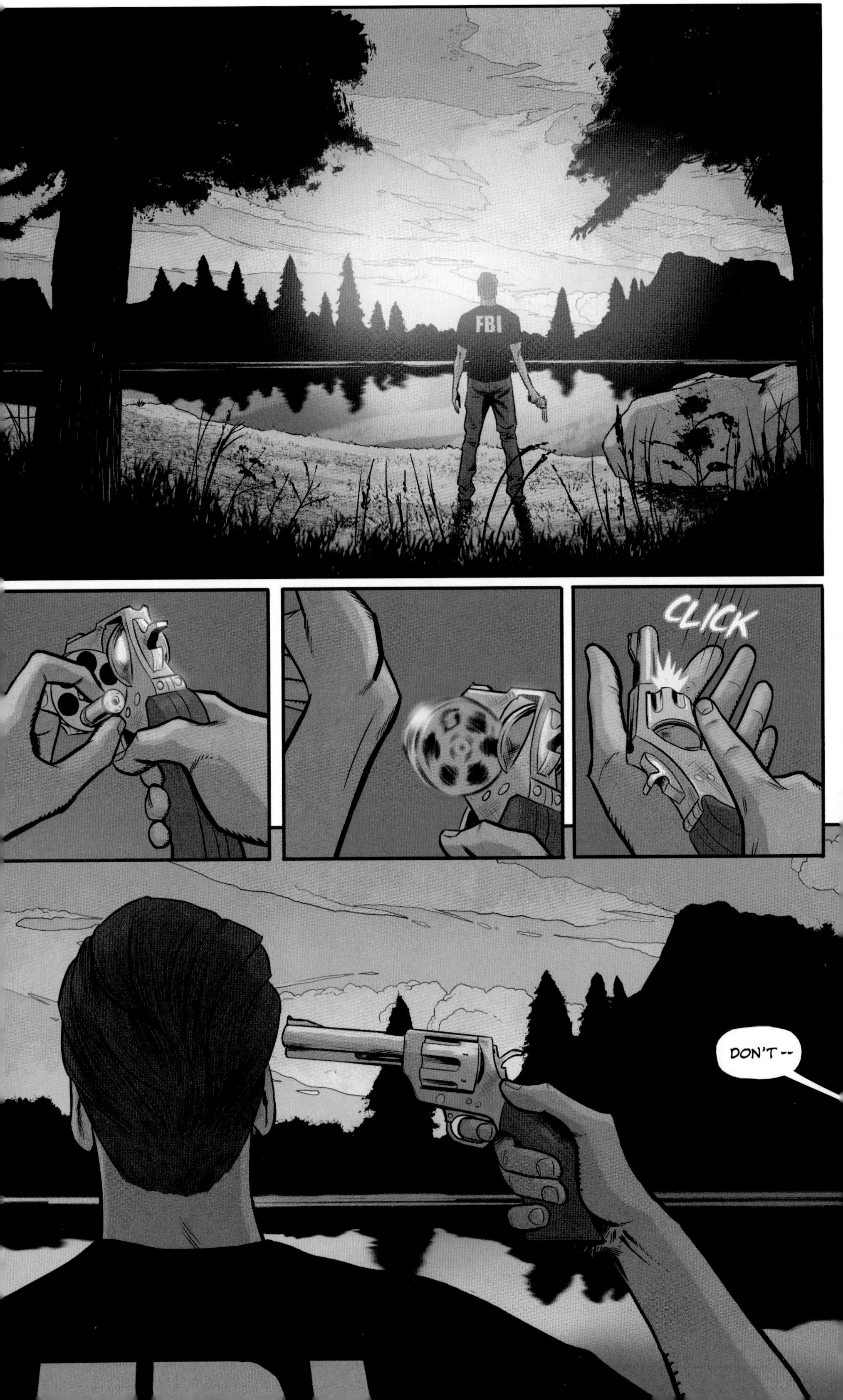
FBI
CLICK
DON'T --

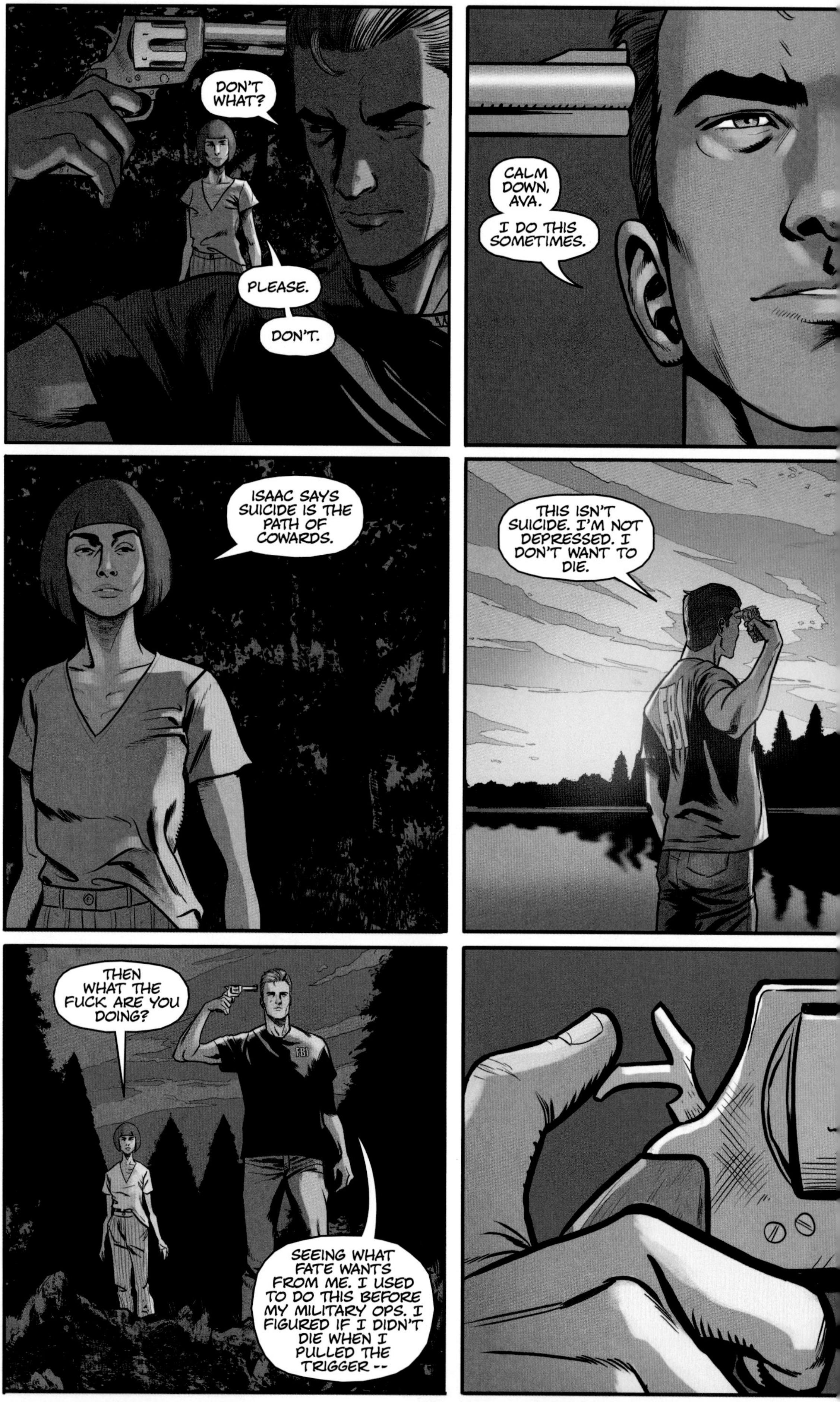
DON'T WHAT?
PLEASE.
DON'T.
CALM DOWN, AVA.
I DO THIS SOMETIMES.
ISAAC SAYS SUICIDE IS THE PATH OF COWARDS.
THIS ISN'T SUICIDE. I'M NOT DEPRESSED. I DON'T WANT TO DIE.
FBI
THEN WHAT THE FUCK ARE YOU DOING?
FBI
SEEING WHAT FATE WANTS FROM ME. I USED TO DO THIS BEFORE MY MILITARY OPS. I FIGURED IF I DIDN'T DIE WHEN I PULLED THE TRIGGER --

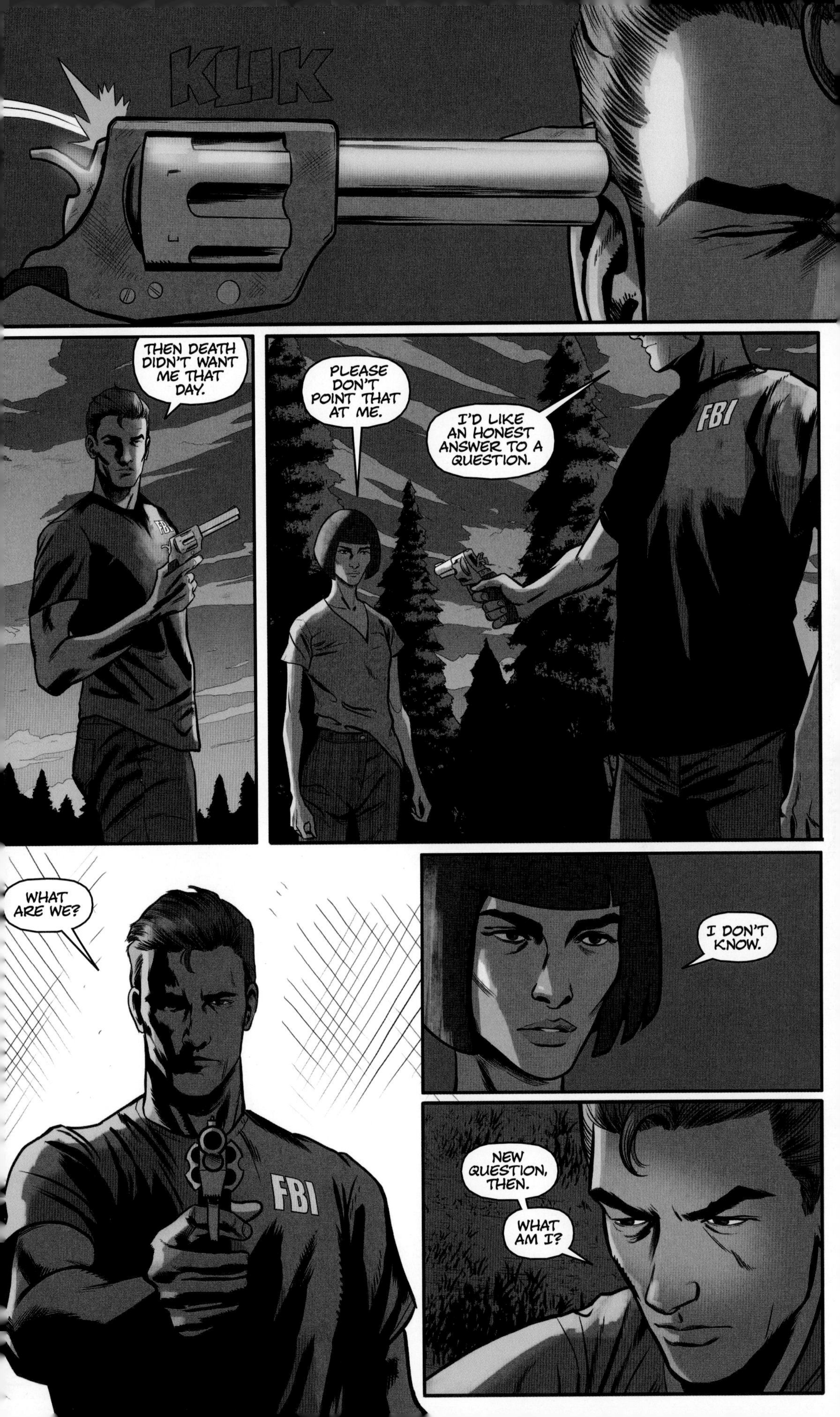
KLIK
THEN DEATH DIDN'T WANT ME THAT DAY.
PLEASE DON'T POINT THAT AT ME.
I'D LIKE AN HONEST ANSWER TO A QUESTION.
FBI
WHAT ARE WE?
FBI
I DON'T KNOW.
NEW QUESTION, THEN.
WHAT AM I?

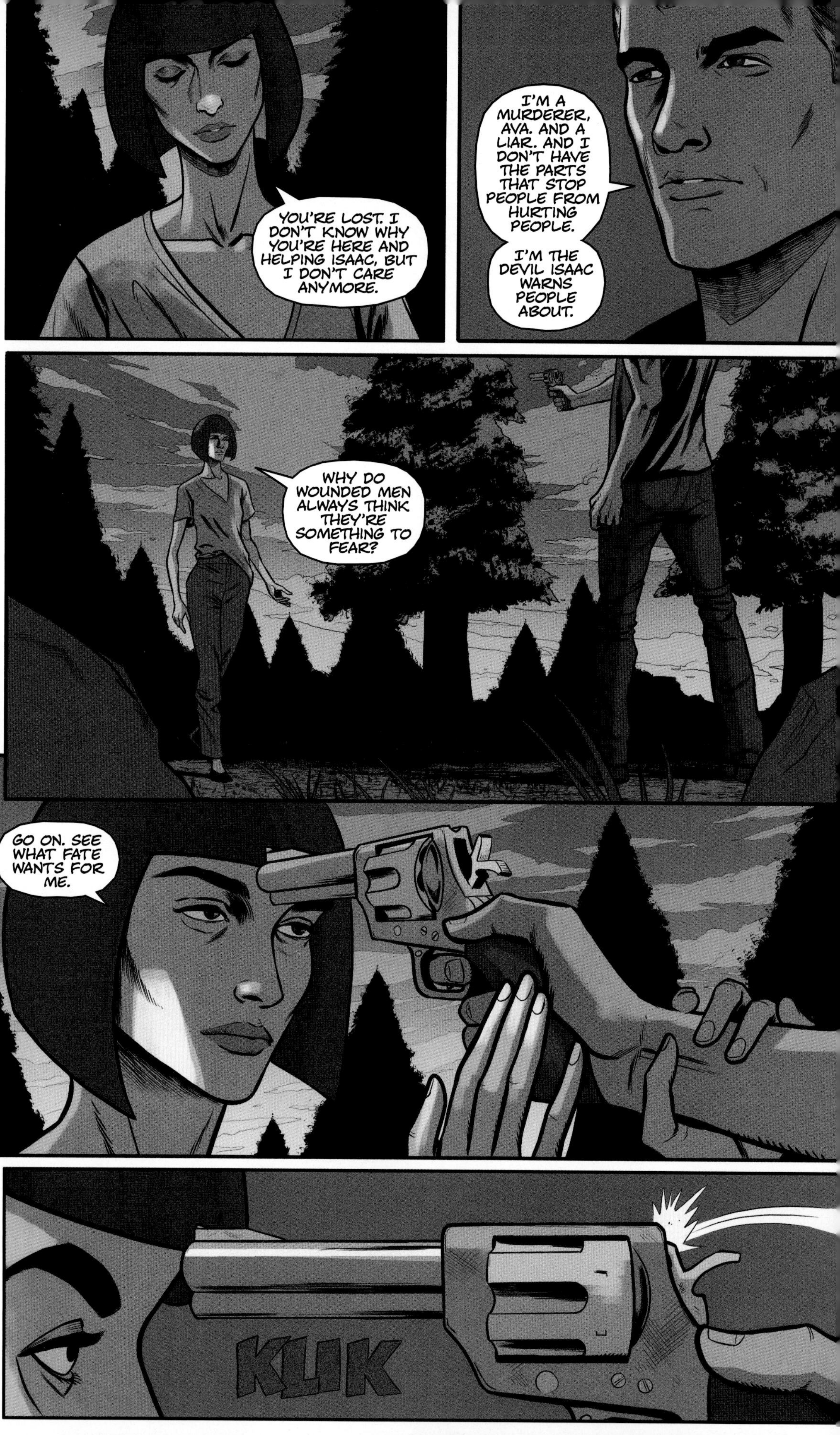
YOU'RE LOST. I DON'T KNOW WHY YOU'RE HERE AND HELPING ISAAC, BUT I DON'T CARE ANYMORE.
I'M A MURDERER, AVA. AND A LIAR. AND I DON'T HAVE THE PARTS THAT STOP PEOPLE FROM HURTING PEOPLE.
I'M THE DEVIL ISAAC WARNS PEOPLE ABOUT.
WHY DO WOUNDED MEN ALWAYS THINK THEY'RE SOMETHING TO FEAR?
GO ON. SEE WHAT FATE WANTS FOR ME.
KLIK

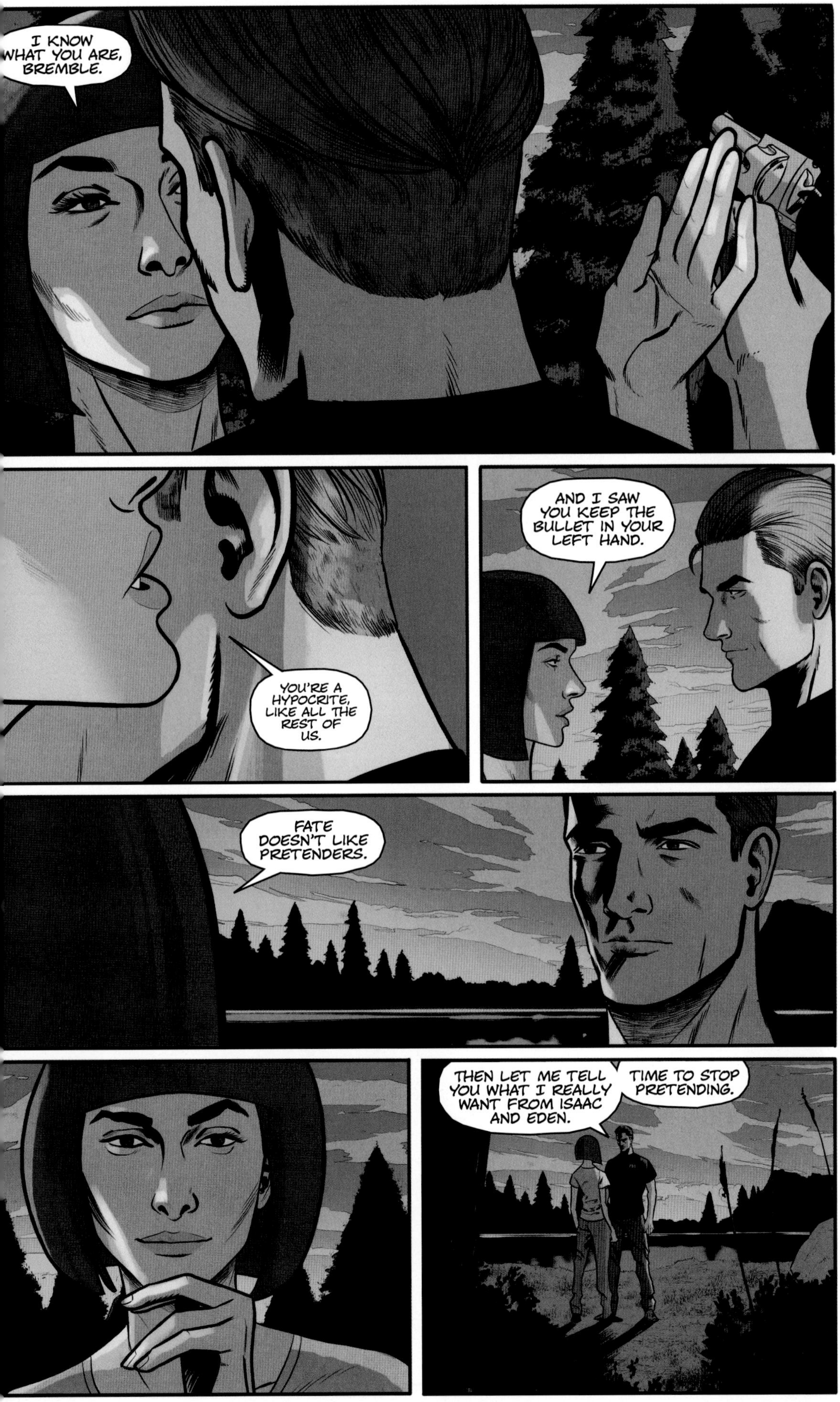
I KNOW WHAT YOU ARE, BREMBLE.
YOU'RE A HYPOCRITE, LIKE ALL THE REST OF US.
AND I SAW YOU KEEP THE BULLET IN YOUR LEFT HAND.
FATE DOESN'T LIKE PRETENDERS.
TIME TO STOP PRETENDING.
THEN LET ME TELL YOU WHAT I REALLY WANT FROM ISAAC AND EDEN.

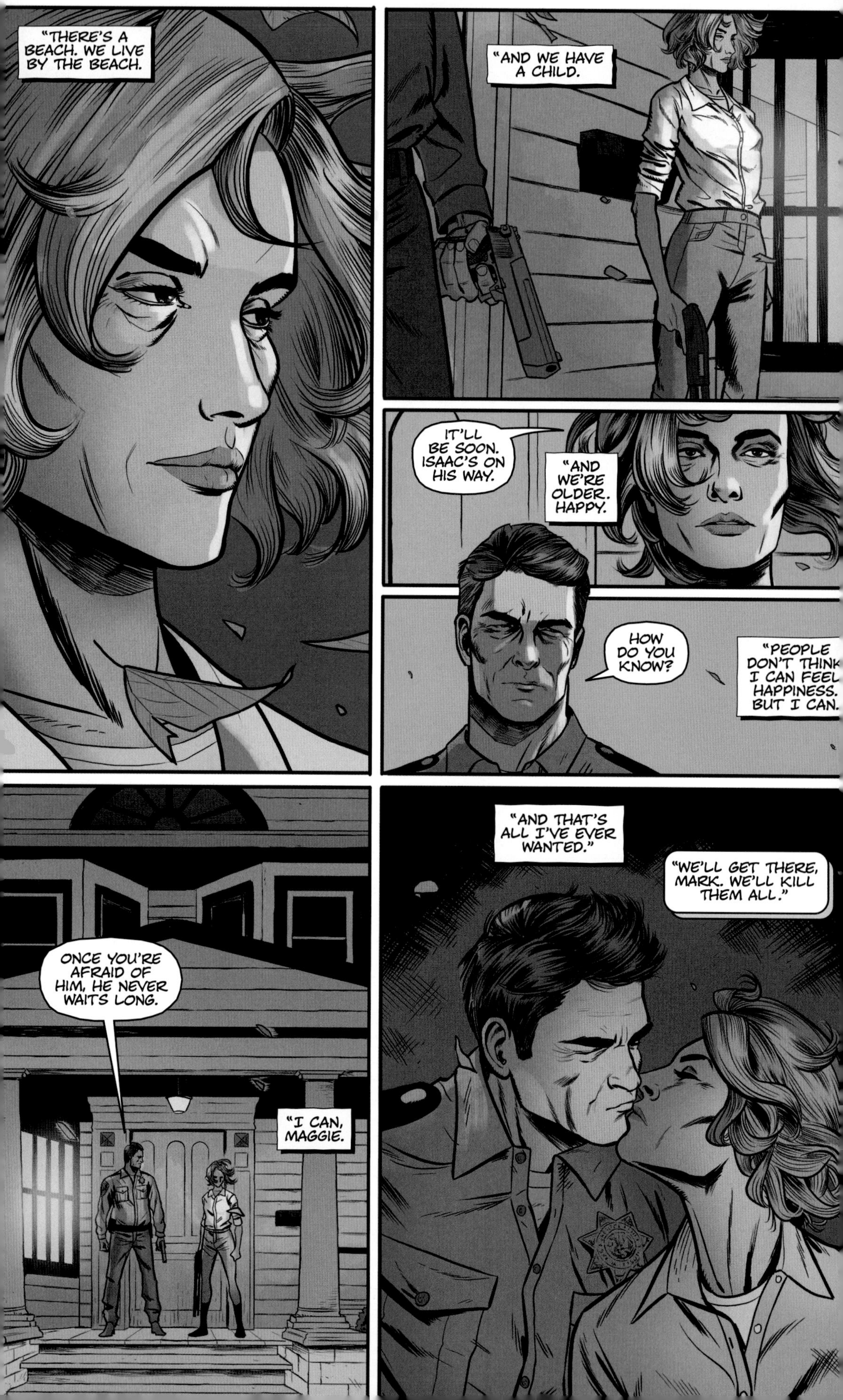
"THERE'S A BEACH. WE LIVE BY THE BEACH.
"AND WE HAVE A CHILD.
IT'LL BE SOON. ISAAC'S ON HIS WAY.
"AND WE'RE OLDER. HAPPY.
HOW DO YOU KNOW?
"PEOPLE DON'T THINK I CAN FEEL HAPPINESS. BUT I CAN.
ONCE YOU'RE AFRAID OF HIM, HE NEVER WAITS LONG.
"I CAN, MAGGIE.
"AND THAT'S ALL I'VE EVER WANTED."
"WE'LL GET THERE, MARK. WE'LL KILL THEM ALL."

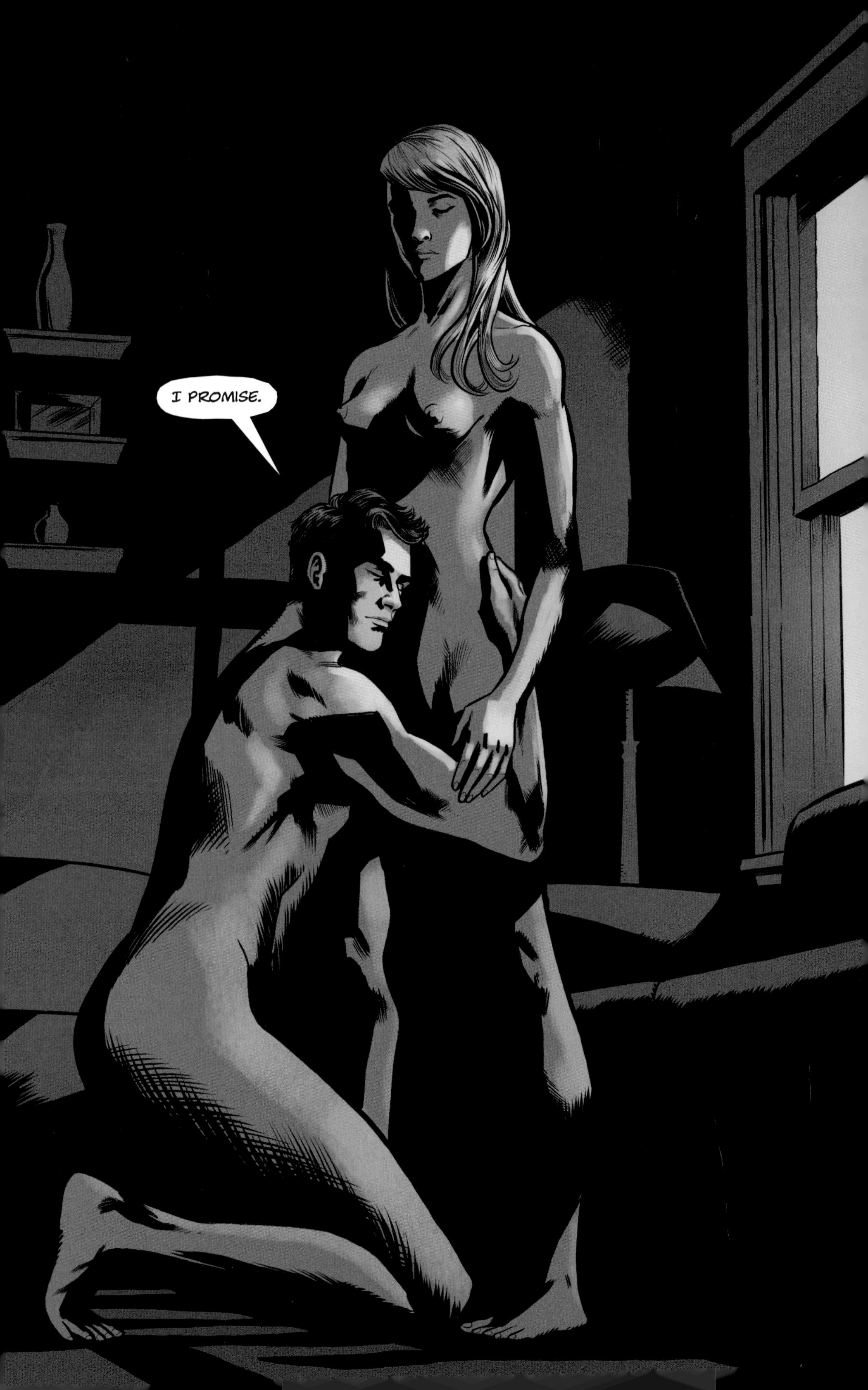
I PROMISE.

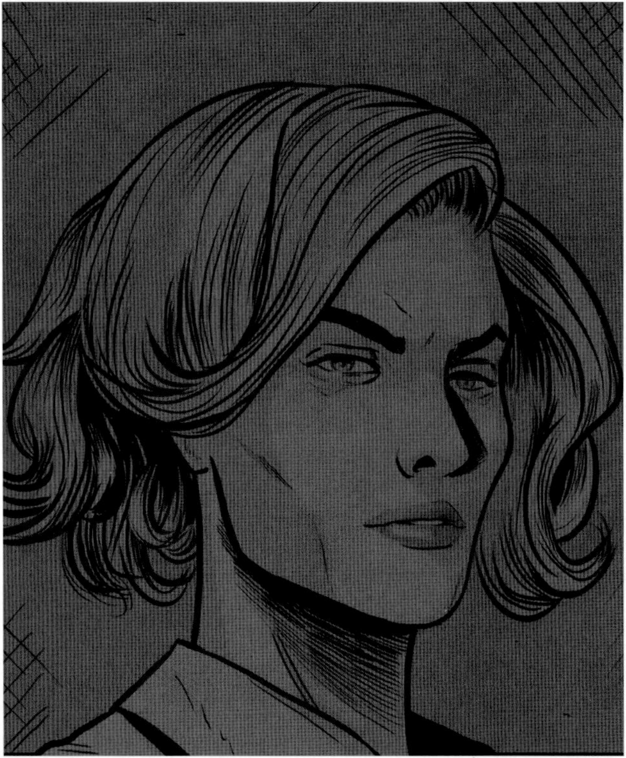

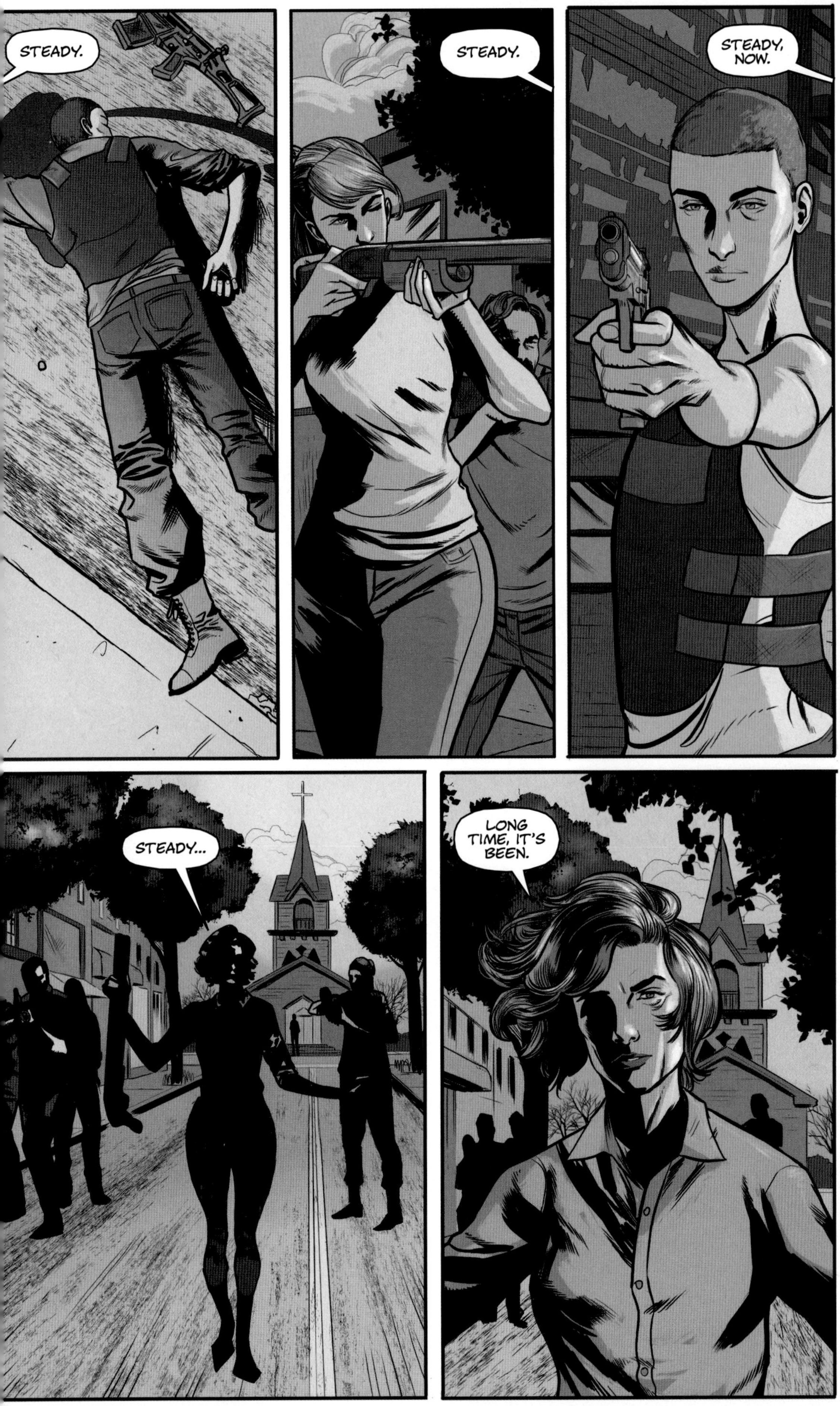
STEADY.
STEADY.
STEADY, NOW.
STEADY...
LONG TIME, IT'S BEEN.

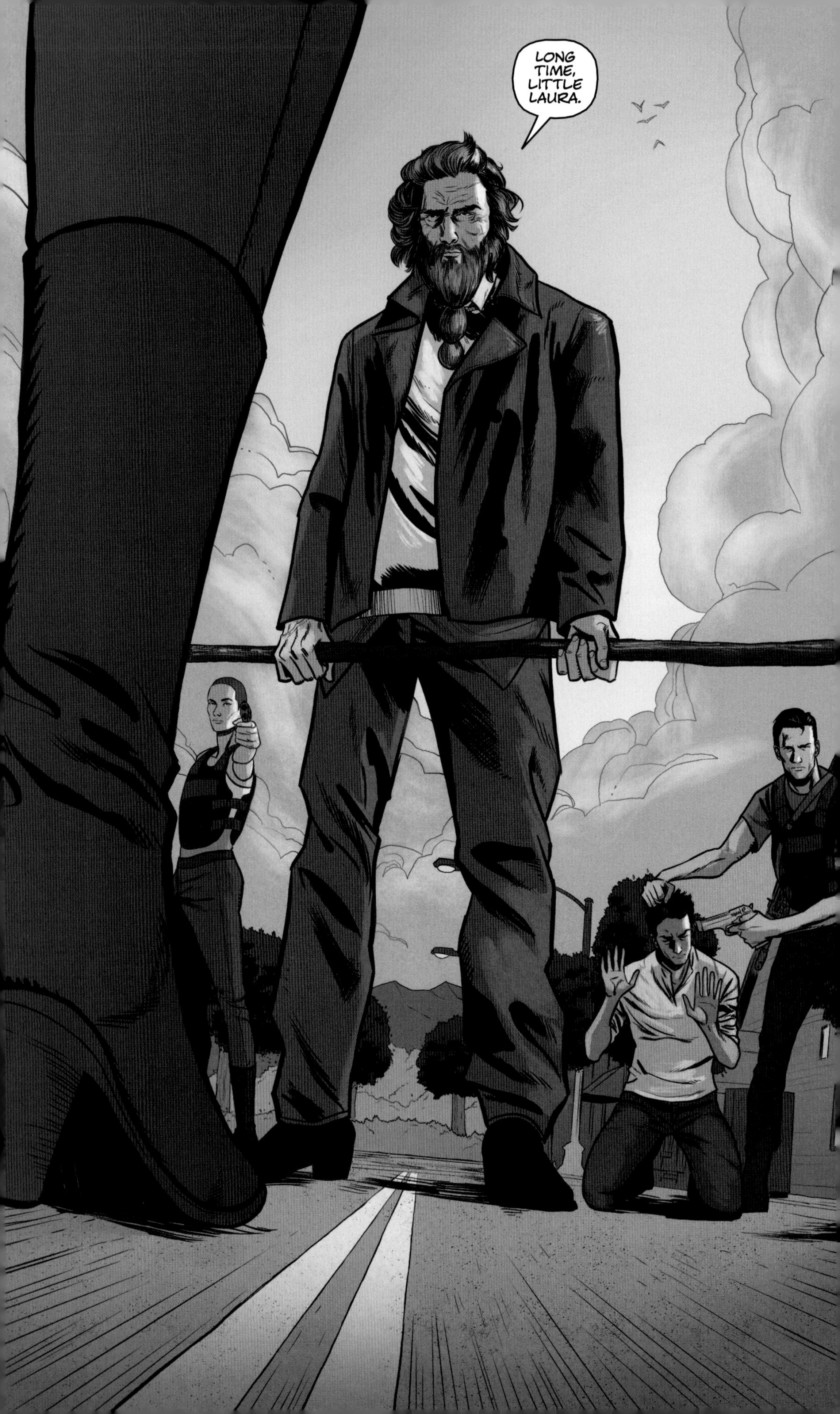
LONG TIME, LITTLE LAURA.

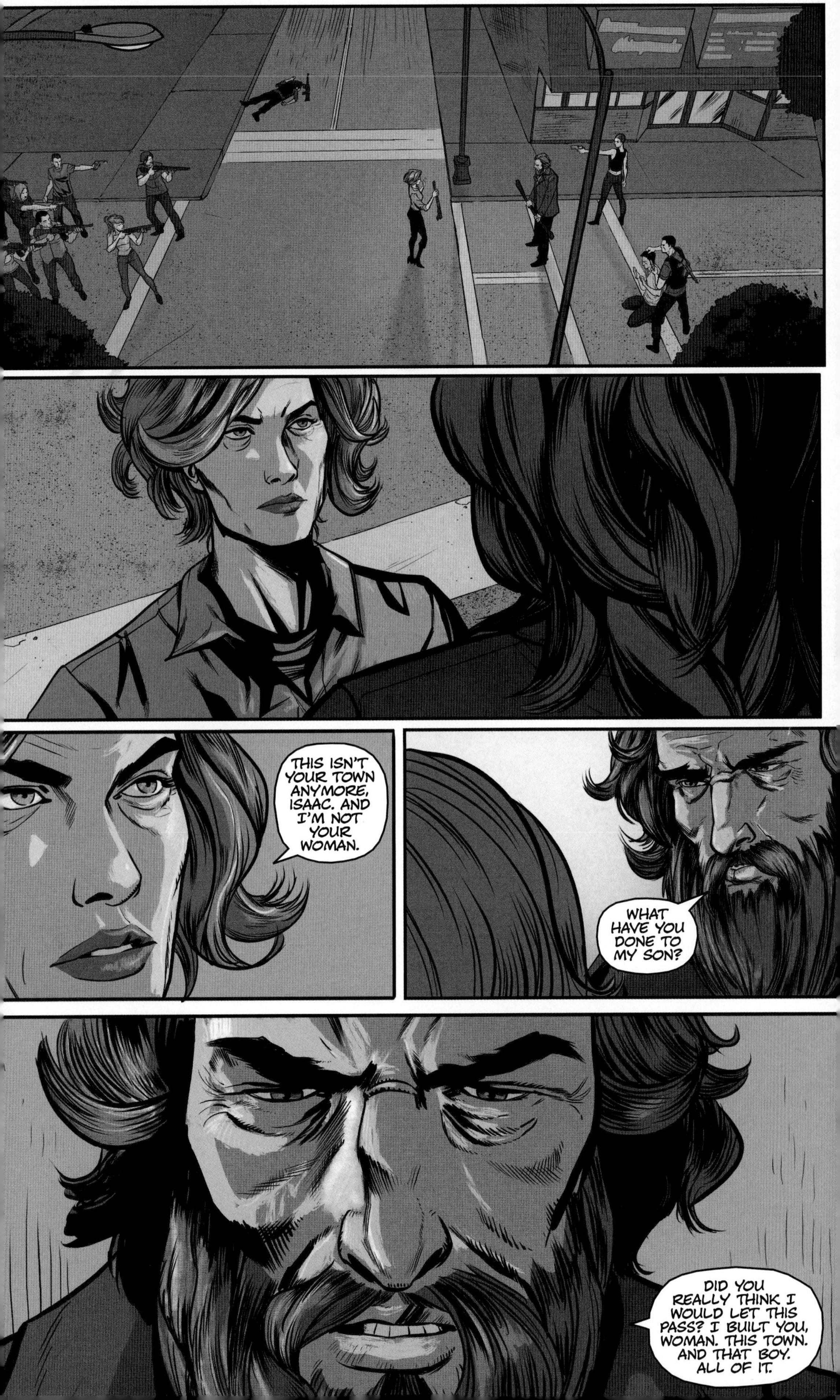
THIS ISN'T YOUR TOWN ANYMORE, ISAAC. AND I'M NOT YOUR WOMAN.
WHAT HAVE YOU DONE TO MY SON?
DID YOU REALLY THINK I WOULD LET THIS PASS? I BUILT YOU, WOMAN. THIS TOWN. AND THAT BOY. ALL OF IT.

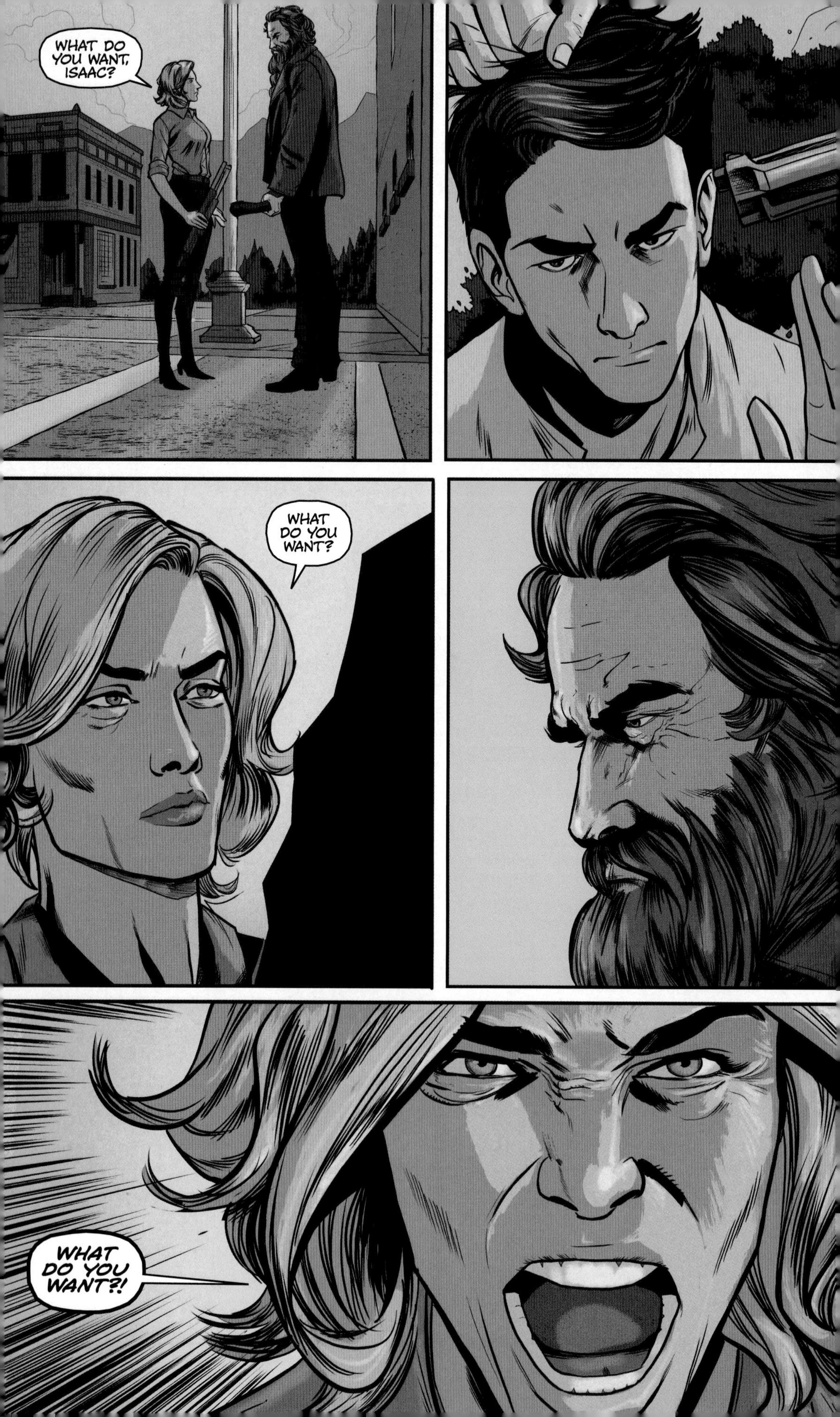
WHAT DO YOU WANT, ISAAC?
WHAT DO YOU WANT?
WHAT DO YOU WANT?!

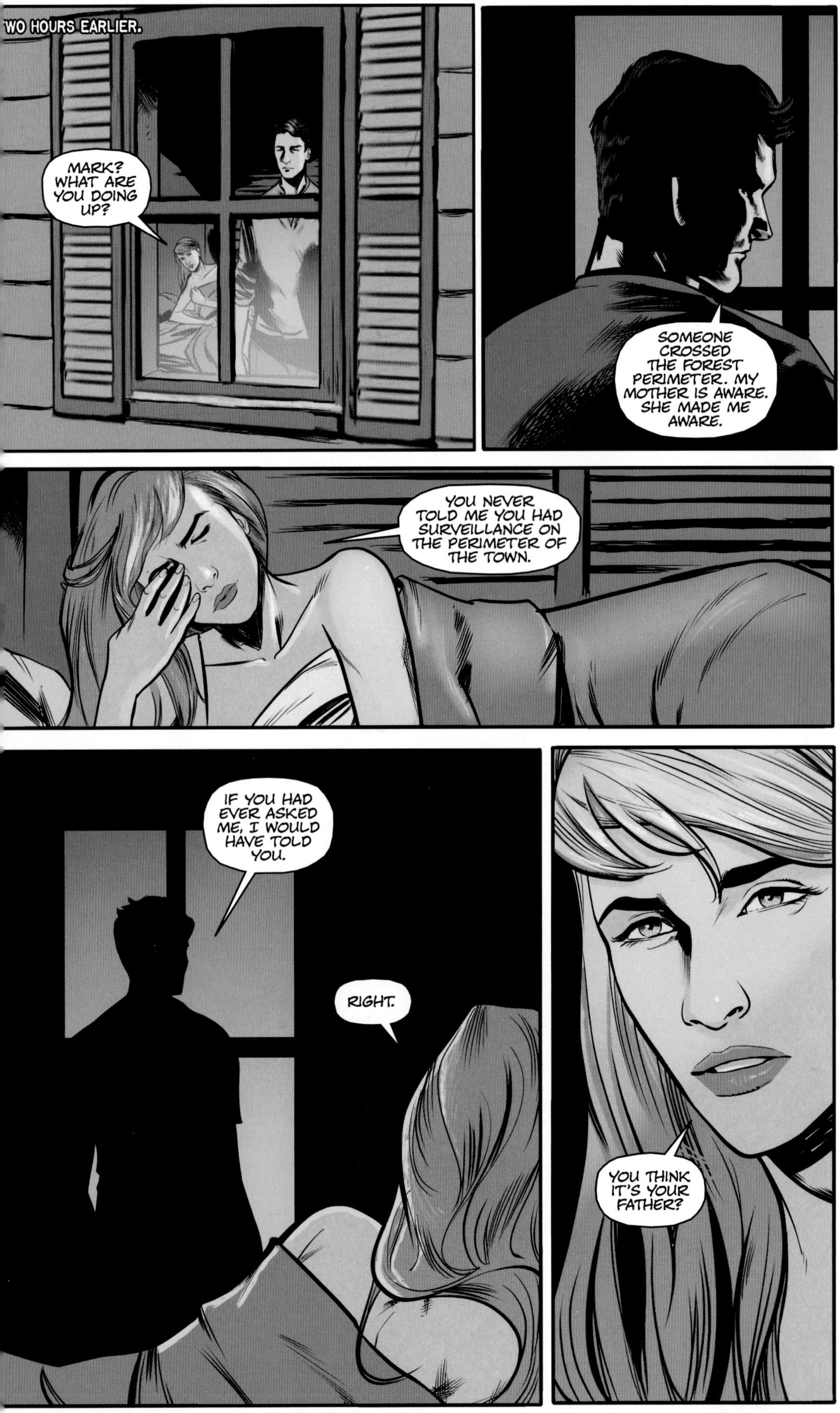
TWO HOURS EARLIER.
MARK? WHAT ARE YOU DOING UP?
SOMEONE CROSSED THE FOREST PERIMETER. MY MOTHER IS AWARE. SHE MADE ME AWARE.
YOU NEVER TOLD ME YOU HAD SURVEILLANCE ON THE PERIMETER OF THE TOWN.
IF YOU HAD EVER ASKED ME, I WOULD HAVE TOLD YOU.
RIGHT.
YOU THINK IT'S YOUR FATHER?

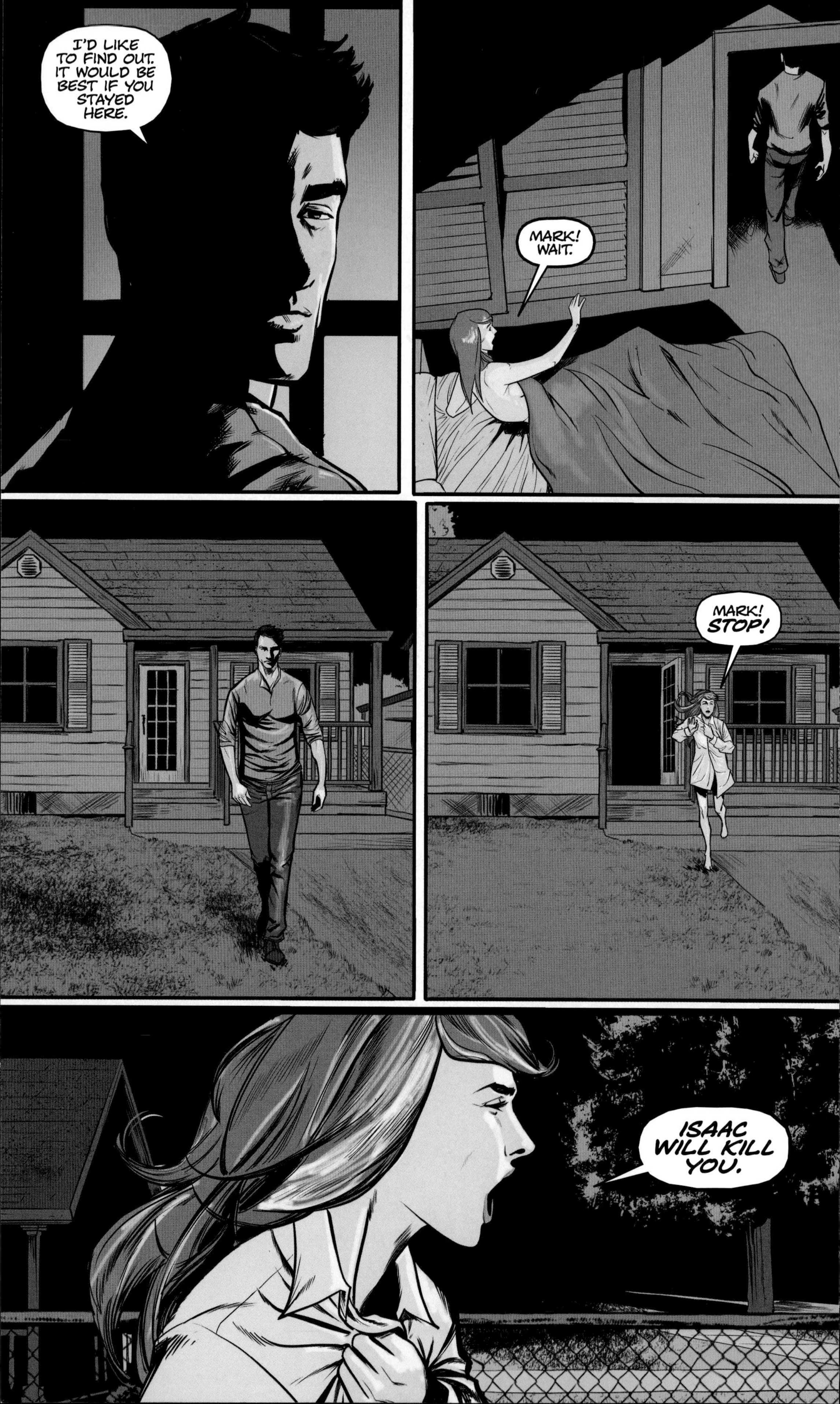
I'D LIKE TO FIND OUT. IT WOULD BE BEST IF YOU STAYED HERE.
MARK! WAIT.
MARK! STOP!
ISAAC WILL KILL YOU.

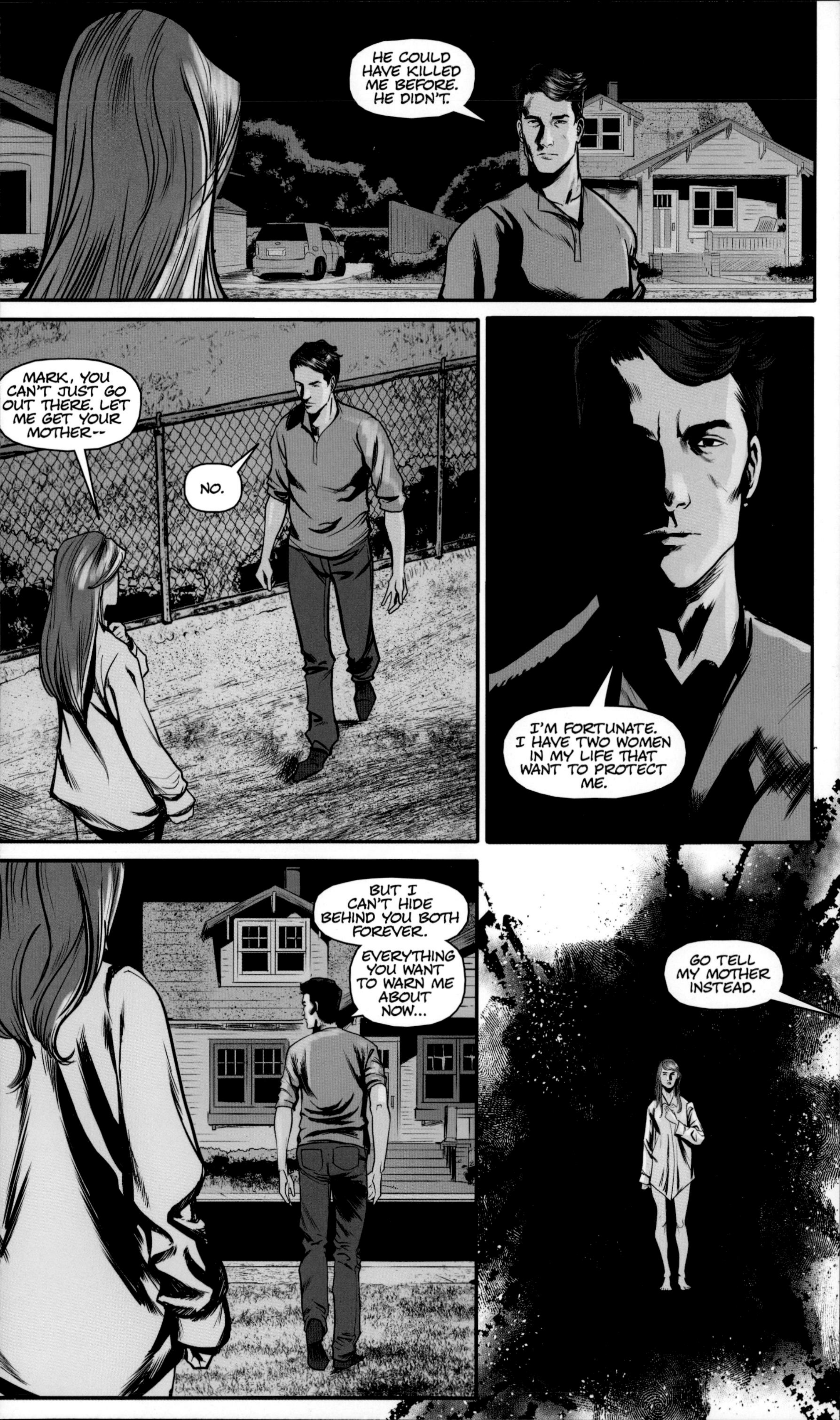
HE COULD HAVE KILLED ME BEFORE. HE DIDN'T.
MARK, YOU CAN'T JUST GO OUT THERE. LET ME GET YOUR MOTHER--
NO.
I'M FORTUNATE. I HAVE TWO WOMEN IN MY LIFE THAT WANT TO PROTECT ME.
BUT I CAN'T HIDE BEHIND YOU BOTH FOREVER.
EVERYTHING YOU WANT TO WARN ME ABOUT NOW...
GO TELL MY MOTHER INSTEAD.

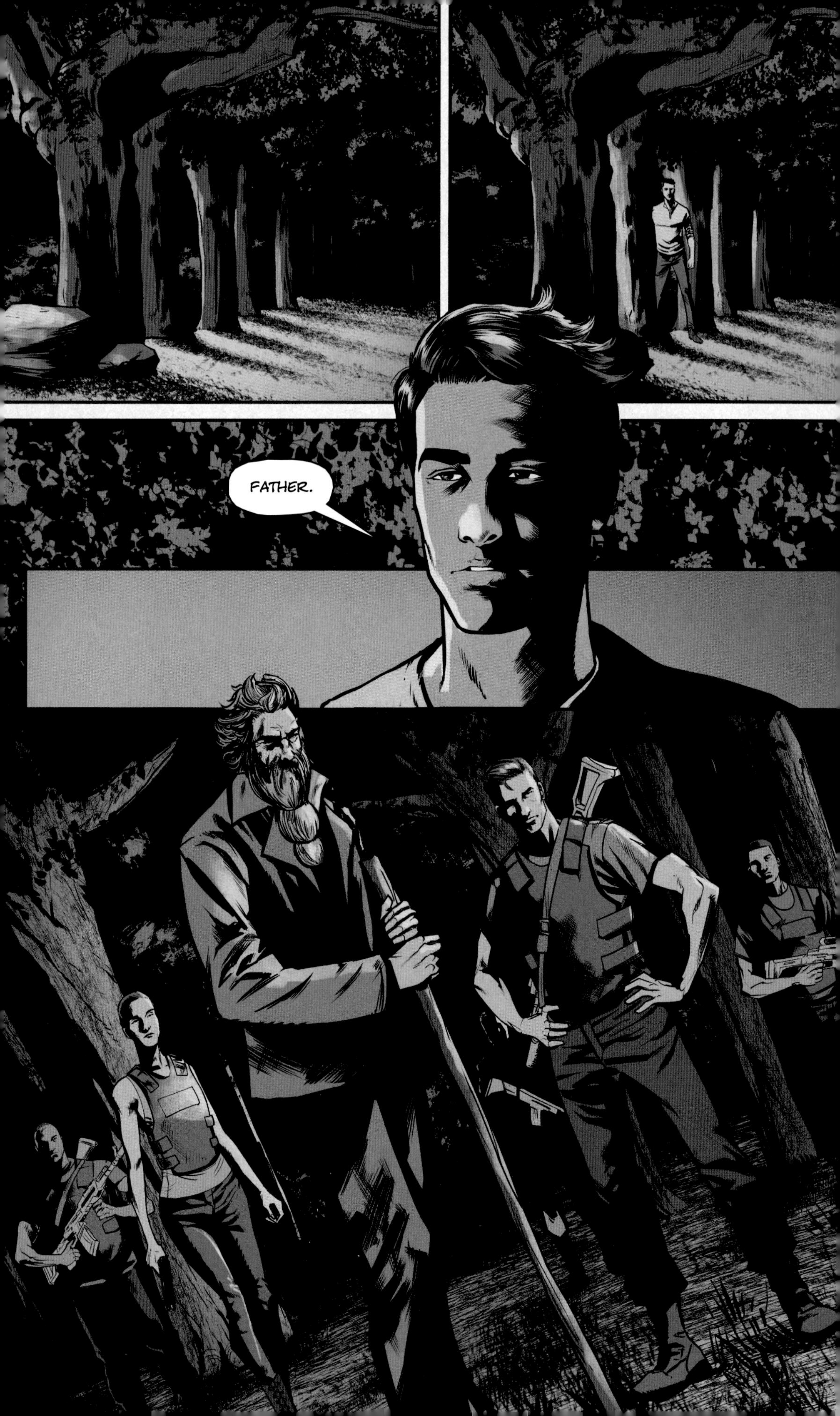
FATHER.

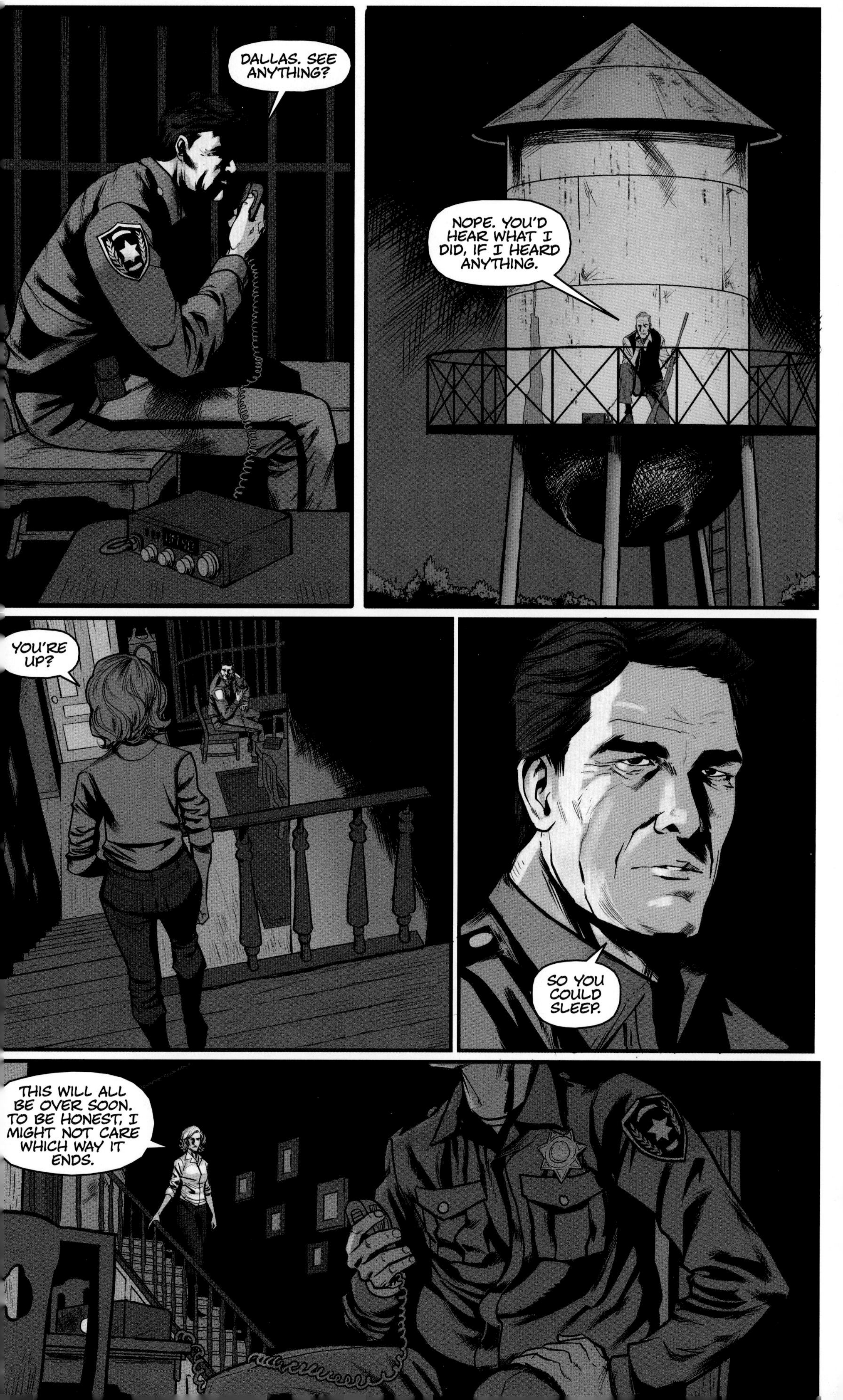
DALLAS. SEE ANYTHING?
NOPE. YOU'D HEAR WHAT I DID, IF I HEARD ANYTHING.
YOU'RE UP?
SO YOU COULD SLEEP.
THIS WILL ALL BE OVER SOON. TO BE HONEST, I MIGHT NOT CARE WHICH WAY IT ENDS.

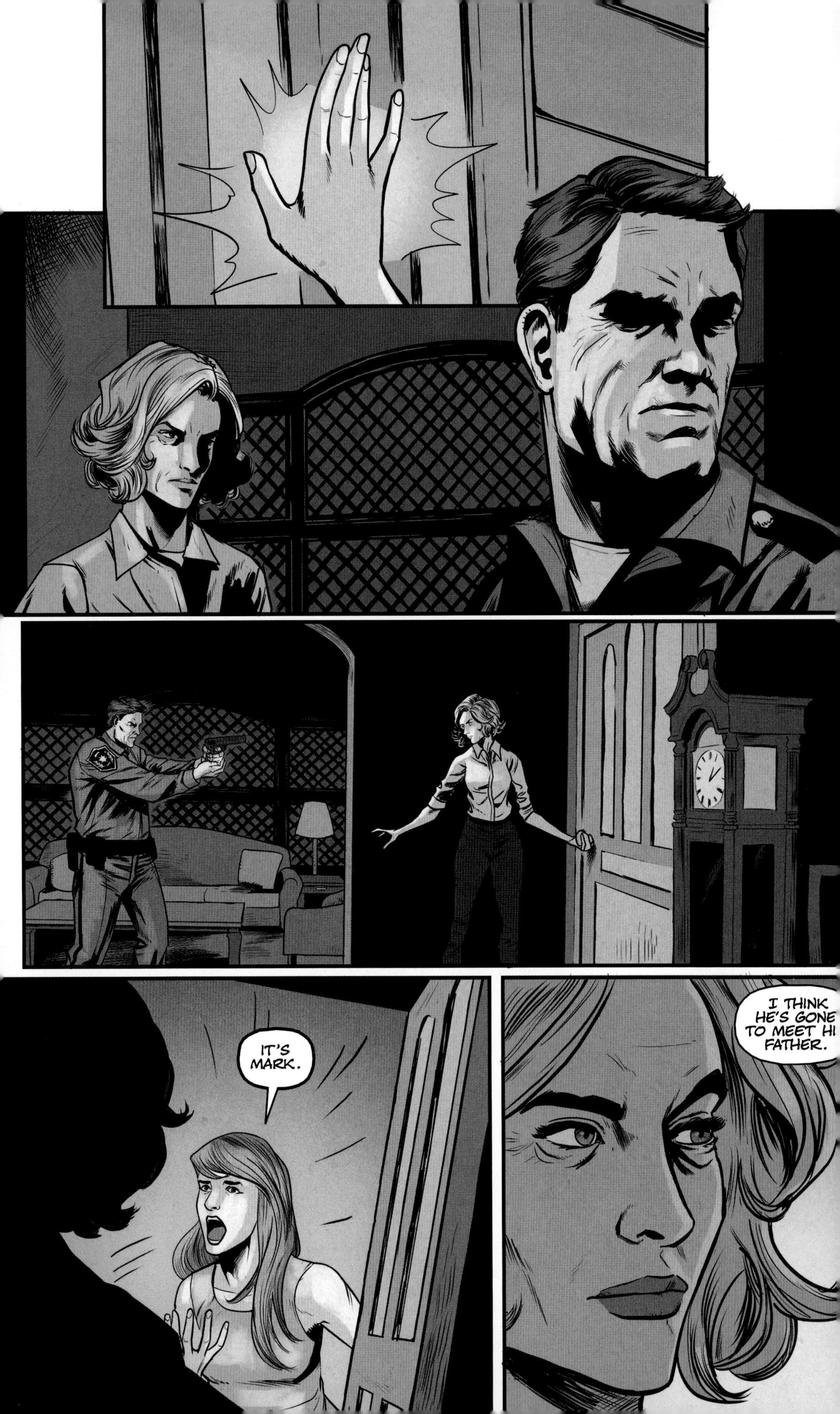
IT'S MARK.
I THINK HE'S GONE TO MEET HI FATHER.

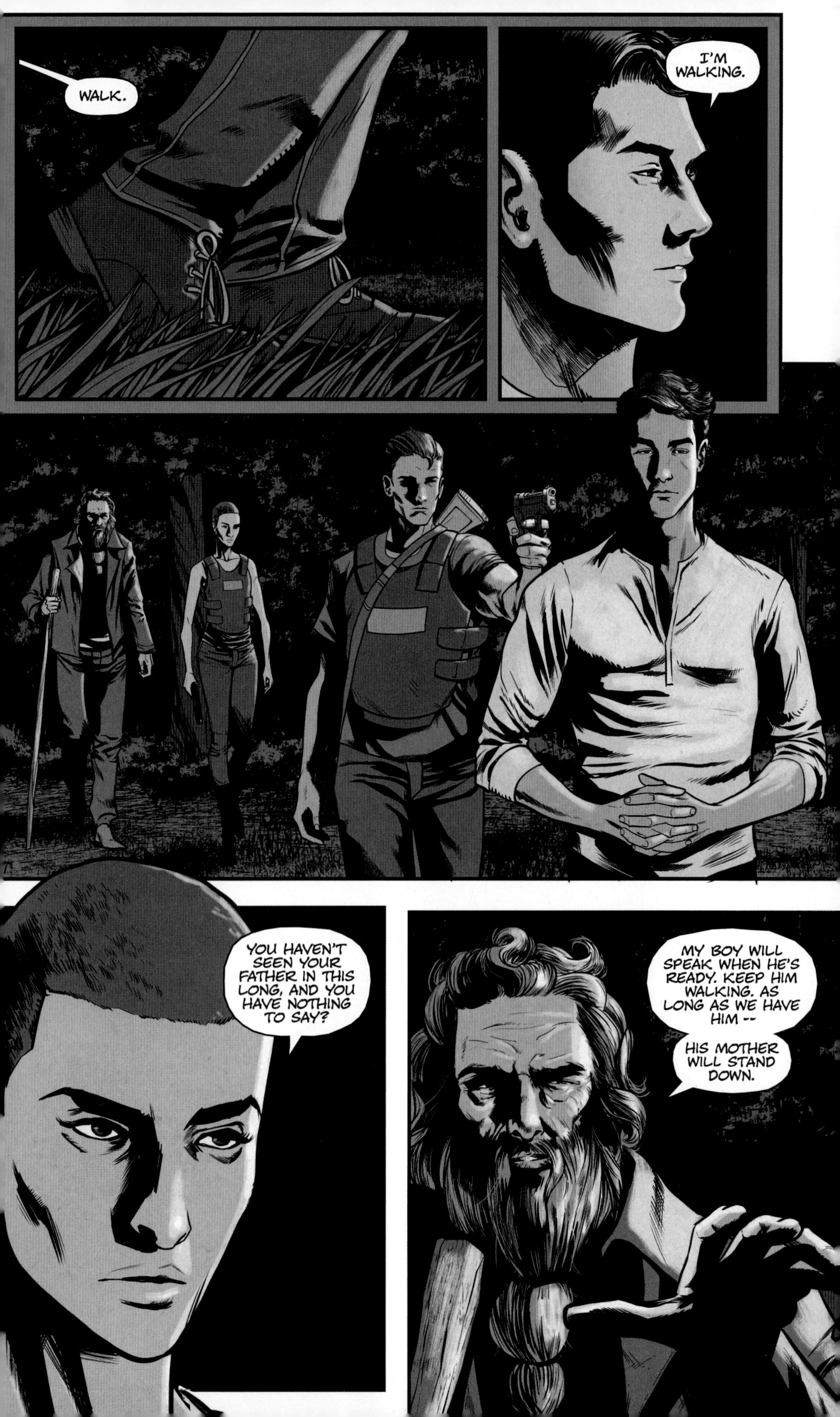
WALK.
I'M WALKING.
YOU HAVEN'T SEEN YOUR FATHER IN THIS LONG, AND YOU HAVE NOTHING TO SAY?
MY BOY WILL SPEAK WHEN HE'S READY. KEEP HIM WALKING. AS LONG AS WE HAVE HIM --
HIS MOTHER WILL STAND DOWN.

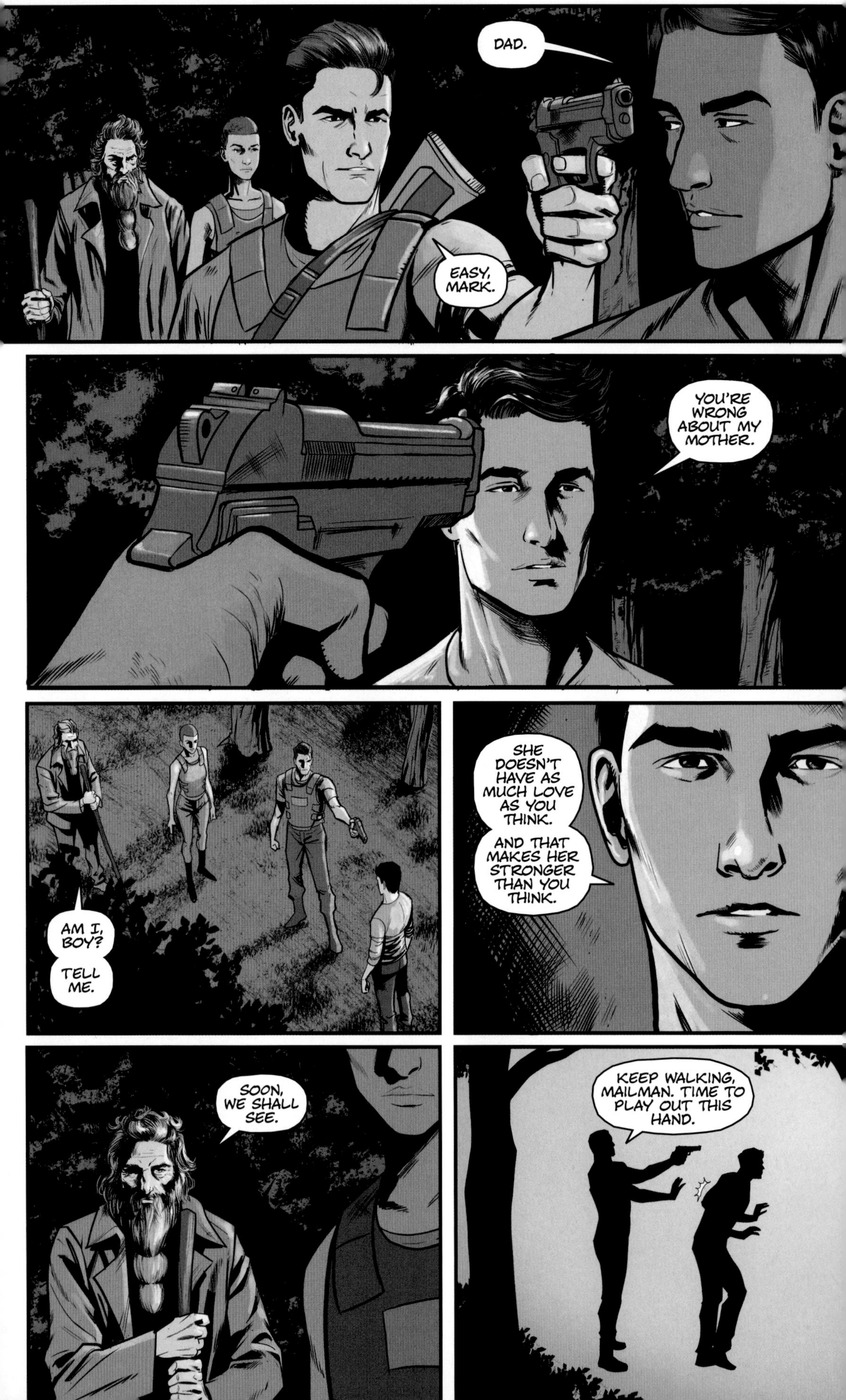
DAD.
EASY, MARK.
YOU'RE WRONG ABOUT MY MOTHER.
AM I, BOY?
TELL ME.
SHE DOESN'T HAVE AS MUCH LOVE AS YOU THINK.
AND THAT MAKES HER STRONGER THAN YOU THINK.
SOON, WE SHALL SEE.
KEEP WALKING, MAILMAN. TIME TO PLAY OUT THIS HAND.

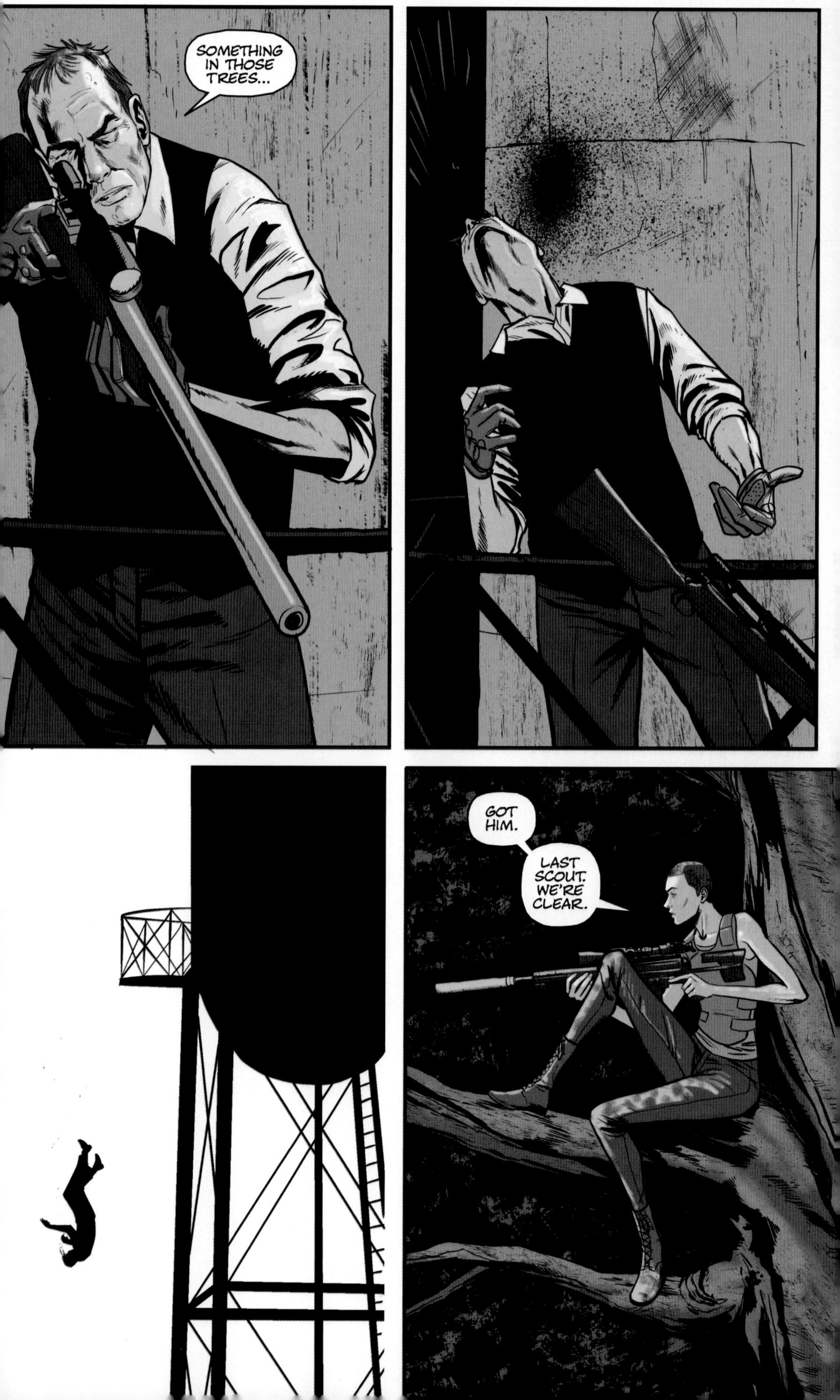
SOMETHING IN THOSE TREES...
GOT HIM.
LAST SCOUT. WE'RE CLEAR.

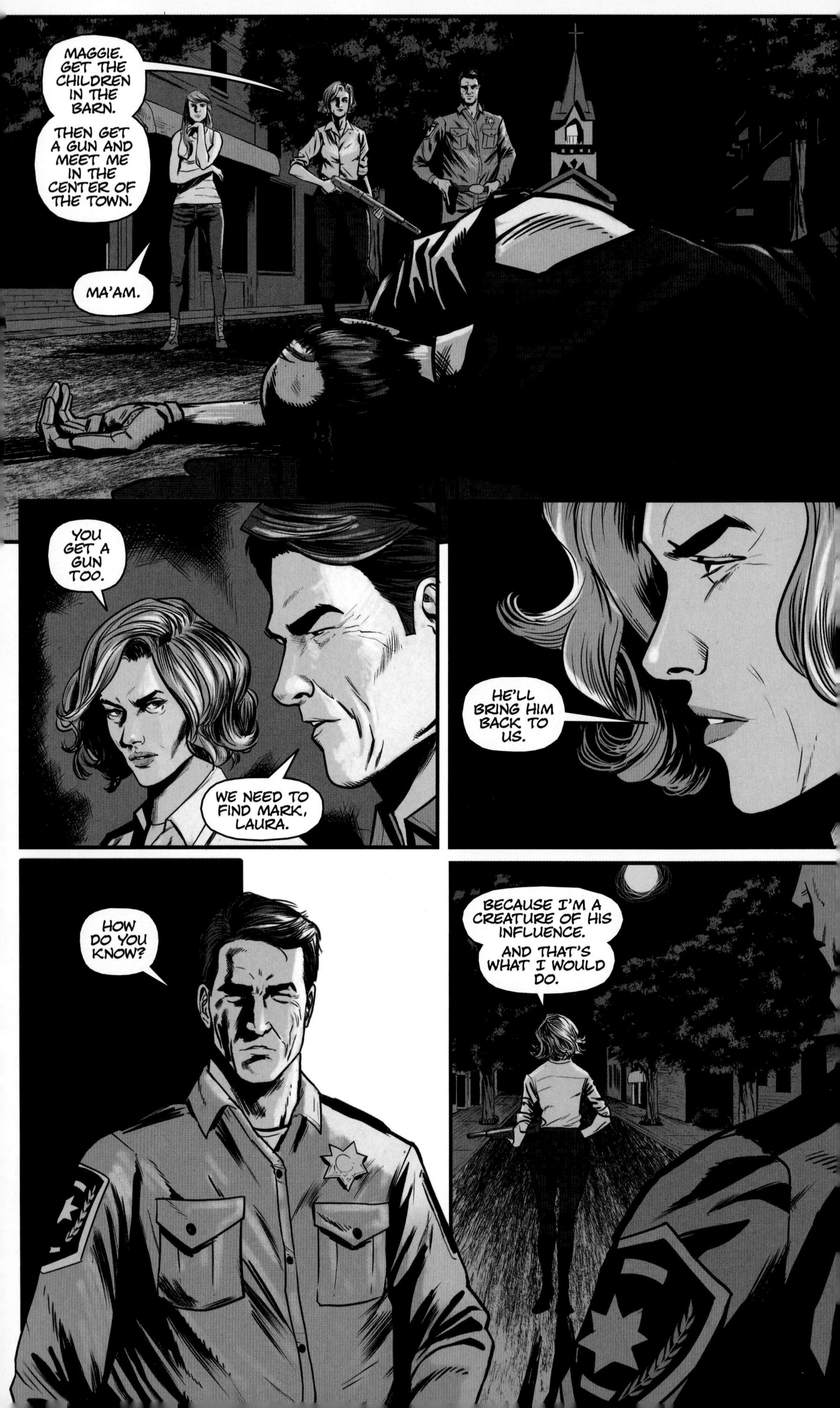
MAGGIE. GET THE CHILDREN IN THE BARN.
THEN GET A GUN AND MEET ME IN THE CENTER OF THE TOWN.
MA'AM.
YOU GET A GUN TOO.
WE NEED TO FIND MARK, LAURA.
HE'LL BRING HIM BACK TO US.
HOW DO YOU KNOW?
BECAUSE I'M A CREATURE OF HIS INFLUENCE.
AND THAT'S WHAT I WOULD DO.

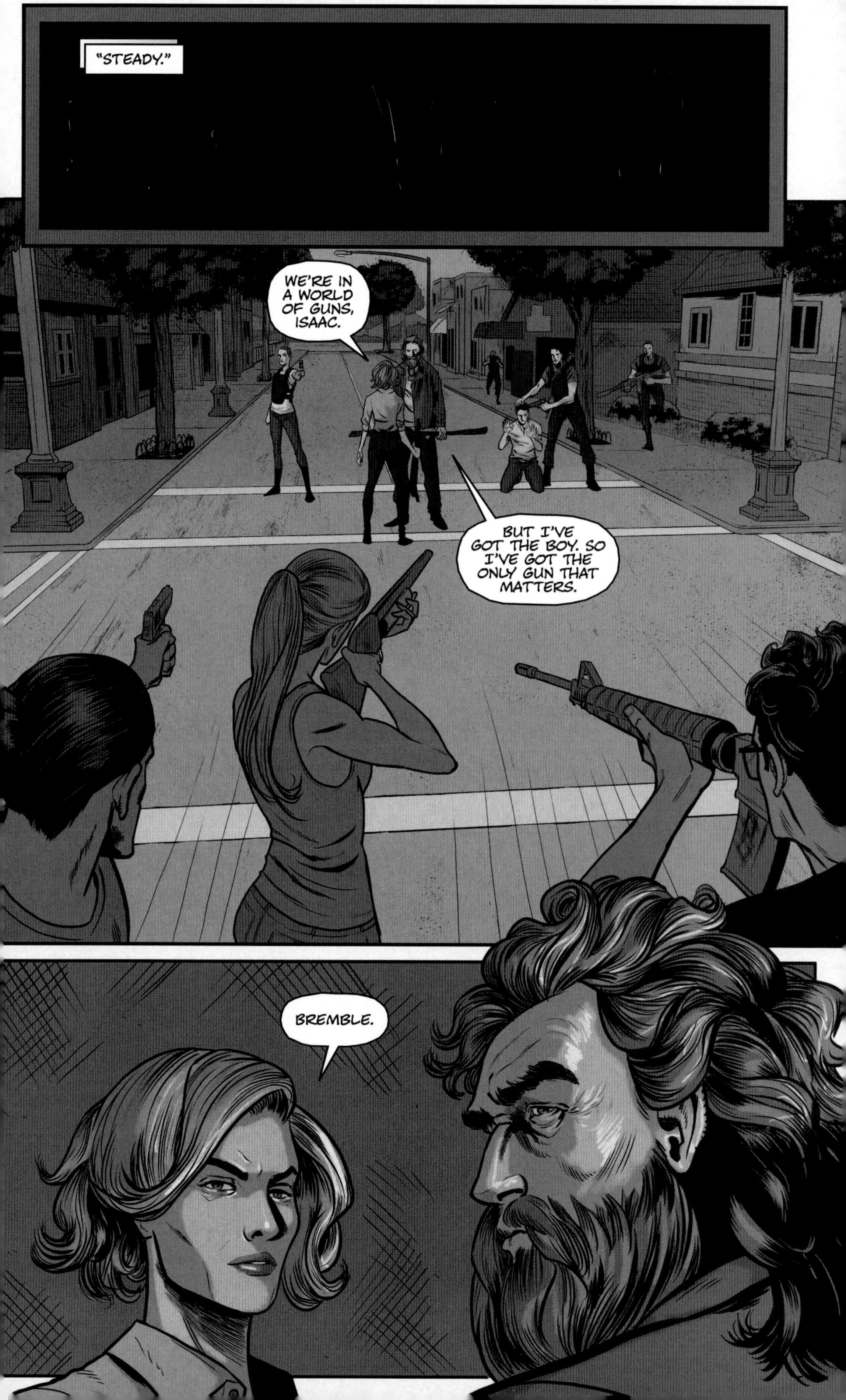
"STEADY."
WE'RE IN A WORLD OF GUNS, ISAAC.
BUT I'VE GOT THE BOY. SO I'VE GOT THE ONLY GUN THAT MATTERS.
BREMBLE.

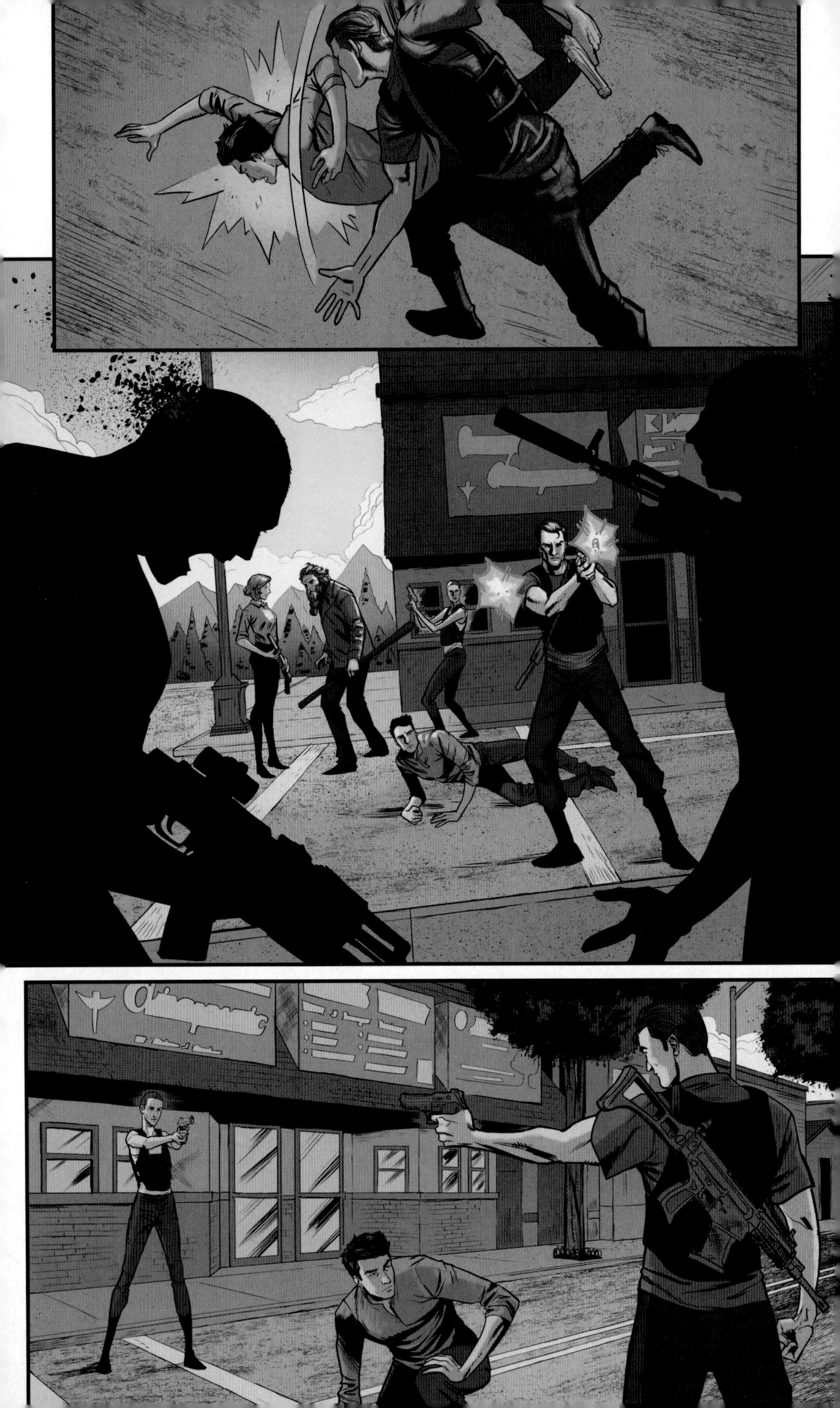

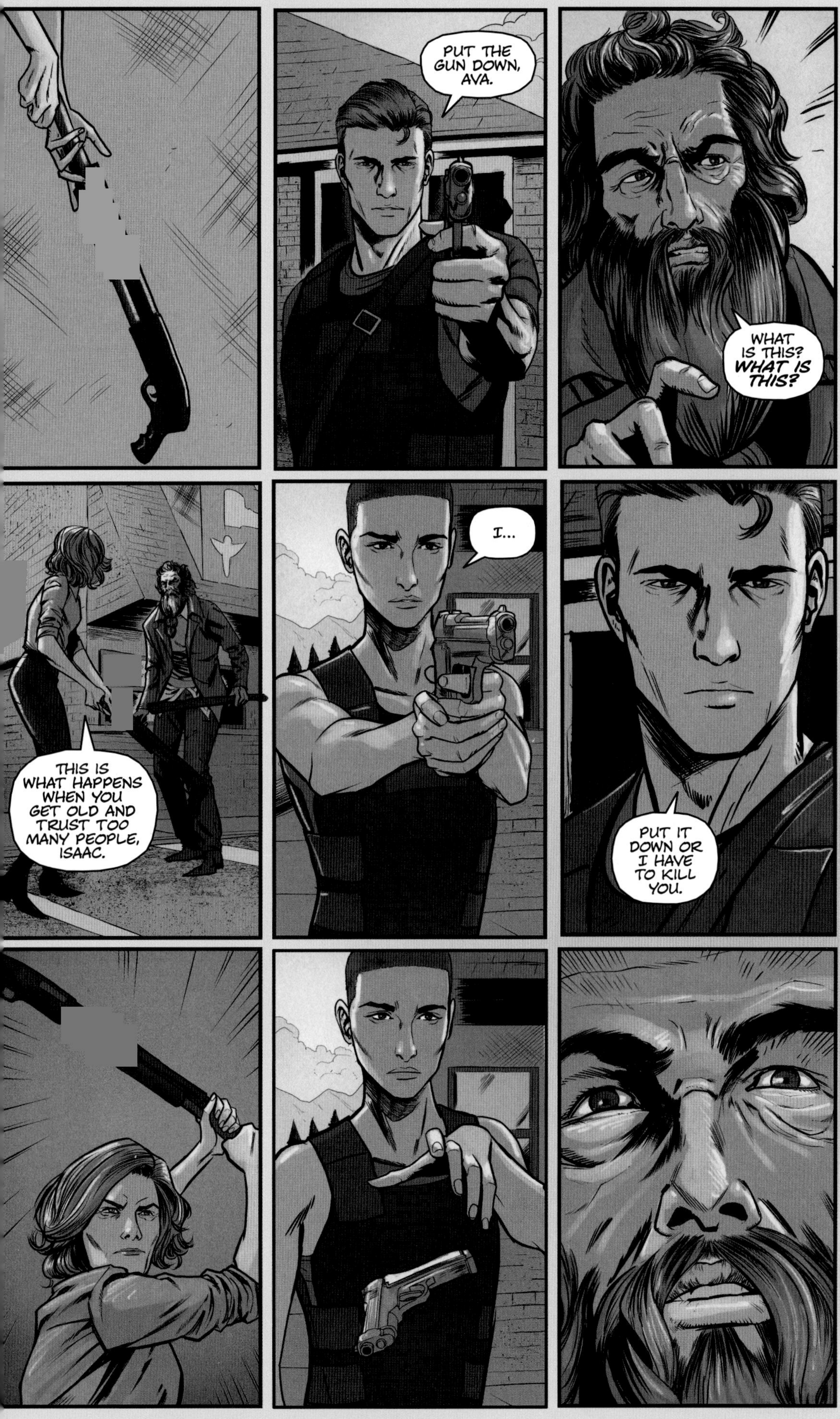
PUT THE GUN DOWN, AVA.
WHAT IS THIS? *WHAT IS THIS?*
THIS IS WHAT HAPPENS WHEN YOU GET OLD AND TRUST TOO MANY PEOPLE, ISAAC.
I...
PUT IT DOWN OR I HAVE TO KILL YOU.

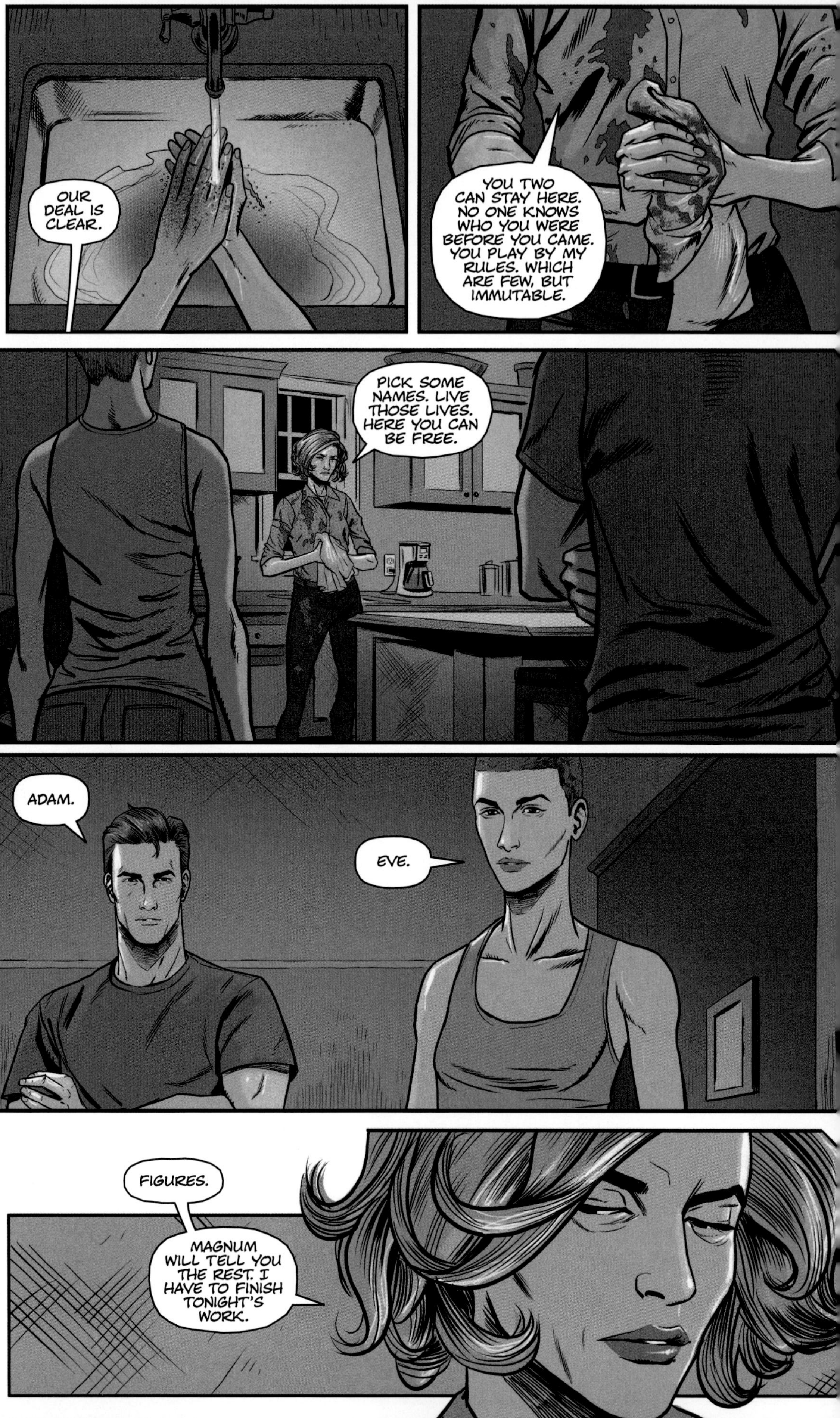
OUR DEAL IS CLEAR.
YOU TWO CAN STAY HERE. NO ONE KNOWS WHO YOU WERE BEFORE YOU CAME. YOU PLAY BY MY RULES. WHICH ARE FEW, BUT IMMUTABLE.
PICK SOME NAMES. LIVE THOSE LIVES. HERE YOU CAN BE FREE.
ADAM.
EVE.
FIGURES.
MAGNUM WILL TELL YOU THE REST. I HAVE TO FINISH TONIGHT'S WORK.

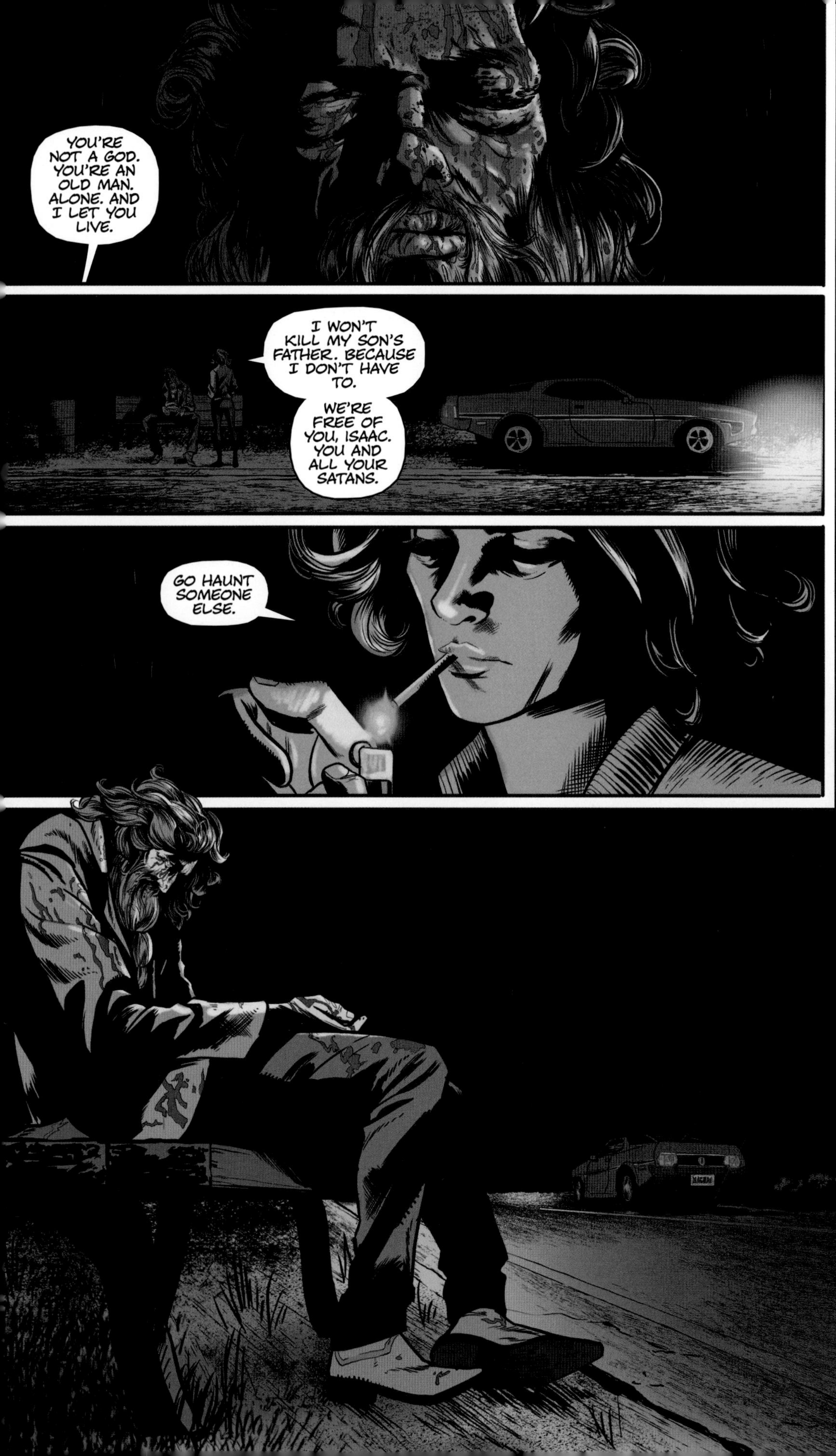
YOU'RE NOT A GOD. YOU'RE AN OLD MAN. ALONE. AND I LET YOU LIVE.
I WON'T KILL MY SON'S FATHER. BECAUSE I DON'T HAVE TO.
WE'RE FREE OF YOU, ISAAC. YOU AND ALL YOUR SATANS.
GO HAUNT SOMEONE ELSE.

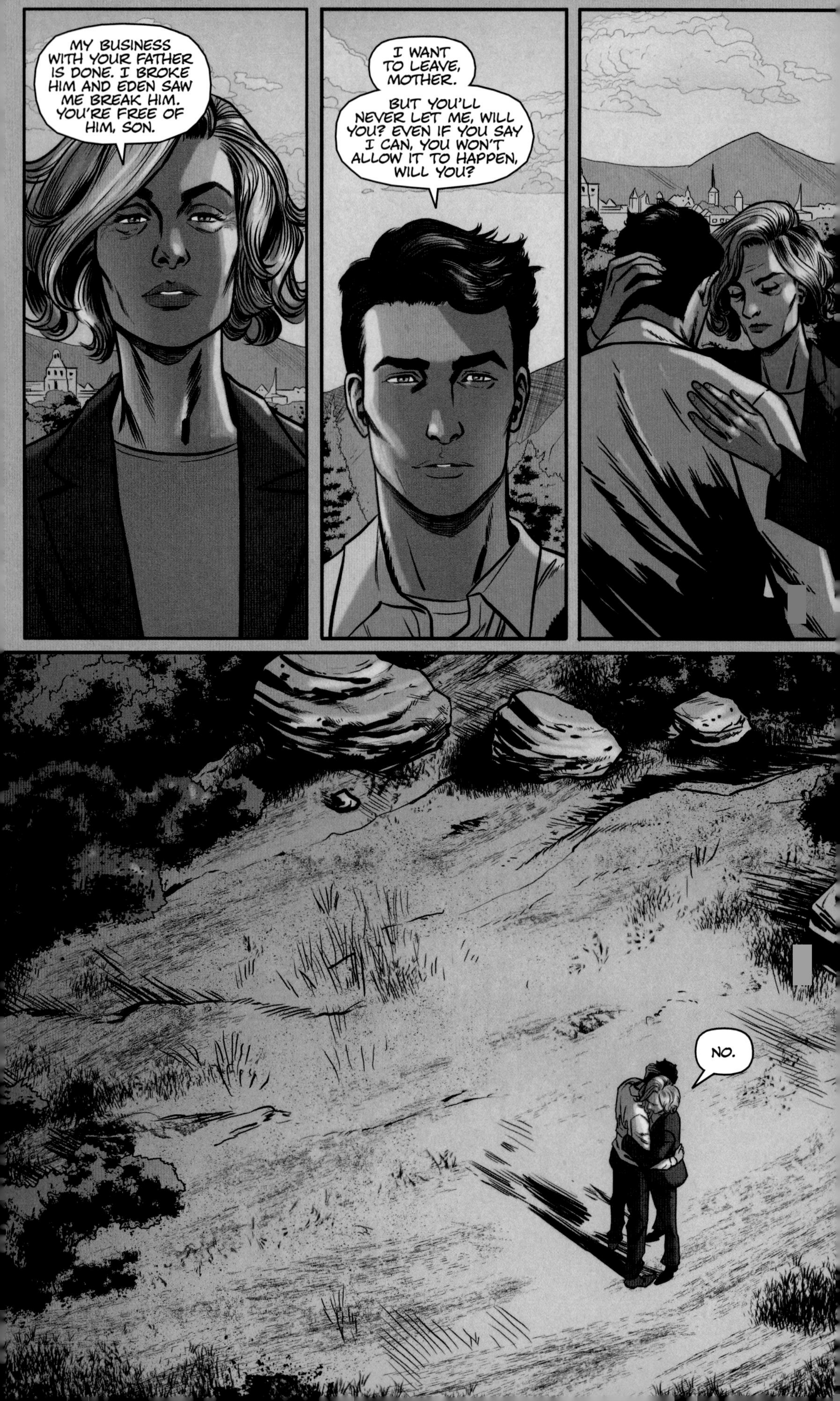
MY BUSINESS WITH YOUR FATHER IS DONE. I BROKE HIM AND EDEN SAW ME BREAK HIM. YOU'RE FREE OF HIM, SON.
I WANT TO LEAVE, MOTHER.
BUT YOU'LL NEVER LET ME, WILL YOU? EVEN IF YOU SAY I CAN, YOU WON'T ALLOW IT TO HAPPEN, WILL YOU?
NO.

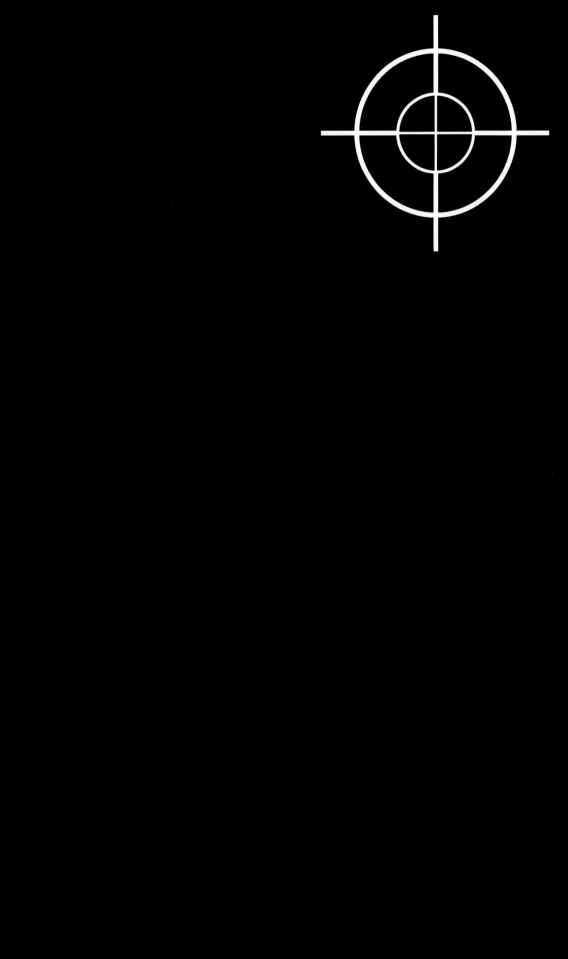

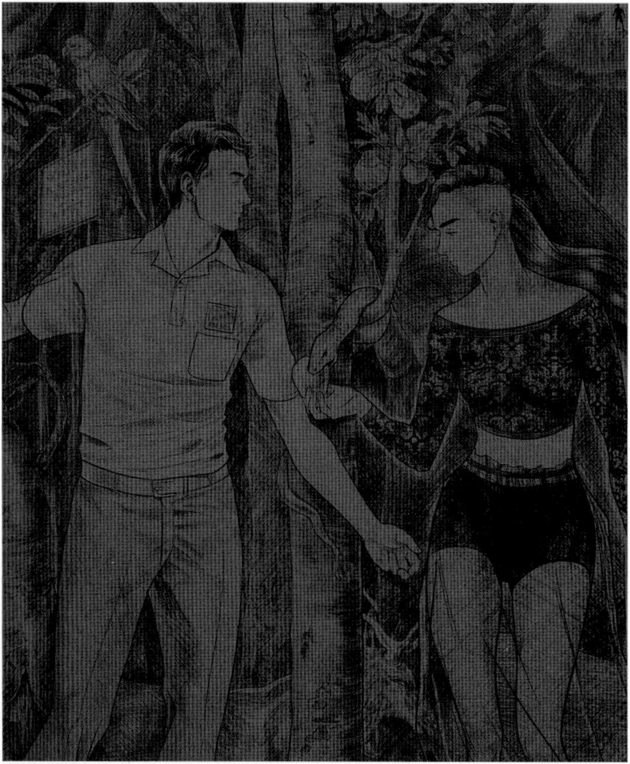

Postal #21
Linda Sejic

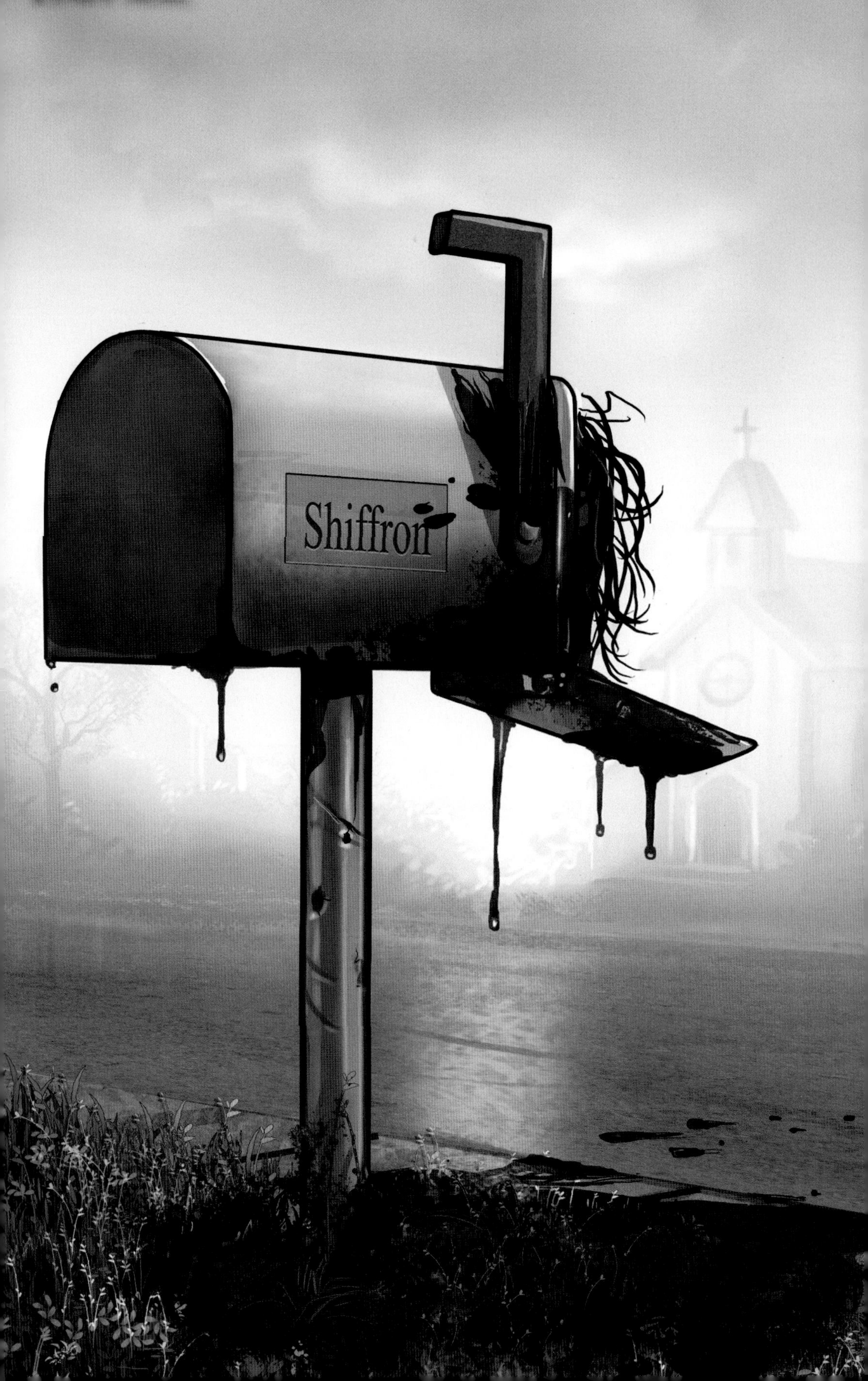
Shiffron

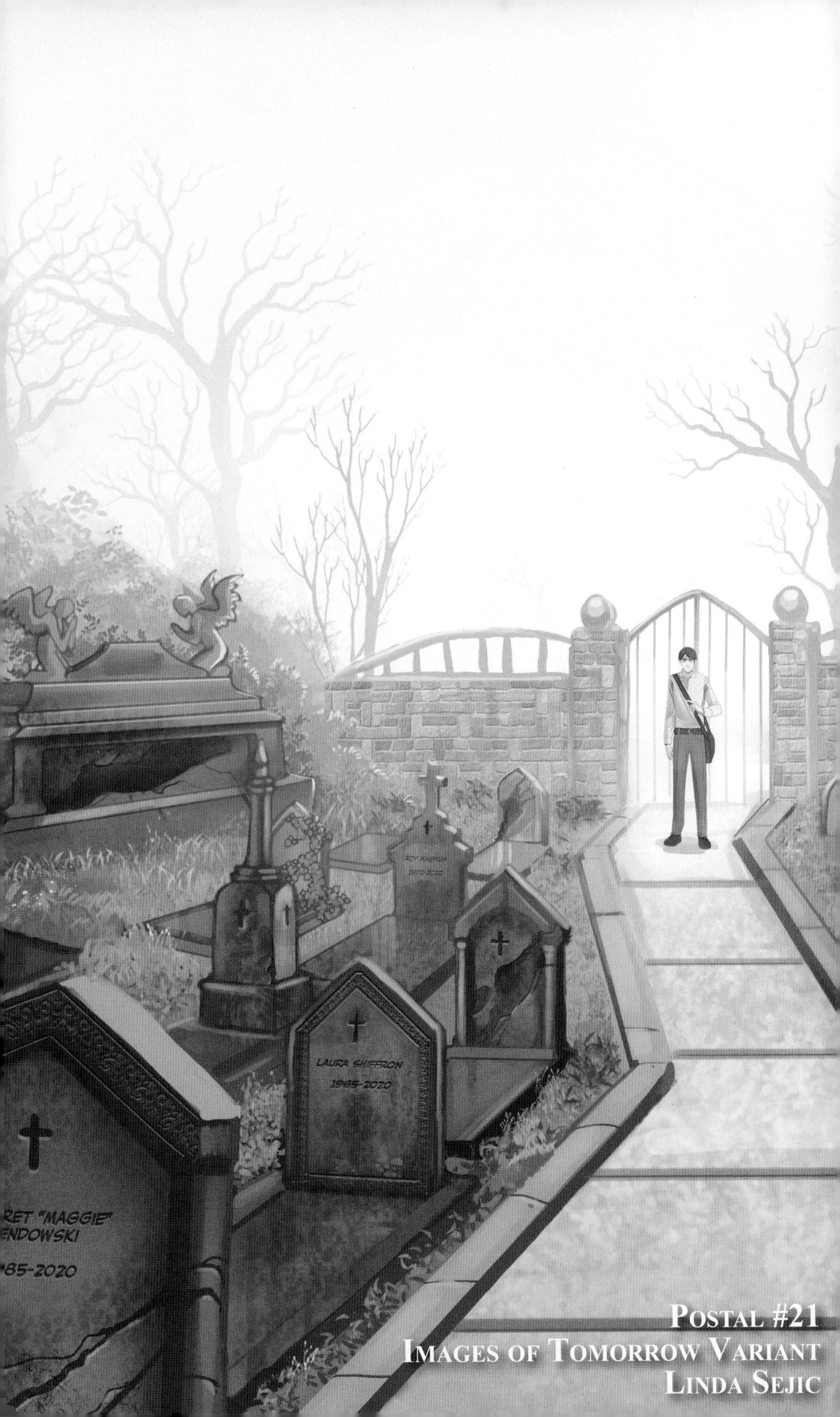
LAURA SHIFFRON
1965-2020
RET "MAGGIE"
ENDOWSKI
85-2020

Postal #21
Images of Tomorrow Variant
Linda Sejic

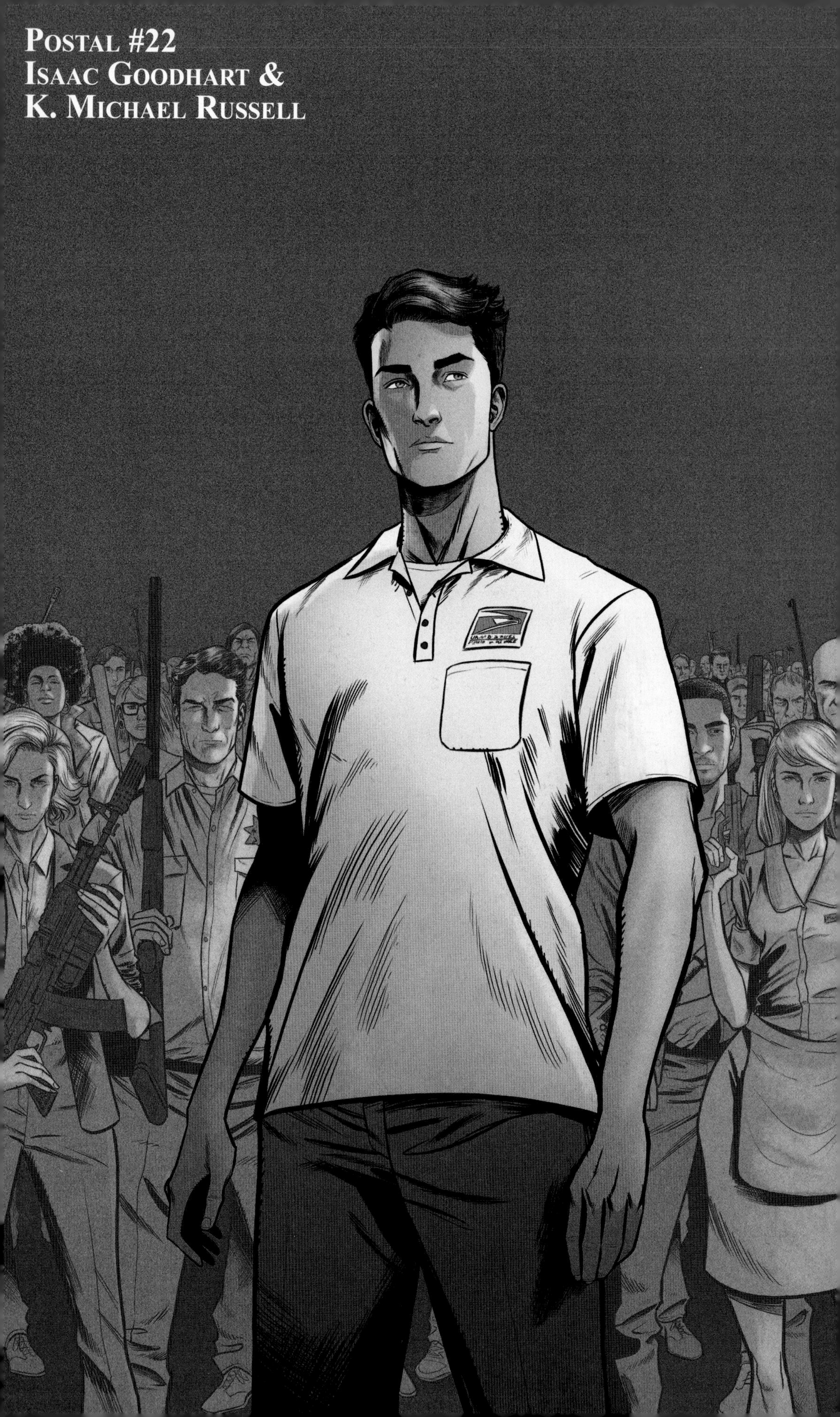

POSTAL #22
ISAAC GOODHART &
K. MICHAEL RUSSELL

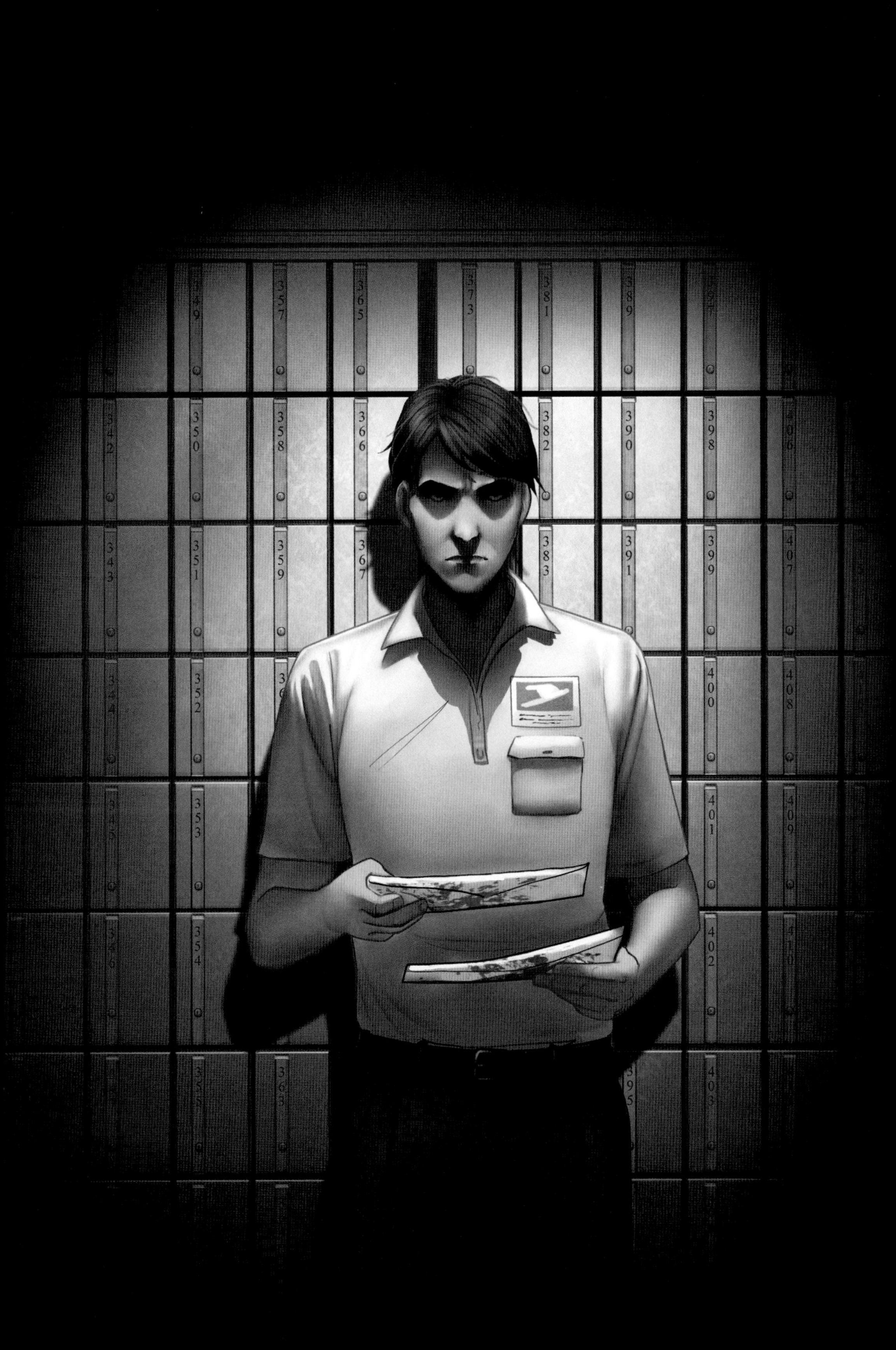

Postal #23
Linda Sejic

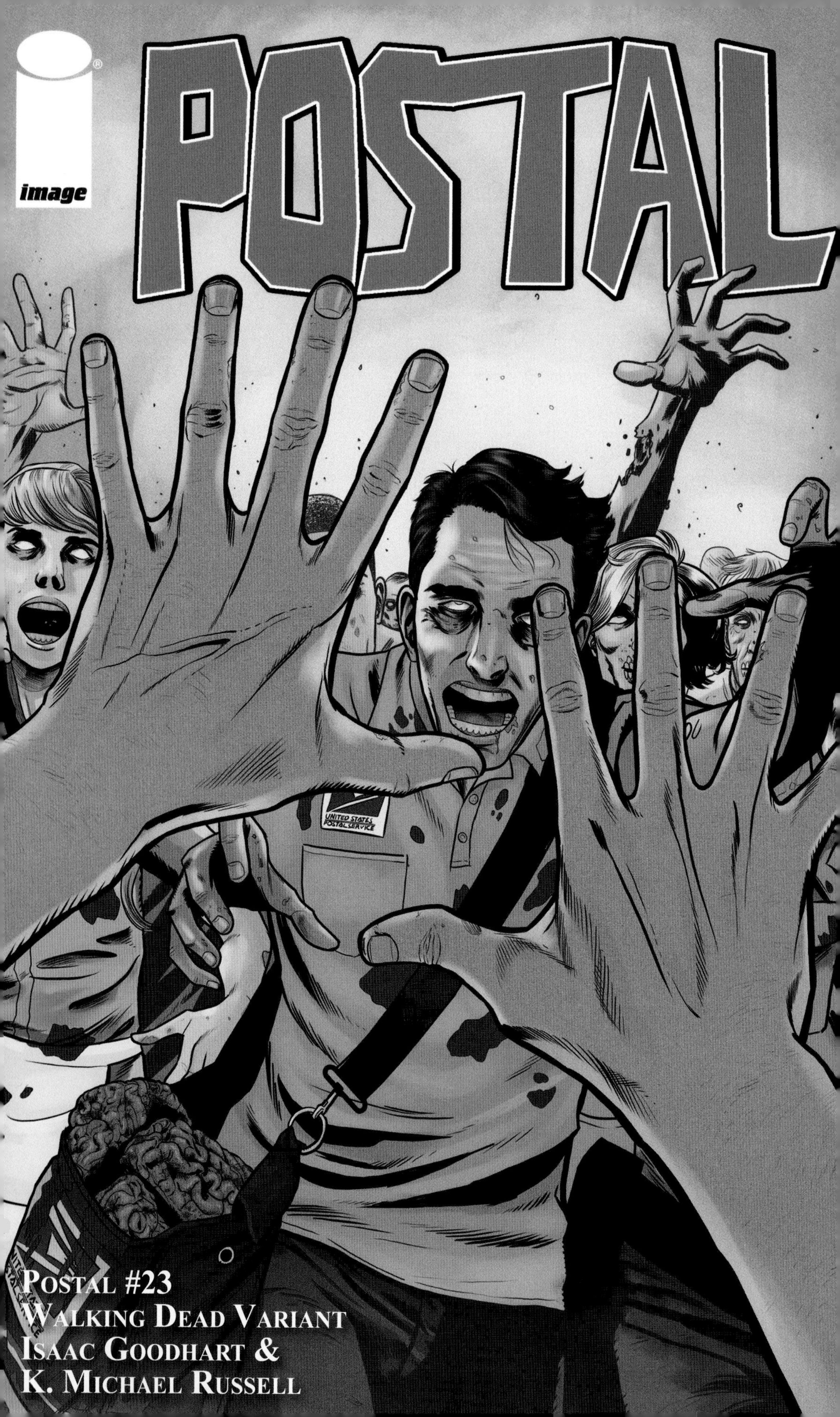
POSTAL
image
UNITED STATES POSTAL SERVICE
POSTAL #23
WALKING DEAD VARIANT
ISAAC GOODHART &
K. MICHAEL RUSSELL

Postal #24
Isaac Goodhart
& K. Michael Russell

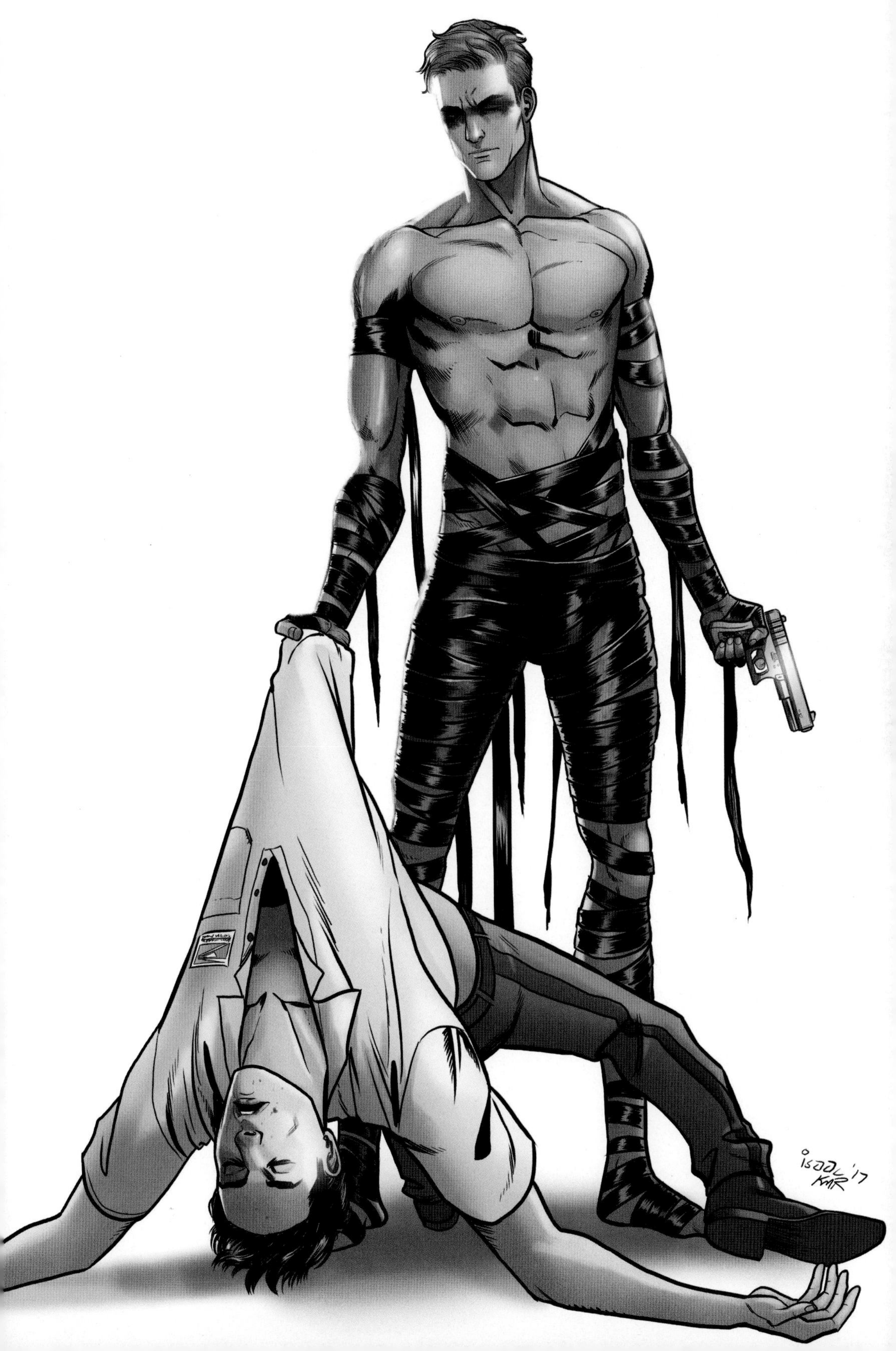

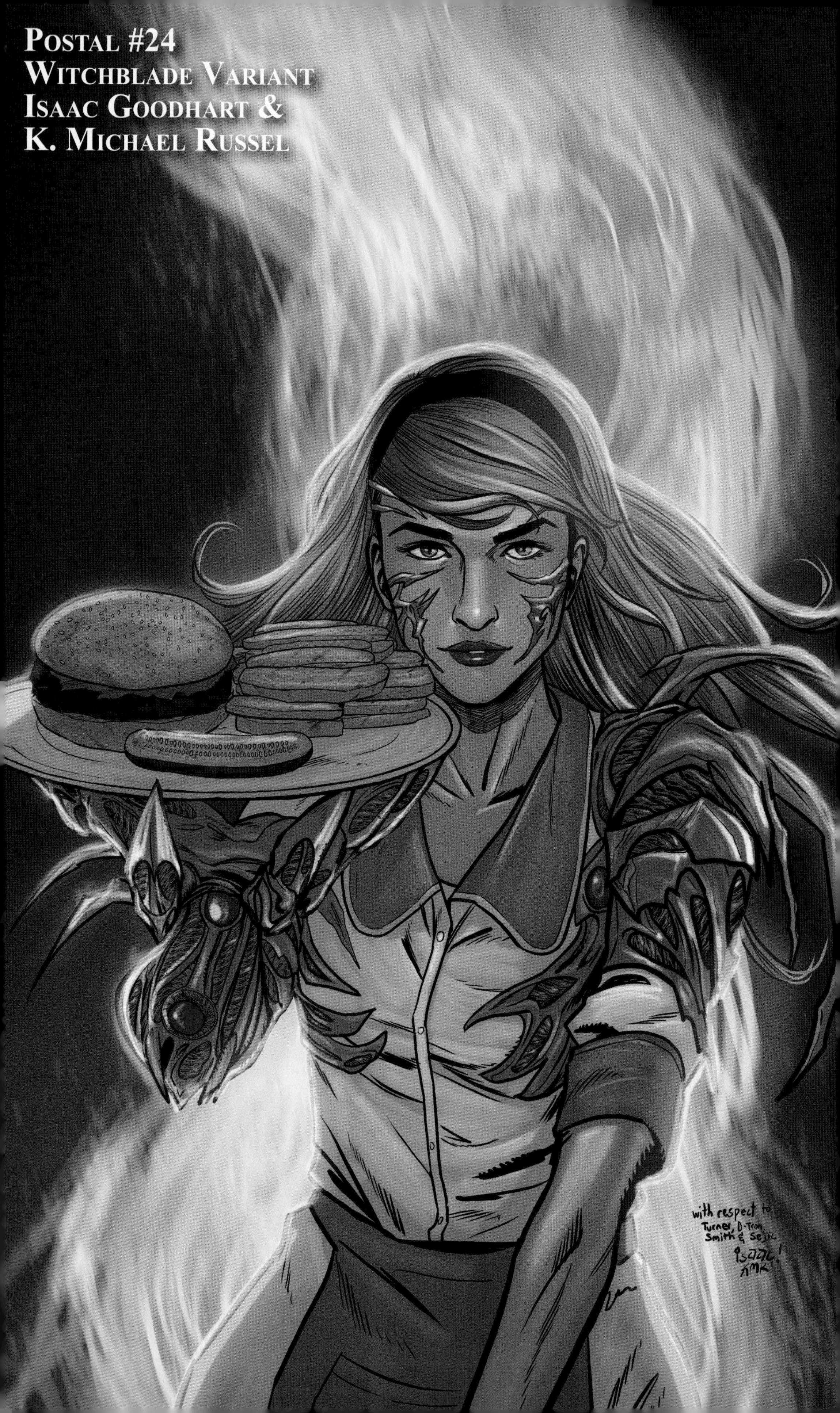
POSTAL #24
WITCHBLADE VARIANT
ISAAC GOODHART &
K. MICHAEL RUSSEL
with respect to
Turner, D-Tron, Smith & Sejic
KMR

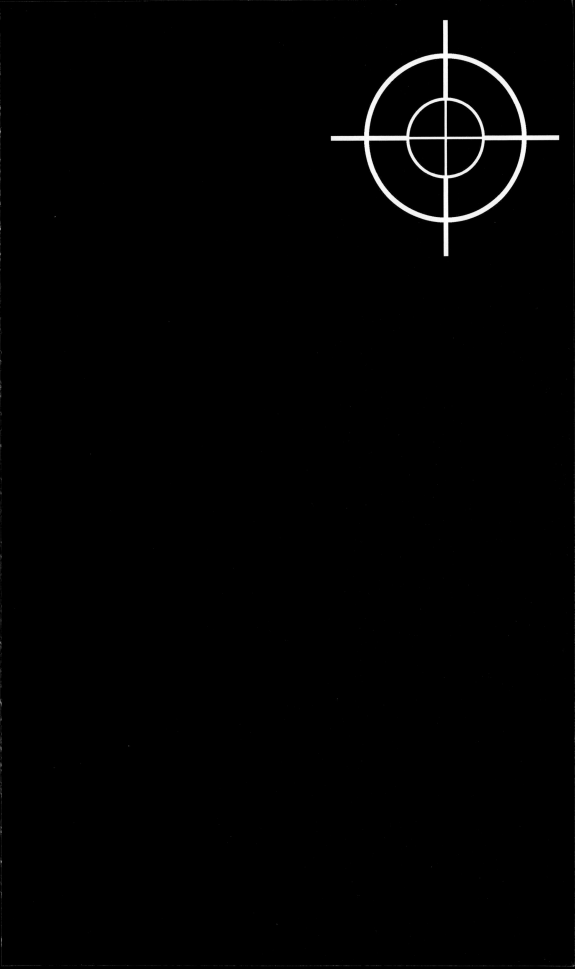

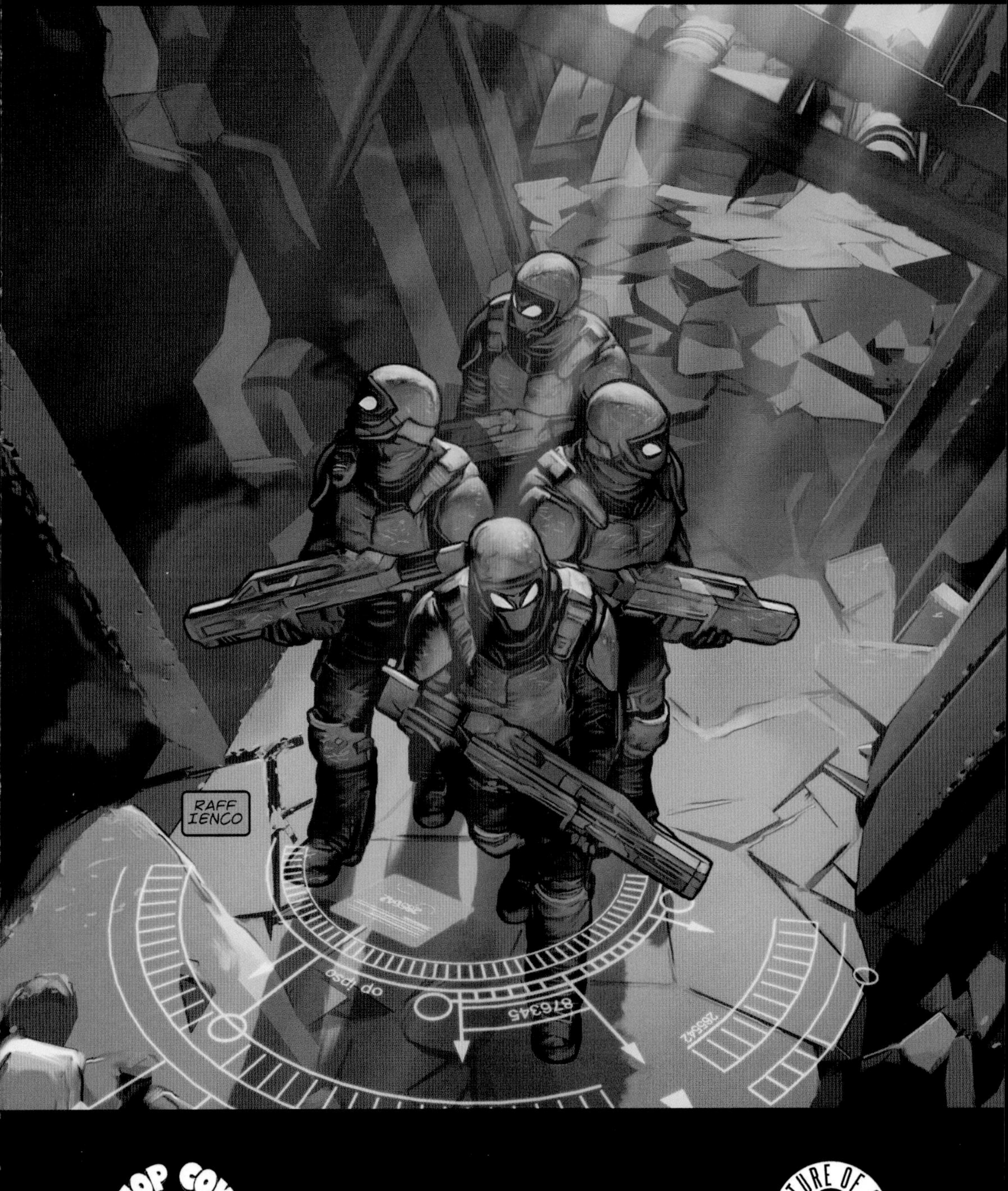
RAFF IENCO
876345

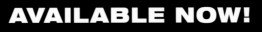

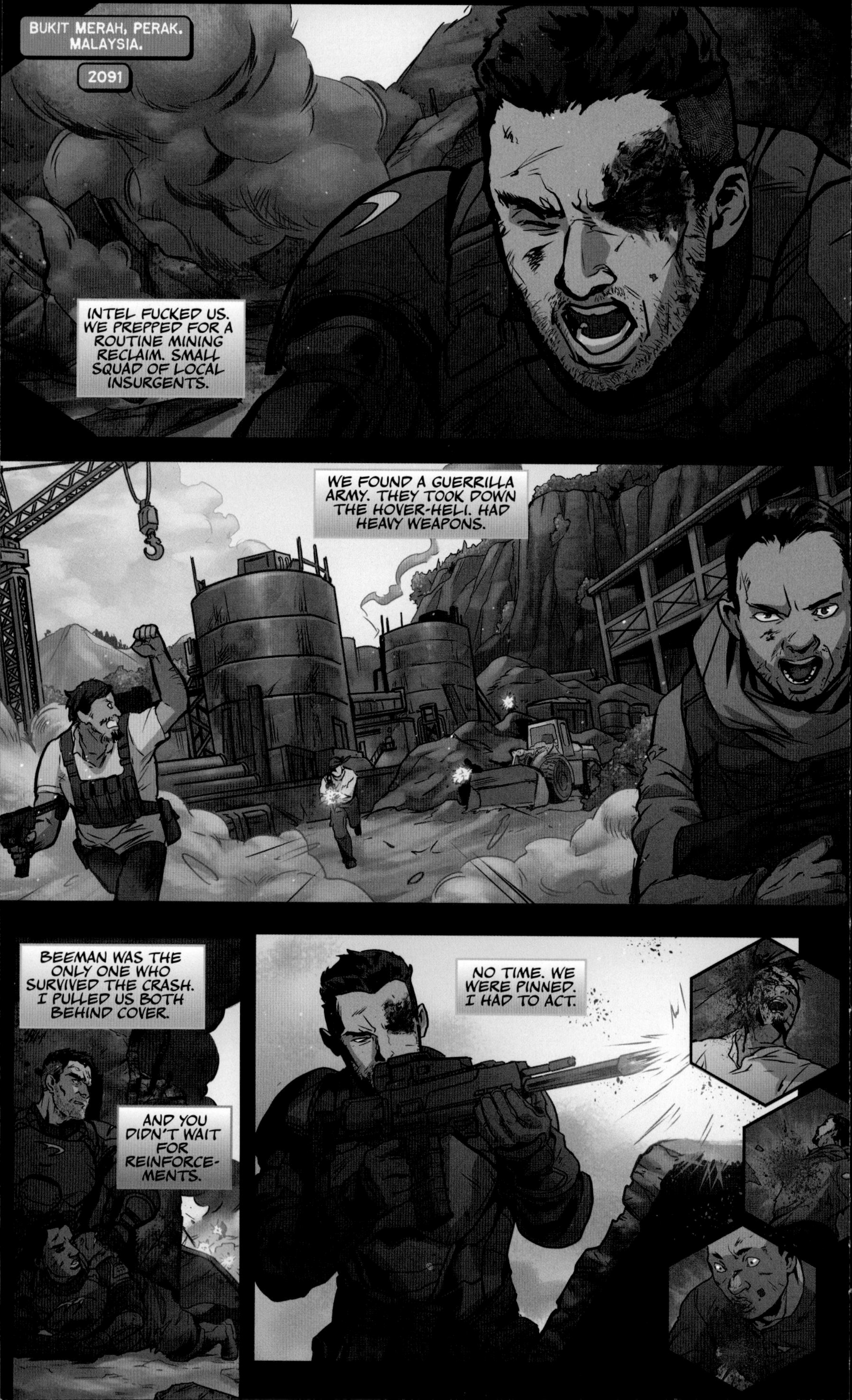
BUKIT MERAH, PERAK. MALAYSIA.
2091
INTEL FUCKED US. WE PREPPED FOR A ROUTINE MINING RECLAIM. SMALL SQUAD OF LOCAL INSURGENTS.
WE FOUND A GUERRILLA ARMY. THEY TOOK DOWN THE HOVER-HELI. HAD HEAVY WEAPONS.
BEEMAN WAS THE ONLY ONE WHO SURVIVED THE CRASH. I PULLED US BOTH BEHIND COVER.
AND YOU DIDN'T WAIT FOR REINFORCE-MENTS.
NO TIME. WE WERE PINNED. I HAD TO ACT.

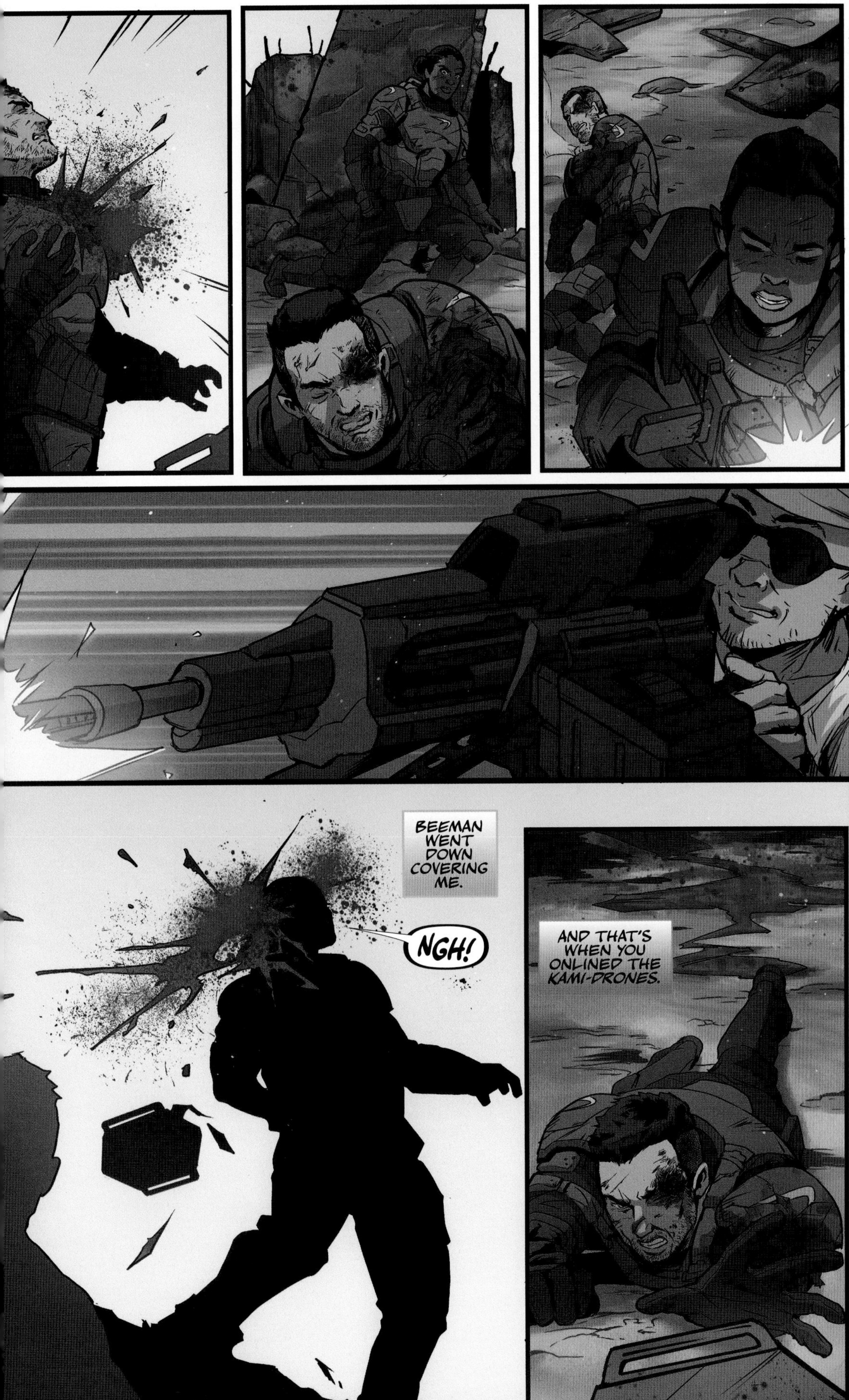
BEEMAN WENT DOWN COVERING ME.
NGH!
AND THAT'S WHEN YOU ONLINED THE KAMI-DRONES.

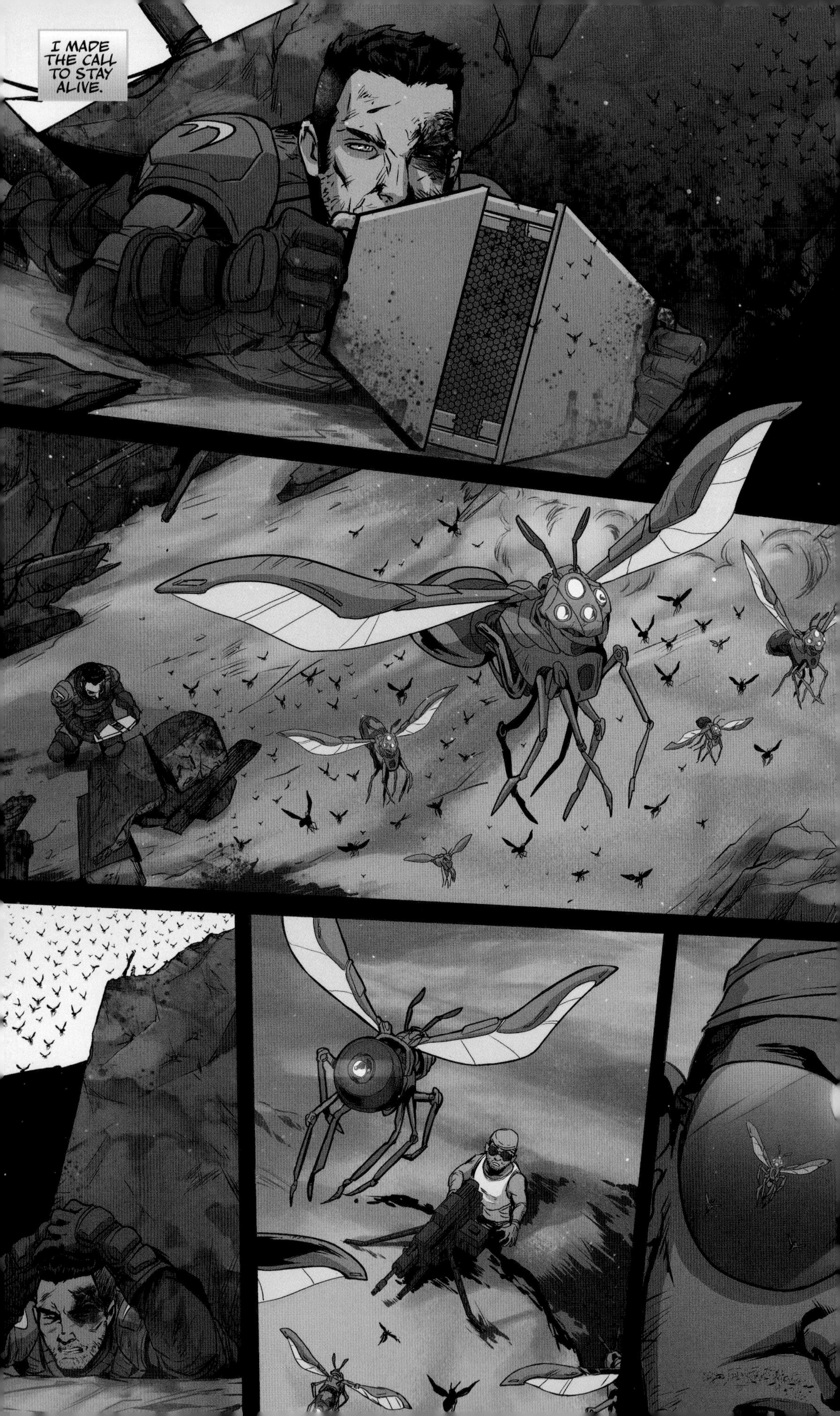
I MADE THE CALL TO STAY ALIVE.

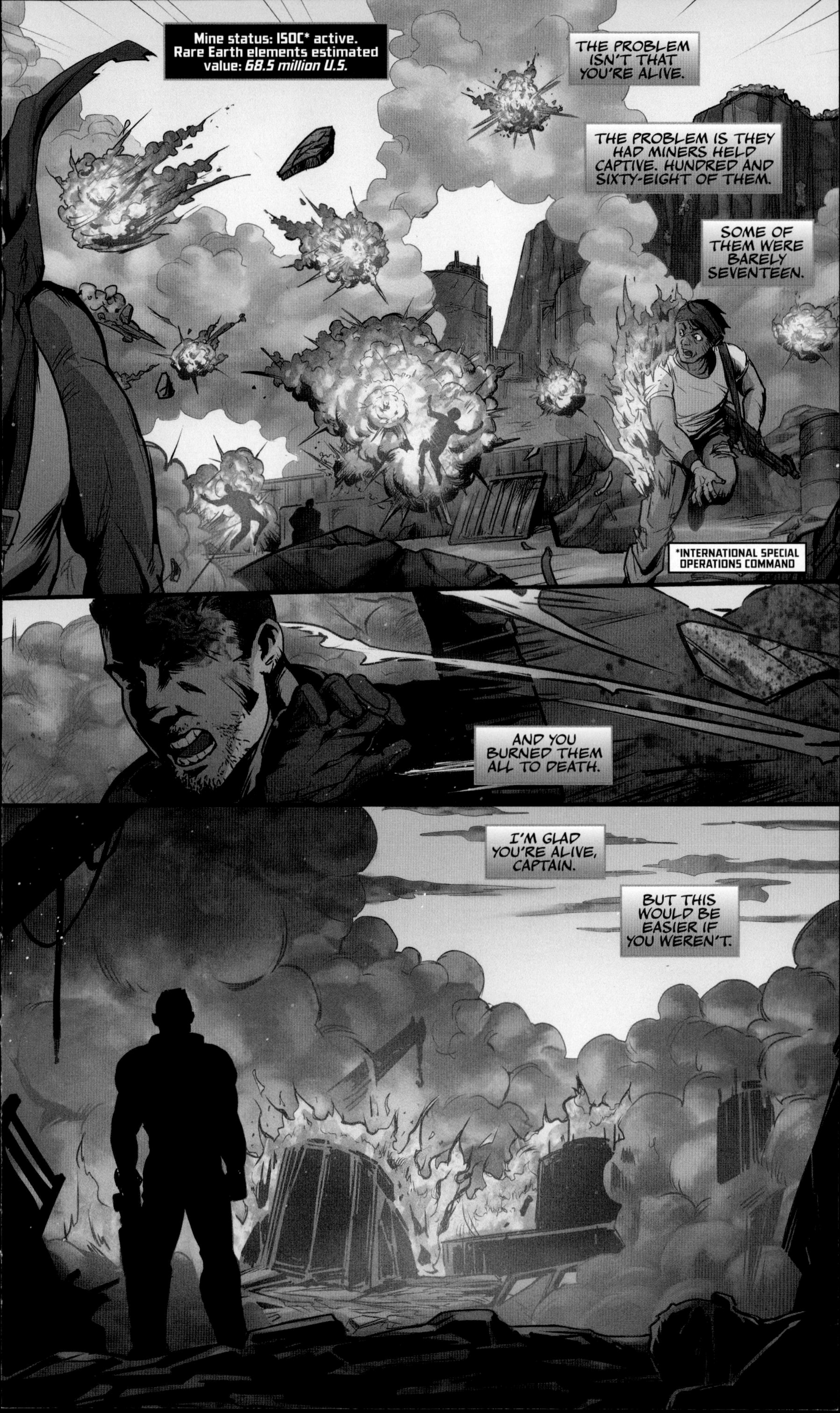
Mine status: ISOC* active. Rare Earth elements estimated value: *68.5 million U.S.*
THE PROBLEM ISN'T THAT YOU'RE ALIVE.
THE PROBLEM IS THEY HAD MINERS HELD CAPTIVE. HUNDRED AND SIXTY-EIGHT OF THEM.
SOME OF THEM WERE BARELY SEVENTEEN.
*INTERNATIONAL SPECIAL OPERATIONS COMMAND
AND YOU BURNED THEM ALL TO DEATH.
I'M GLAD YOU'RE ALIVE, CAPTAIN.
BUT THIS WOULD BE EASIER IF YOU WEREN'T.

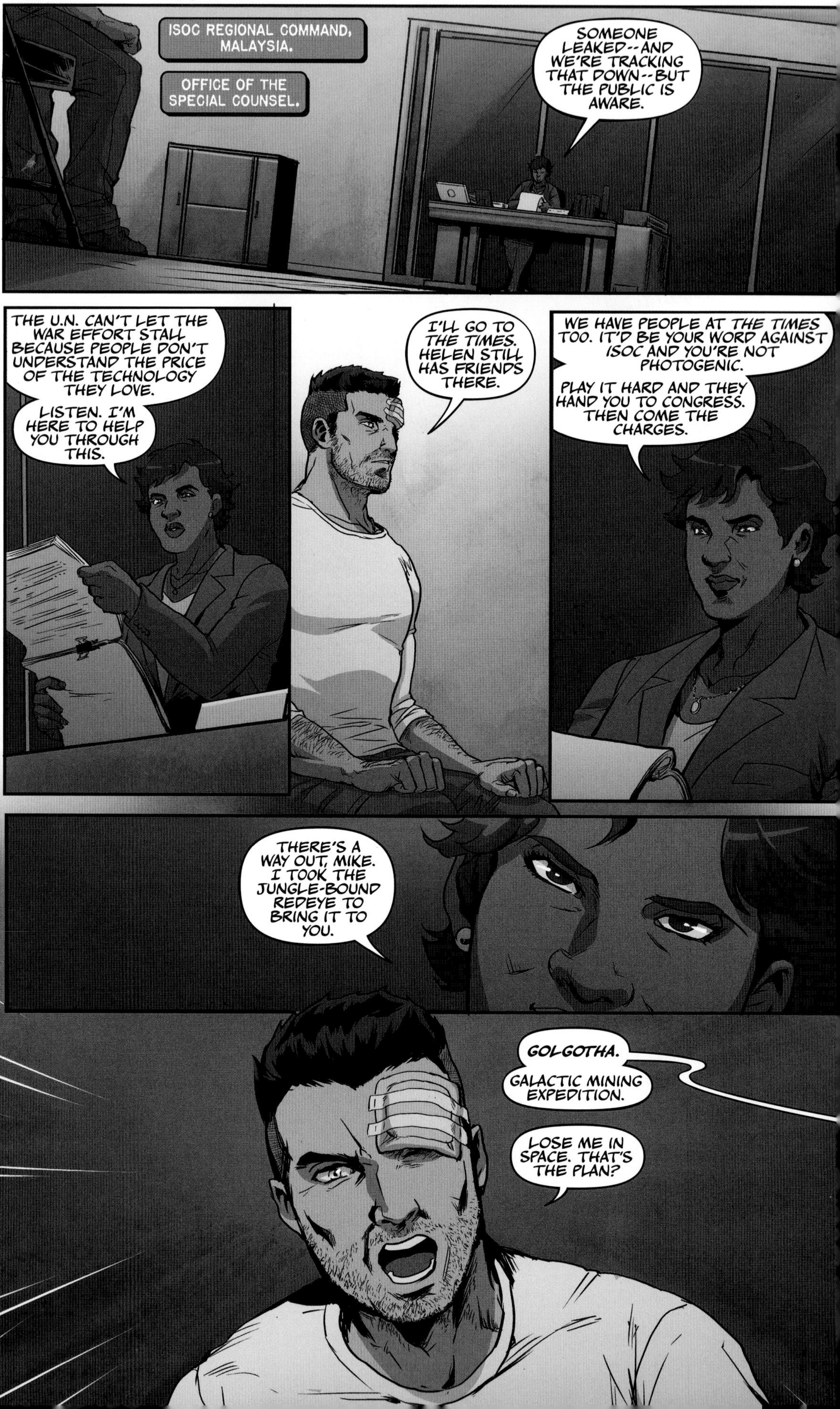

ISOC REGIONAL COMMAND, MALAYSIA.
OFFICE OF THE SPECIAL COUNSEL.
SOMEONE LEAKED--AND WE'RE TRACKING THAT DOWN--BUT THE PUBLIC IS AWARE.
THE U.N. CAN'T LET THE WAR EFFORT STALL BECAUSE PEOPLE DON'T UNDERSTAND THE PRICE OF THE TECHNOLOGY THEY LOVE.
LISTEN. I'M HERE TO HELP YOU THROUGH THIS.
I'LL GO TO *THE TIMES*. HELEN STILL HAS FRIENDS THERE.
WE HAVE PEOPLE AT *THE TIMES* TOO. IT'D BE YOUR WORD AGAINST *ISOC* AND YOU'RE NOT PHOTOGENIC.
PLAY IT HARD AND THEY HAND YOU TO CONGRESS. THEN COME THE CHARGES.
THERE'S A WAY OUT, MIKE. I TOOK THE JUNGLE-BOUND REDEYE TO BRING IT TO YOU.
GOLGOTHA.
GALACTIC MINING EXPEDITION.
LOSE ME IN SPACE. THAT'S THE PLAN?

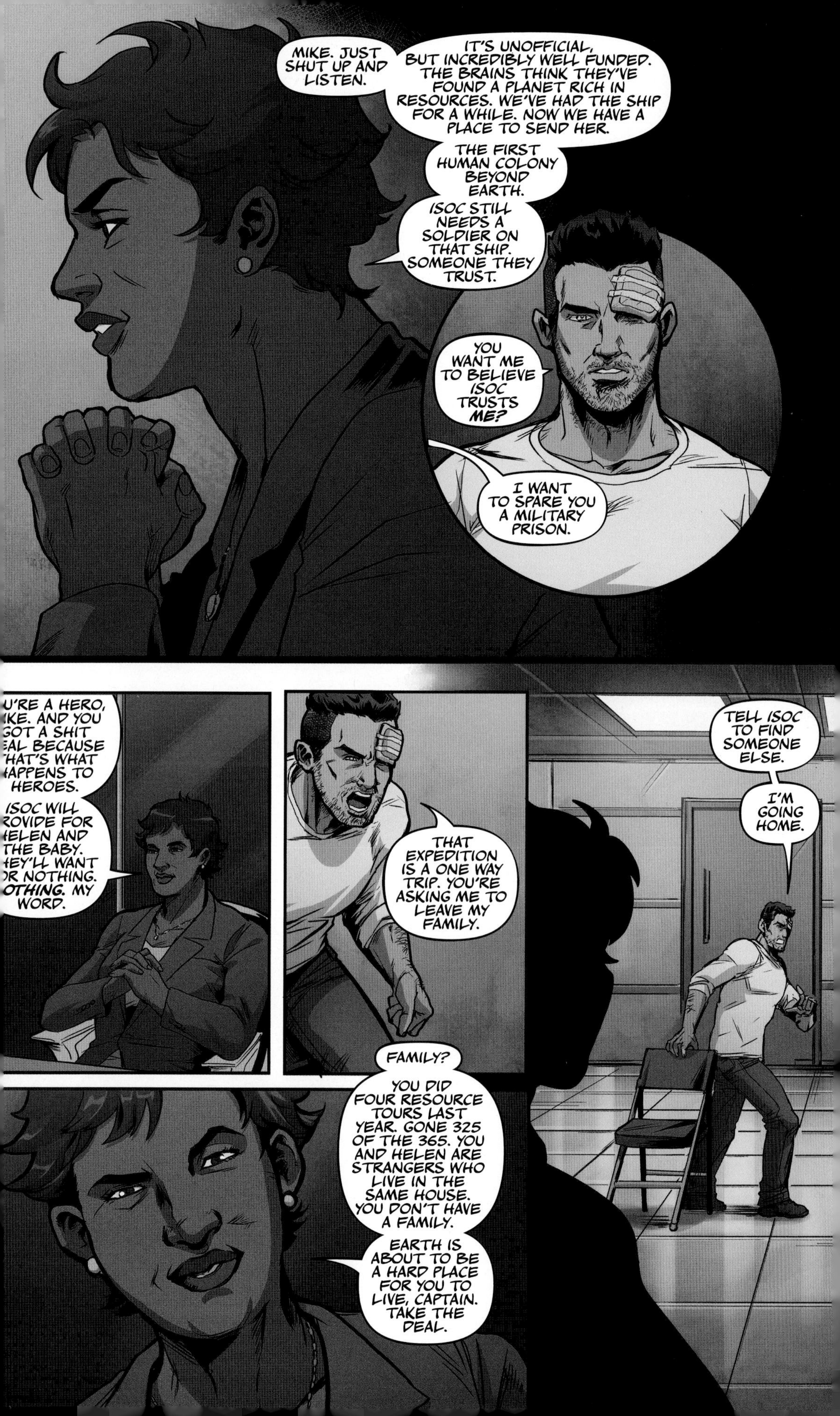
MIKE. JUST SHUT UP AND LISTEN.
IT'S UNOFFICIAL, BUT INCREDIBLY WELL FUNDED. THE BRAINS THINK THEY'VE FOUND A PLANET RICH IN RESOURCES. WE'VE HAD THE SHIP FOR A WHILE. NOW WE HAVE A PLACE TO SEND HER.
THE FIRST HUMAN COLONY BEYOND EARTH.
ISOC STILL NEEDS A SOLDIER ON THAT SHIP. SOMEONE THEY TRUST.
YOU WANT ME TO BELIEVE ISOC TRUSTS *ME?*
I WANT TO SPARE YOU A MILITARY PRISON.
U'RE A HERO, IKE. AND YOU GOT A SHIT EAL BECAUSE THAT'S WHAT HAPPENS TO HEROES.
ISOC WILL ROVIDE FOR HELEN AND THE BABY. HEY'LL WANT OR NOTHING. **OTHING.** MY WORD.
THAT EXPEDITION IS A ONE WAY TRIP. YOU'RE ASKING ME TO LEAVE MY FAMILY.
FAMILY?
YOU DID FOUR RESOURCE TOURS LAST YEAR. GONE 325 OF THE 365. YOU AND HELEN ARE STRANGERS WHO LIVE IN THE SAME HOUSE. YOU DON'T HAVE A FAMILY.
EARTH IS ABOUT TO BE A HARD PLACE FOR YOU TO LIVE, CAPTAIN. TAKE THE DEAL.
TELL ISOC TO FIND SOMEONE ELSE.
I'M GOING HOME.

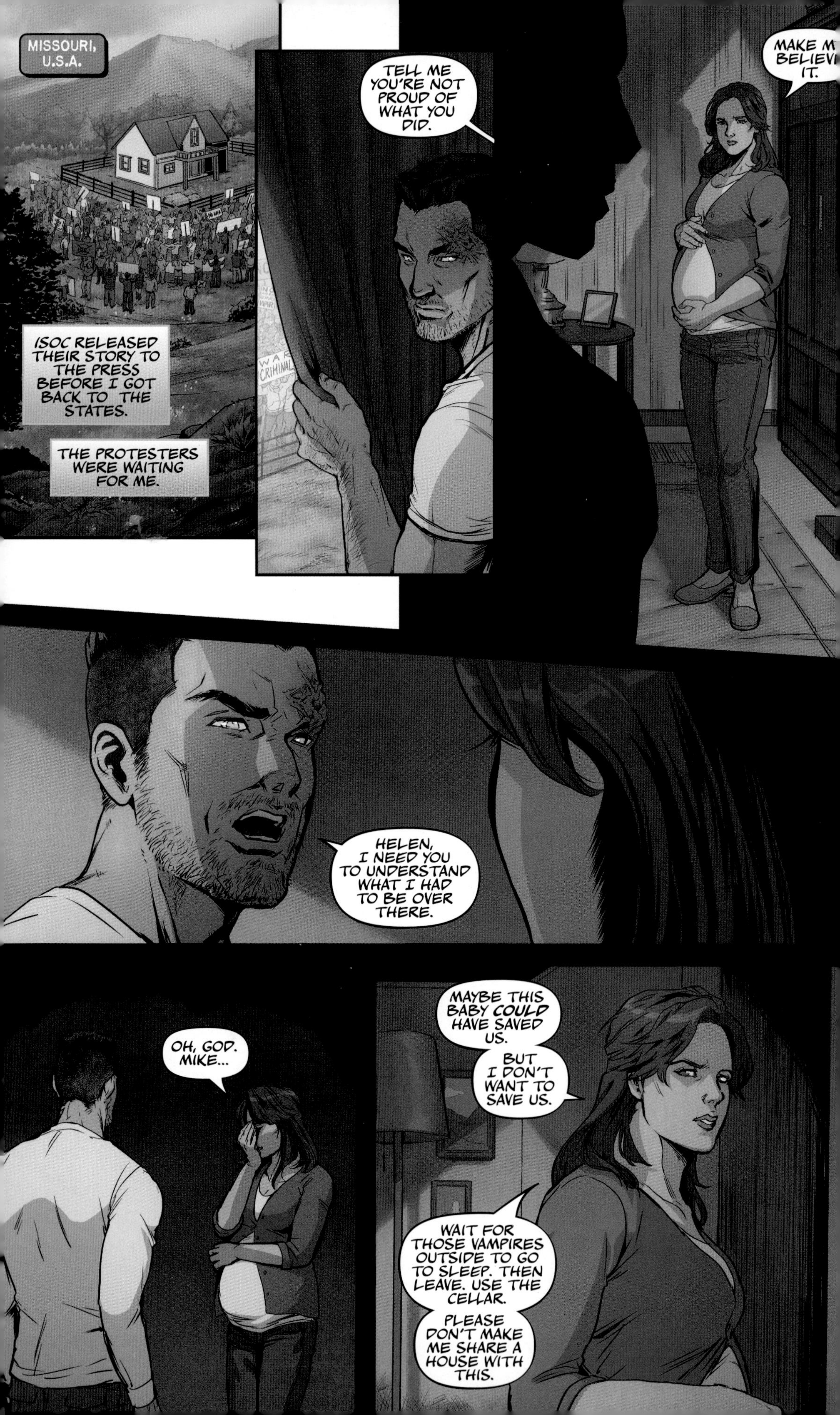
MISSOURI, U.S.A.
ISOC RELEASED THEIR STORY TO THE PRESS BEFORE I GOT BACK TO THE STATES.
THE PROTESTERS WERE WAITING FOR ME.
TELL ME YOU'RE NOT PROUD OF WHAT YOU DID.
WAR CRIMINAL
MAKE M BELIEV IT.
HELEN, I NEED YOU TO UNDERSTAND WHAT I HAD TO BE OVER THERE.
OH, GOD. MIKE...
MAYBE THIS BABY *COULD* HAVE SAVED US.
BUT I DON'T WANT TO SAVE US.
WAIT FOR THOSE VAMPIRES OUTSIDE TO GO TO SLEEP. THEN LEAVE. USE THE CELLAR.
PLEASE DON'T MAKE ME SHARE A HOUSE WITH THIS.

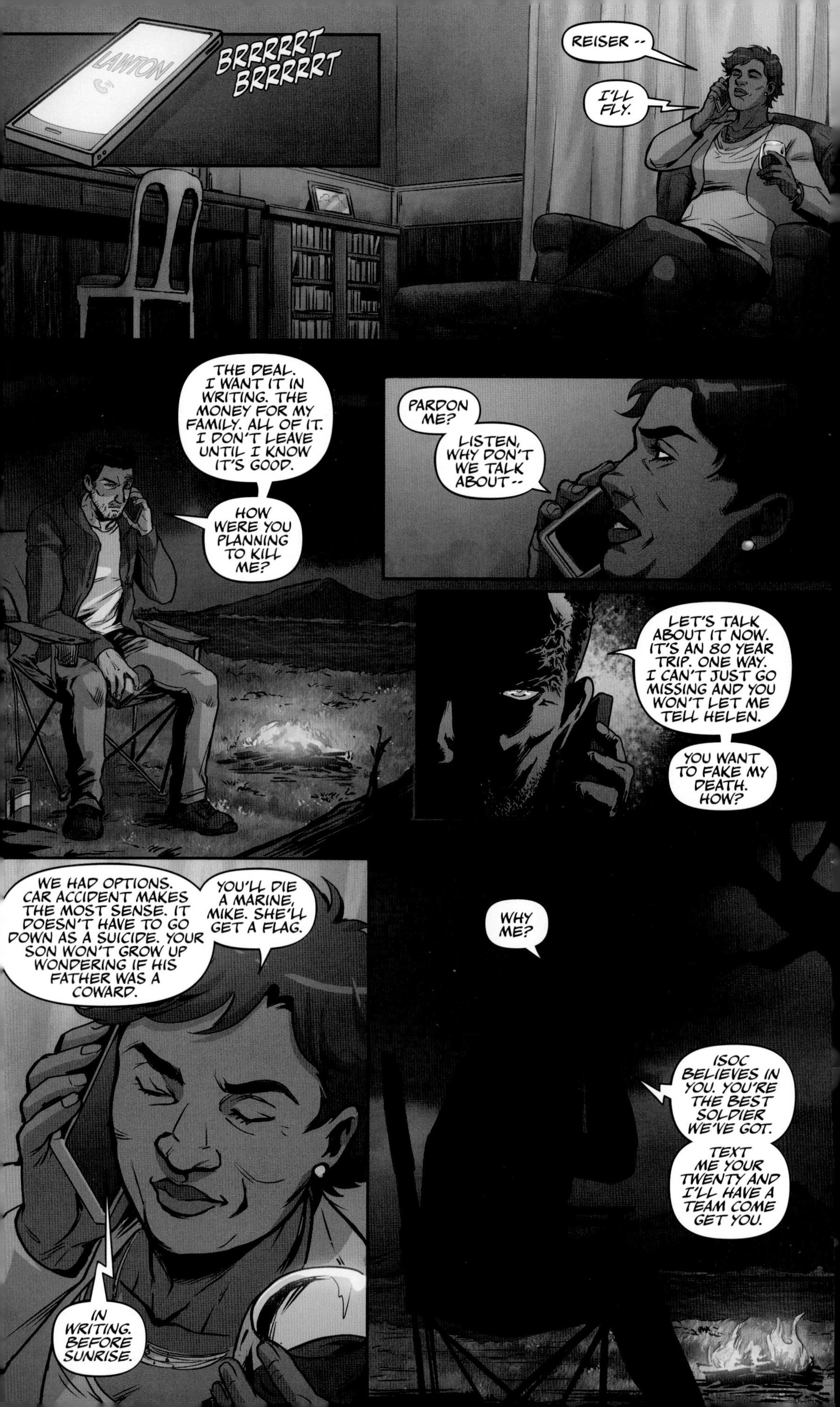
LAWTON
BRRRRRT BRRRRRT
REISER --
I'LL FLY.
THE DEAL. I WANT IT IN WRITING. THE MONEY FOR MY FAMILY. ALL OF IT. I DON'T LEAVE UNTIL I KNOW IT'S GOOD.
HOW WERE YOU PLANNING TO KILL ME?
PARDON ME?
LISTEN, WHY DON'T WE TALK ABOUT --
LET'S TALK ABOUT IT NOW. IT'S AN 80 YEAR TRIP. ONE WAY. I CAN'T JUST GO MISSING AND YOU WON'T LET ME TELL HELEN.
YOU WANT TO FAKE MY DEATH. HOW?
WE HAD OPTIONS. CAR ACCIDENT MAKES THE MOST SENSE. IT DOESN'T HAVE TO GO DOWN AS A SUICIDE. YOUR SON WON'T GROW UP WONDERING IF HIS FATHER WAS A COWARD.
YOU'LL DIE A MARINE, MIKE. SHE'LL GET A FLAG.
WHY ME?
ISOC BELIEVES IN YOU. YOU'RE THE BEST SOLDIER WE'VE GOT.
TEXT ME YOUR TWENTY AND I'LL HAVE A TEAM COME GET YOU.
IN WRITING. BEFORE SUNRISE.

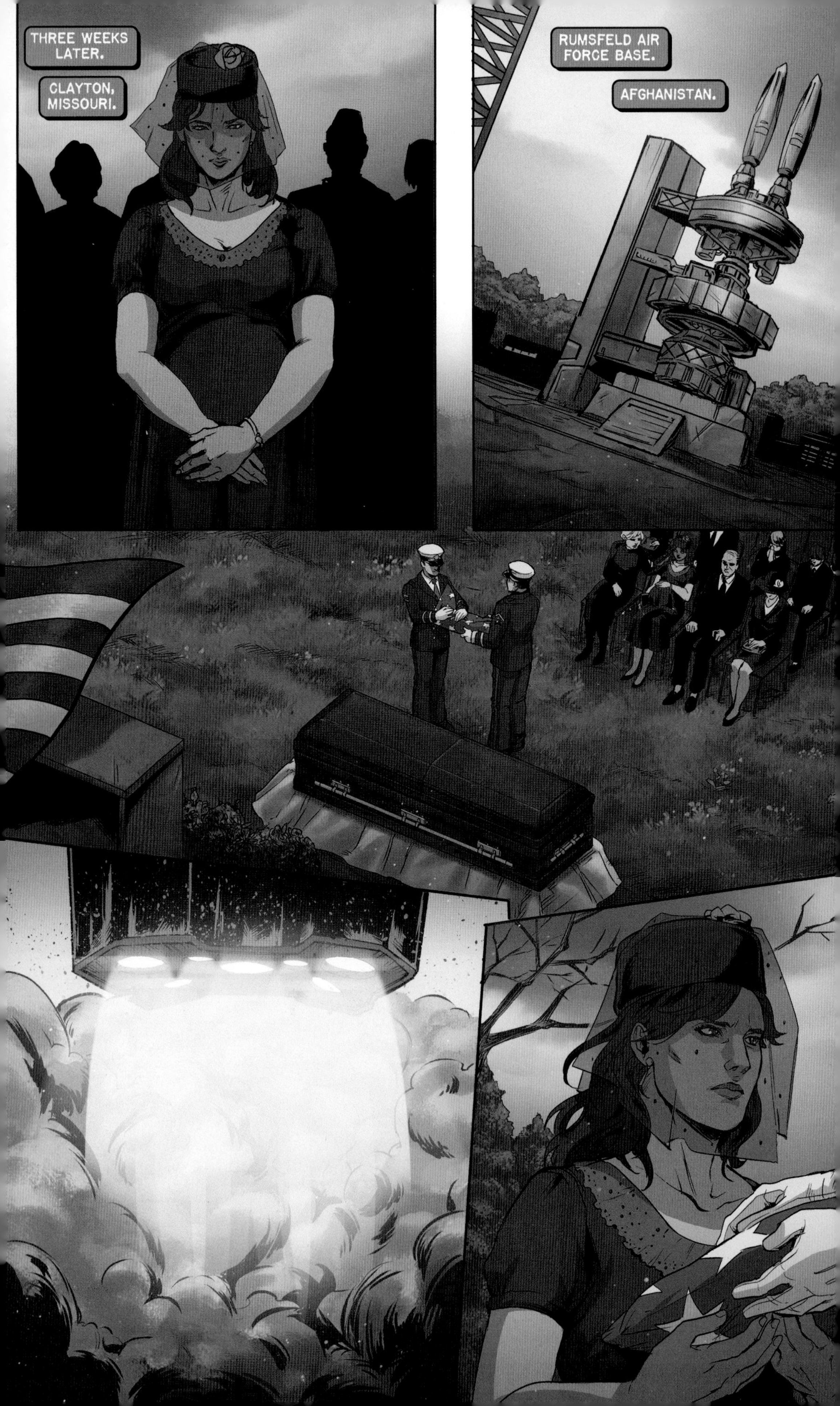
THREE WEEKS LATER.
CLAYTON, MISSOURI.
RUMSFELD AIR FORCE BASE.
AFGHANISTAN.

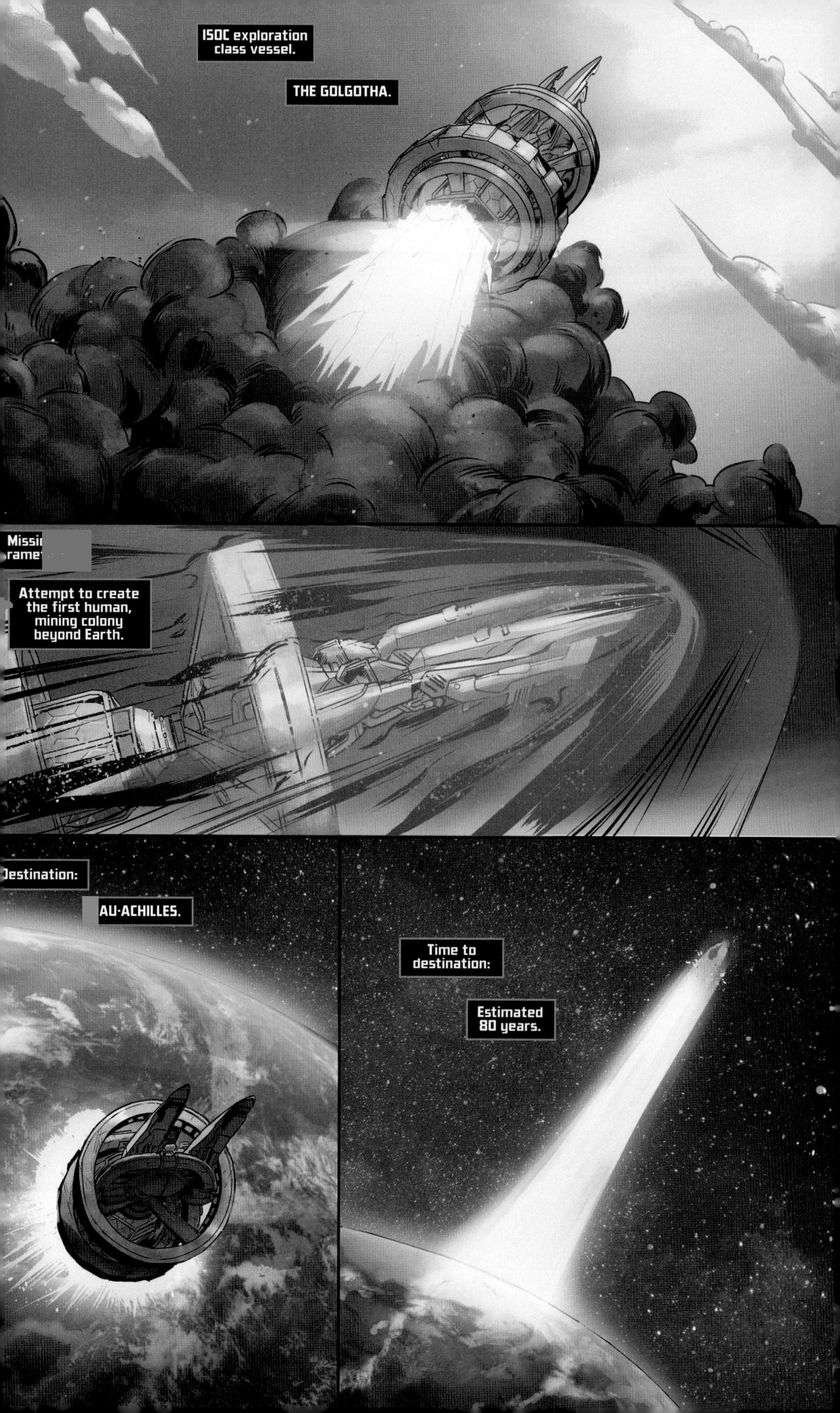
ISOC exploration class vessel.
THE GOLGOTHA.
Attempt to create the first human, mining colony beyond Earth.
Destination:
AU-ACHILLES.
Time to destination:
Estimated 80 years.

Meet the Creators of Postal

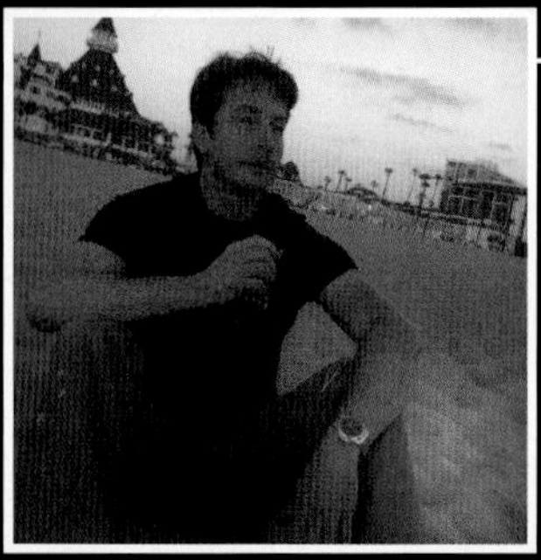

MATT HAWKINS

A veteran of the initial Image Comics launch, Matt started his career in comic book publishing in 1993 and has been working with Image as a creator, writer, and executive for over twenty years. President/COO of Top Cow since 1998, Matt has created and written over thirty new franchises for Top Cow and Image including *Think Tank, Necromancer, VICE, Lady Pendragon,* and *Aphrodite IX* as well as handling the company's business affairs.

BRYAN HILL

Writes comics, writes movies, and makes films. He lives and works in Los Angeles. @bryanedwardhill | Instagram/bryanehill

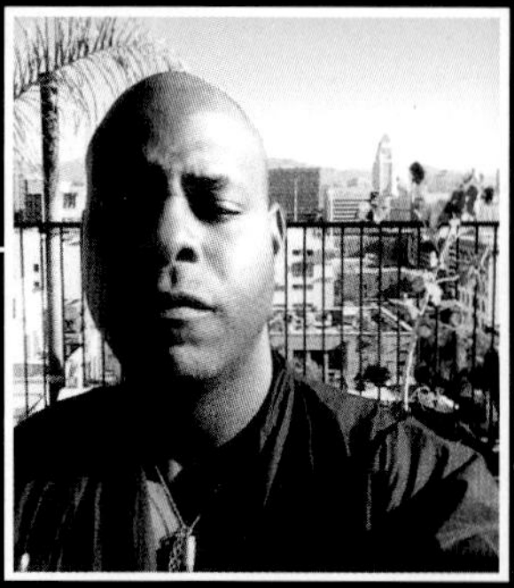

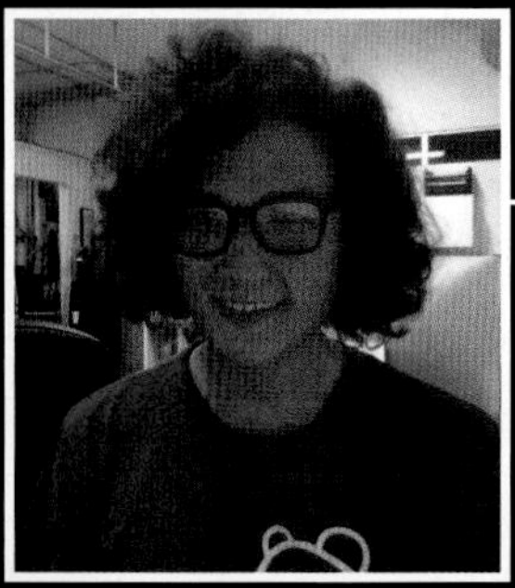

ISAAC GOODHART

A life-long comics fan, Isaac graduated from the School of Visual Arts in New York in 2010. In 2014, he was one of the winners for Top Cow's annual talent hunt. He currently lives in Los Angeles where he storyboards and draws comics.

K. MICHAEL RUSSELL

Michael has been working as a comic book color artist since 2011. His credits include the Image series *Glitterbomb* with *Wayward* and *Thunderbolts* writer Jim Zub, *Hack/Slash*, *Judge Dredd*, and the Eisner and Harvey-nominated *In the Dark: A Horror Anthology*. He launched an online comic book coloring course in 2014 at ColoringComics.com and maintains a YouTube channel dedicated to coloring tutorials. He lives on the coast in Long Beach, Mississippi, with his wife of sixteen years, Tina. They have two cats. One is a jerk. @kmichaelrussell

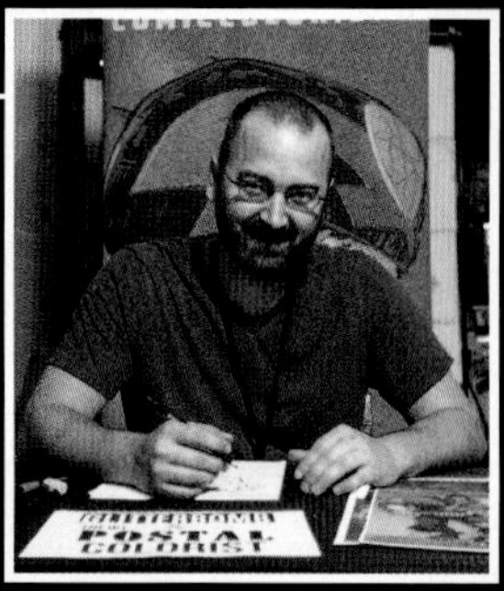

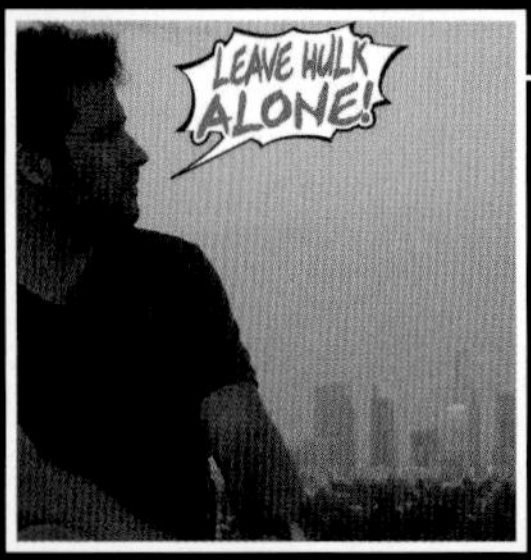
LEAVE HULK ALONE!

TROY PETERI

Starting his career at Comicraft, Troy Peteri lettered titles such as *Iron Man*, *Wolverine*, and *Amazing Spider-Man*, among many others. He's been lettering roughly 97% of all Top Cow titles since 2005. In addition to Top Cow, he currently letters comics from multiple publishers and websites, such as Image Comics, Dynamite, and Archaia. He (along with co-writer Tom Martin and artist Dave Lanphear) is currently writing (and lettering) *Tales of Equinox*, a webcomic of his own creation for www.Thrillbent.com. (Once again, www.Thrillbent.com.) He's still bitter about no longer lettering *The Darkness* and wants it back on stands immediately.

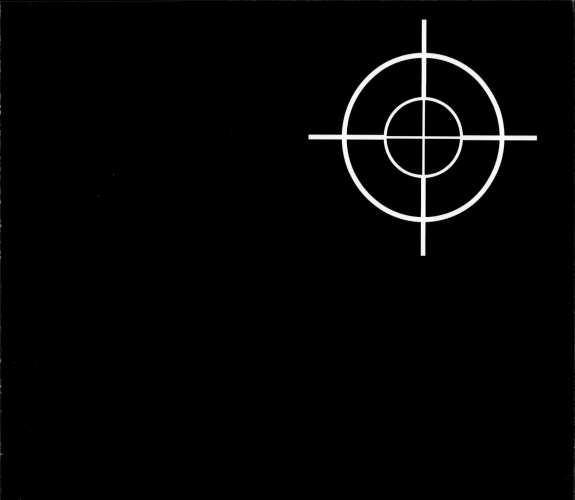

The Top Cow essentials checklist:

IXth Generation, Volume 1
(ISBN: 978-1-63215-323-4)

Aphrodite IX: Complete Series
(ISBN: 978-1-63215-368-5)

Artifacts Origins: First Born
(ISBN: 978-1-60706-506-7)

Bloodstain, Volume 1
(ISBN: 978-1-63215-544-3)

Cyber Force: Rebirth, Volume 1
(ISBN: 978-1-60706-671-2)

The Darkness: Origins, Volume 1
(ISBN: 978-1-60706-097-0)

The Darkness: Rebirth, Volume 1
(ISBN: 978-1-60706-585-2)

Death Vigil, Volume 1
(ISBN: 978-1-63215-278-7)

Eclipse, Volume 1
(ISBN: 978-1-5343-0038-5)

Eden's Fall, Volume 1
(ISBN: 978-1-5343-0065-1)

Genius, Volume 1
(ISBN: 978-1-63215-223-7)

Magdalena: Reformation
(ISBN: 978-1-5343-0238-9)

Postal, Volume 1
(ISBN: 978-1-63215-342-5)

Rising Stars Compendium
(ISBN: 978-1-63215-246-6)

Romulus, Volume 1
(ISBN: 978-1-5343-0101-6)

Sunstone, Volume 1
(ISBN: 978-1-63215-212-1)

Symmetry, Volume 1
(ISBN: 978-1-63215-699-0)

The Tithe, Volume 1
(ISBN: 978-1-63215-324-1)

Think Tank, Volume 1
(ISBN: 978-1-60706-660-6)

Witchblade: Redemption, Volume 1
(ISBN: 978-1-60706-193-9)

Witchblade: Rebirth, Volume 1
(ISBN: 978-1-60706-532-6)

Witchblade: Borne Again, Volume 1
(ISBN: 978-1-63215-025-7)

For more ISBN and ordering information on our latest collections go to:
www.topcow.com
Ask your retailer about our catalogue of collected editions,
digests, and hard covers or check the listings at:
Barnes and Noble, Amazon.com,
and other fine retailers.

To find your nearest comic shop go to:
www.comicshoplocator.com